SPEAK

ITS

NAME

Speak Its Name

Kathleen Jowitt

2016

Published by Kathleen Jowitt

This book is a work of fiction and any resemblance to any person living or dead is entirely coincidental. Stancester, its university, students' union and affiliated organisations, the Federation of Student Christian Societies, and the churches depicted in this book, are all fictitious.

First Printing: 2016

Printed in 9- and 11-point Palatino Linotype

ISBN 978-0-9935339-0-7

www.kathleenjowitt.com

CONTENTS

Acknowledgements

I am extremely grateful for the encouragement and enthusiasm of many offline and online friends, including the groups popularly known as Pico, Swoop and the Readlist. In particular I should like to thank Alex Brett, Tony Evershed, A.J. Hall, Nicola Janke, Mthr Jo Kershaw, Kate Lambert, Susan Lanigan and Ankaret Wells for their excellent and constructive advice. Any errors or infelicities that remain are attributable to my own stubbornness.

Michaelmas Term

Chapter 1

Anglican, Methodist and United Reformed Church Society – AngthMURC is a small, friendly Christian society which welcomes everyone who is interested in exploring both the joyful and the challenging aspects of faith. We meet at 7.30pm on Wednesdays in the Chaplaincy Centre – why not come along to Evensong in the University Chapel (5.30pm) and/or the bring-and-share meal (6.45pm) first? We have strong links with Campus Quakers and Cathsoc.

Catholic Society – We're a relaxed group of (mostly!) Catholic students who meet to share friendship, faith and fun. Stancester's international community is well represented here. Mass is held on Tuesdays at 7pm in the Catholic Chapel (Markham Grange); our meetings are at 8pm in the Chaplaincy Centre.

Christian Fellowship – Stancester's Christian society, committed to spreading the Good News of Jesus Christ to everyone on campus and beyond. All welcome at our main meeting at the Venue in the Union Building every Monday night at 8pm. If you have questions about Christianity, we'll answer them at our Big Tent in Freshers' Week. See our programme for this year online at www.stancester-su.org.uk/societies/christianfellowship

- selected extracts from *Stancester University Students' Union Handbook*

'Well, then,' Lydia said to the empty room. 'Let's get started.' But all her motivation seemed to have evaporated.

This slice of attic was one of the most desirable bedrooms in Richmond Hall, and Richmond was one of the University of Stancester's more desirable halls of residence, a three-storey Victorian mansion whose once-spacious bedrooms had been subdivided into narrow cubicles, just big enough to sleep and study in. Empty, however, it did not show itself to its best advantage. Fractious September sunshine, trapped by the locked window, made the room uncomfortably stuffy; a couple of dead flies lay on the windowsill, legs in the air. The walls were peppered with drawing-pin holes and blu-tack stains, and a blob of chewing gum had got itself trodden into the carpet. A whiff of illegal cigarette smoke (or worse) in the corridor must be a legacy of the summer school that had vacated the place this morning. The silence was unsettling.

Lydia looked at the motley collection of cardboard boxes and polythene bags, and wondered where to start. She ought to unpack as quickly as possible. She ought to make her room neat and tidy and welcoming. She ought to start wandering the halls looking for Freshers, introduce herself to them as their Christian Fellowship Hall Officer, identify four or five committed believers who might form the nucleus of a group, and generally let the Spirit of God work through her.

She couldn't be bothered.

It was not a good start to the new year. She had, she reproved herself, looked forward to this for so long, relishing the challenge that the responsibility would bring, privately grateful to be staying in catered halls. Now, however, she was wishing she could be on the other side of town, with Mel and Rose in their new, exciting student house (and she could, she knew, so easily have been part of it). By now they would be settling in and catching up and having a laugh. A glum wave of envy washed over her as she thought of it: a household full of Christians, sharing teaching and faith and fellowship together, like the early Church. Meanwhile, here she was, all alone atop the hill, setting out on a mission for which she felt spectacularly unprepared. The sense of *déjà vu* was oppressive; she felt as if she were starting all over again, as if she had learned nothing, changed nothing. She had thought, a year ago, that she would find freedom in Stancester, but she was as constrained as ever by her own fears and scruples, and the secrets she tried to keep even from herself.

The smallest box was the one marked *sponge bag and wash stuff*. She dumped it in the basin and saw her own face flash through the mirror as she straightened up: a curl of sun-streaked brown hair, brown eyes, sharp nose, strained mouth. She could, she supposed, text Rose and see whether they would be up for a drink after dinner. No. Freshers really would be turning up by then, and it was her duty to be there to welcome them. Well, then: perhaps she could go out for a walk, just as far as the off-licence on the corner of Dorchester Road, to get some air and buy some Fresher-welcoming biscuits...

'No,' she told herself sternly. 'Not until you've unpacked.' She sighed and turned to the boxes. Winter clothes; this semester's books; a month's worth of Bible notes: unpacking seemed to take forever, and by the time she had finished it was already dinner time. She pulled on her official Hall Officer hoodie and trudged down to the dining room, where fifteen or twenty Freshers were already seated. It was subdued compared to what would follow when Richmond Hall was up to its full complement of residents, but after a summer spent with her uncommunicative family the clatter of plates and cutlery and the excited bellow of conversation were deafening.

She accompanied a gaggle of Freshers to the Curzon Arms afterwards, but failed to recruit anyone to the hall group.

Still, tomorrow was another day, and God's mercies are new every morning. The Freshers' Week Guide reported that, should any Freshers wish to attend church, representatives of the various congregations would be waiting outside the Union to show them the way, and Lydia had volunteered on behalf of St Mark's.

The air was crisp, the grass lush and dewy as she walked down after breakfast. A representative cluster had already gathered. She recognised James (there on behalf of the Baptist church, she supposed), Rory (Centrepoint Church) and Ellie (St Mark's). The Catholics had printed R.C.: CHAPLAINCY and R.C.: SACRED HEART out on pieces of sturdy cardboard and were holding them up like taxi drivers at an airport. Two other students were squabbling over a pad of ruled A4 paper and a marker pen; she did not know either the tall, skinny, black Anglican *(UNIVERSITY CHAPEL AND ASK ME ABOUT ALL SAINTS)* or the short dark-haired Methodist *(WARDLE STREET)* with him. She smiled at them warily and went to join Rory and Ellie.

'Hey, Lydia,' Rory said. 'How's things?'

Lydia looked to see what cheesy message was on today's T-shirt. *I follow a man who is tougher than nails.* They always looked slightly incongruous on him: he was a slight, intense-looking man, with close-set eyes, bushy dark eyebrows and a long nose. 'Good, thanks,' she said. 'Settling back into halls. You?'

'Yeah, it's good. I'm out on Balton Street with these guys this year.' He nodded at Ellie.

'With Mel and Rose,' Lydia said. 'I know.'

'Yes, and Jake, too, of course,' Ellie said reverently, lest anyone forget that she lived with the President of the Christian Fellowship.

'Of course. How was your summer?' Lydia asked her.

Ellie beamed; she pushed her sunglasses up her forehead, where they tangled in her hair. 'Yeah, it was great! I went to Rwanda with this group from my home church.'

Lydia nodded. 'Oh, yes, I remember you talking about that before the holidays. How did it go?'

Ellie laid a confiding hand on Lydia's arm. 'Really, really well. We did ministry after this football match – this guy Dave, he's one of the pastors at my church, preached about a football boot – but it was *relevant* – and they were all following us around, because we were *white*, but that was fine – and about forty people came to Jesus.'

'Wow,' Lydia said, dutifully. She almost thought she saw the Anglican rep rolling his eyes at his Methodist friend. (Had Ellie offended him?) She glanced away, fast.

'But what about *you*?' Ellie asked. 'How are you feeling about being a hall officer?'

'I don't know...' A proper Christian would of course have answered, 'excited', and 'nervous'. These were acceptable responses, expected of a Christian student who had been appointed by the Christian Fellowship and deemed worthy of the privilege of living in university accommodation for the duration of her academic career to provide Christian support and Christian teaching to Christian Freshers.

'Mm?' An expectant smile flickered across Ellie's face.

'Oh. Excited. Nervous.' Feeling guilty, she fell silent. The eight of them stood for some minutes in the cool sunshine before Freshers appeared. Some sorted themselves into the Catholic group. Two of them were asking ASK ME ABOUT ALL SAINTS about St Mark's. 'These ladies, I think,' he said, waving at Lydia and Ellie.

Ellie nodded frostily to him. 'Thank you, Peter,' she said, and then, to the new pair, 'Hello – I'm Ellie Ford, I'm a third-year Theology student. This is Lydia Hawkins, she does English and she's hall officer for Richmond. What are your names?'

'Louise,' said one.

'Ben,' said the other.

'Great to meet you both. Have you heard about the Christian Fellowship here at Stancester?' (Ellie was so gifted in this welcoming ministry, Lydia thought. She was so confident, so friendly.) 'We meet at the Venue, which is the big meeting room in the Students' Union building, every Monday night.'

'No,' Louise said, 'but I have now. My minister said I should look out for the Christian Union – I guess this is the equivalent?'

'Tomayto, tomahto,' Lydia said, and felt stupid. She was distracted by the arrival of a gaggle from Richmond. She resolved to talk to them later about joining the hall group. One of them, Simon, had sought her out over breakfast. Two others she recognised. (One girl headed straight for the Chapel guy; well, she supposed, that was allowed, even if the Chapel lot were a bit weird.)

Lydia looked at her watch. Quarter to ten. 'Had we better move off?' she asked Ellie.

'I suppose we should. We've got further to go than this lot. Right, everyone!' she called. 'Let's go! I'm afraid you've got a long walk, but there's a great church at the end of it!'

Lydia followed Ellie and their trio of Freshers off campus, down the hill, and into the city. The houses in the student quarter were sleepy but mostly inhabited. The church bells were ringing in St Andrew's peculiar octagonal tower. Behind her, the tall, elegant finger of the Sciences Block was flashing insolently white. The morning sun was turning the cathedral to warm honey, and glinting off the swift, silent river.

All the way to church she pointed out the places that it might be useful for the new students to know. The off-licence on Dorchester Road. The Curzon Arms, which they would refer to as 'Curzon's' soon enough whether or not they were the type to spend any time in there. Southview, the good shopping street, and Broadway, the rubbish shopping street. The only really safe spot to cross Western Road, if you worried about that. All the other churches that they could have chosen to go to (but St Mark's really was the best choice).

And there it was. Certainly not the oldest church in Stancester, definitely not the easiest to get to from campus, and hardly the most beautiful, but *her* church, and the soundest. Chris was standing at the door wearing his loudest shirt and his widest smile, ready to welcome the new intake. Ellie led the new crowd in and showed them to the reserved seats; Lydia followed with an undeniable sense of pride, and, satisfied at last, sat down for the few minutes before the band started up.

Dear Lord Jesus, she prayed, *please help me to get a hall group together. And please change me. You can change me. You know what I struggle with. Please show me the way to be.*

Chapter 2

Like all Stancester's catered halls, Richmond holds monthly formal dinners. These 'formals' offer an opportunity to socialise with the people you live with, and an excuse to dress up a bit! A £20 supplement is charged to cover wine, upgrade to the 'deluxe' menu for the evening, and the entertainment – we're sure you'll agree it's worth it! For more information, you can talk to your Hall President.

Welcome to the University of Stancester (Richmond Hall edition)

Lydia woke the morning after the first formal dinner of term with an undeserved headache and an hour to prepare for her first hall group meeting.

An hour. She could do it in an hour. *Wide Sargasso Sea* would have to wait until afterwards. Guiltily conscious of how much time she could have spent preparing for both the first hall group meeting of term and for Monday's seminar, and how little she now had left to do either, Lydia drew the 'Week 1' sheet from the glossy folder and groaned.

Matthew 5:48. *Be perfect, therefore, as your heavenly Father is perfect.*

Well, she had to say this for God: He had a sense of humour. She was not feeling remotely perfect today.

Chewing the end of her pencil, Lydia tried to recall the 'Perfection?' talk from way back in first year. Was it the Freshers' Week talk, even? No, it must have been a few weeks into term, because she had already started worrying about literary criticism; had already become scared of looking too closely at a text; had already felt, uncomfortably close, the potential of the Bible to dissolve into meaningless marks and trickle away before her eyes, and for her faith to go with it. She remembered the terrifying sense of freedom, too: the heady consciousness that she could do anything she wanted now, and her parents and her church need never know about it.

Anything she wanted.

Her cheeks were hot. Had she really been thinking about *that* so specifically, back then? She would not have known where to start. No. God had protected her from that, kept her from temptation. She had considered skipping the talk. Perfection? The thought had seemed a challenge too great to bear at that moment; she had feared she would buckle under its impossible demands. She had gone, though, unable to justify the omission to herself, and it had not been nearly as bad as she had expected. The speaker had even opened by saying, 'None of us are perfect.'

She remembered the relief crashing through her. Acknowledgement that it was difficult – *impossible* – to be perfect, that they were all struggling with the knowledge that they had done sinful things, hurt other people, grieved God; confirmation that everyone was tempted now and again; reassurance that what she had been taught by her church and her parents stood as solid as ever. Most of all, encouragement to be strong in the faith – because it was true, it was worthwhile, and whatever challenging new ideas they might be coming across in the course of their studies, they would meet nothing to compare with what they already knew, the ultimate truth of Jesus Christ.

Which, she thought now, was all very well, but some of us are less perfect than others. Could she cheat, and see how the officers for the other halls had handled it? She knew she was the last one to run this week's module. The others had been debriefing each other via email. It could not hurt to have a look... She switched her laptop on, and skimmed the rest of the sheet while it booted up.

The word 'perfect' implies something that doesn't change, something that has no need to change. How can we seek out perfection in a world that's changing dramatically? How can we find perfection in our own lives as we deal with massive changes?

Lydia turned her attention to her emails. She had meant only to look at the trail that ran between the hall officers, but an unfamiliar name snatched her attention, and she clicked, and read:

Christians Together at Stancester University
'Will you watch with me one hour?'

The night before he died, Jesus prayed that his followers might be one (John 17:21). We are a group of Christian students of all denominations looking to join our brothers and sisters in Christ, acknowledging our differences, and pray together for love, understanding and unity between all Christians.

We're looking to hold an ecumenical prayer event this autumn and would love all the Christian groups on campus to be involved. If you're interested, come along to the Chaplaincy Centre at 12.30pm next Wednesday for an initial meeting. All very welcome – all we ask is that you approach the project in a spirit of trust, generosity and inclusivity.

With very best wishes,

in Christ,

Peter Nathan

Vice-President and Ecumenical Representative

Anglican, Methodist and United Reformed Church Society, Stancester University

Ha, Lydia thought, and wondered how far *acknowledging our differences* went. Was any Christian on campus quite so different as she was? All the same, she felt an unwilling groundswell of hope rising through her distrust. Suddenly she wanted, quite desperately, to be part of it.

It was stupid. This was a circular email, sent by someone who would not recognise her if he saw her, to everyone whose email address was on the Fellowship website; and yet it reached into her loneliness like a friendly, reliable hand pulling her to safety.

But she *was* safe, she told herself angrily; she wasn't lonely; she was already part of an amazing organisation in the Christian Fellowship, and she had no right to be feeling like this. And yet there was something about this idea that promised a greater hope and a wider faith, and for the sake of her new group and for her imperfect self she wanted to make Fellowship a part of it.

The living room at Balton Street was cosy at the best of times, and felt very full today. Lydia and Rose occupied the hideous red leather sofa ('our landlady's choice,' Ellie said, 'and she evidently regretted it') with *Wide Sargasso Sea* and the associated notes spread between them. Rose was flushed pink with the warmth, her blonde hair dishevelled. Ellie sat cross-legged on the floor, emptying a box-file of Fellowship papers around herself. Jake sat in the armchair, Bible at his elbow. Mugs and plates dotted the shag-pile rug.

Jake finished reading the email and shook his head. 'I'm not sure that this is what God is leading us to do at this time.'

'But I thought it sounded great!' Lydia said, dismayed. 'Why do you say that?'

'It's just that... well, we have to be careful,' Jake said regretfully. 'We don't want to get involved with anything that's not promoting sound scriptural doctrine.' He said it with granite immovability, but spoiled the effect by glancing at Ellie for confirmation.

Lydia, greatly daring, ventured, 'But isn't it? I think this is exactly what God wants. I mean, this Peter guy is quoting Jesus here – praying that they "might be one". What could be wrong with that?'

'Have you met Peter Nathan?' Ellie asked, darkly. 'To speak to, I mean?'

'No.'

'Well, then.' Ellie beamed as if she had proved her point.

'But –'

'The thing is,' Jake said, trying his best to be very patient, 'that even though these other groups do call themselves "Christian", they don't necessarily recognise, or teach, Biblical Christianity. Think of Cathsoc, for example. The Catholic Church has all sorts of heresy mixed up in its teachings. It wouldn't be responsible of us to encourage our members to attend an event where they might be asked to pray to Mary.'

'I'm sure they wouldn't do that,' Lydia said, doubtfully. She was conscious that she walked on thin ice, and she could not quite work out where the cracks were. 'If I were organising something like this, I'd make sure not to include anything that would offend people.'

'It's not about *offending*,' Ellie admonished her gently. 'It's about Biblical truth. It's about authority. It's the really *important* stuff. We have to get it right – you particularly, in your position as hall officer.'

'In any case,' Rose put in, with a treacherous smile, 'it would have to go to Fellowship Exec. They've got the final say in anything like this. It's not for you and me to decide.'

'I suppose not,' Lydia said, irritated. There was no particular reason why Rose should take her side on this, but it stung, all the same.

Jake nodded. 'Look, Lydia,' he said. 'I will take it to the committee, because you're right, actually, it is a lovely idea, and it would be nice if we could get the other groups to work with us. I think, though, that the committee will agree, quite rightly, that we can only be involved in this so long as the other organisers are prepared to sign our Statement of Belief, to ensure that nothing unscriptural gets included. And I'll email this Peter guy to say so.'

'That seems reasonable,' Lydia said, and, feeling somehow cheated, drained her cold tea.

Chapter 3

2. The Bible is the true and infallible word of God, and the sole source of authority recognised by the Christian Church.

[...]

8. Jesus Christ is the Son of God:

a. whose sinless life gives Christians a pattern to follow;

b. whose innocent death upon the cross satisfied the wrath of the Father and redeems sinful humanity.

9. Without faith in Jesus Christ, there is no salvation.

Statement of Belief, Federation of Student Christian Societies

'Hello! On your way to Fellowship?'

Halfway up the steep tarmac path that led to the Students' Union building, Lydia turned to see who had hailed her: Will Seton, a fellow second-year, one of the floppy-hair brigade and pleasant enough in a public-school kind of way. They were a familiar sight at Stancester, which did well out of its reputation as a university for Oxbridge rejects. She was gratified that he had recognised her. 'Hi! Yes, I am – you too?'

He smiled brilliantly. 'That's right. How's it going – Laura, is it?'

'Lydia.'

'Oh, well, that's nearly the same thing.'

She did not really feel that it was, but she said, 'Yes. Have you had a good day?'

He dismissed it with a wave. 'Same old, same old. Law and disorder. How's – what do you do, again?'

'English. Yes, it's going OK. Lots of reading. But I expect you have lots, too.'

'Oh, yeah, a fair amount, yeah.' He lowered his voice. 'Tell me – is it true what they say about the English course here?'

She followed him up the steps. 'What's that?'

His eyes were full of concern. 'That it's, like, really *challenging* for Christian students, because it's deliberately set up to undermine people's faith – like, I've heard you study the Bible and stuff? Here – let me.' He strode ahead and opened the door for her. 'I mean, as if it were just a *book*?'

'Thank you. There's a certain amount of truth in that,' Lydia said carefully. 'We did look at Genesis quite early on in the first term. They like to throw you in at the deep end – using the King James Version and everything; it's quite difficult language.'

'So stupid,' Will said. 'Are they *trying* to, like, put people off? I bet they are.'

'It is difficult,' she admitted. 'I wouldn't object to studying it – if you think about it, it's an opportunity for so many people to hear the Word – but you're also looking at all sorts of different types of theory at the same time. Some of that's really post-modern stuff that wants you to ignore all the author's intentions, and some of it's the other end of the scale and wants everything put in its exact historical context. And you put the Bible alongside all of that, and you end up thinking that either it has no relevance for anyone born less than two thousand years ago, or that none of it actually means anything at all. Or else it's all Freudian.' She grimaced.

'But you're still here.' He beamed, and made a gesture that encompassed the pair of them, the claustrophobic black-painted walls of the Students' Union Venue, and possibly the entire university. 'It obviously didn't get through to you!'

Lydia supposed that was meant to be a compliment. 'Shall we go in?' she said. 'You're welcome to sit with me and my Freshers.'

He waved her through the double doors, but as soon as they were inside he excused himself and was immediately swallowed up in the throng of excited Christians. Lydia caught sight of him talking to Rory a few minutes later. She was faintly relieved; she did not feel that her embryo hall group would be much edified by listening to the pair of them debate the English Literature syllabus. Not that there was any time for that: the band was already hurling itself into *Over All The Earth*. Lydia found four empty chairs and waved at Simon, Zoe and Fiona until they saw and came to join her.

She listened to the announcements with more interest than usual, but there was no mention of the joint prayer event.

She went round to Balton Street the next day, telling herself that she needed to return Rose's *Introduction to 1 Corinthians*. What she actually wanted was to see if Jake had received a reply; it was unlikely that she would hear if she made no effort to find out. (Jake must be very busy, having to keep on top of all the Fellowship stuff as well as his course.) She accepted with alacrity, therefore, when Rose said why didn't she stay and watch *Come Dine With Me*, and was pleased when Jake emerged, laptop in hand, to join them. Even better, he brought up the topic himself and absolved Lydia of worrying whether she was being inappropriately curious.

'I had a response back from that AngthMURC guy, Lyds,' he said, when Rose had gone to make them another pot of tea.

'Oh, right?' She tried not to sound too interested. 'What does he say?'

'Give me a second and I'll get the email up to show you. Not good news, I'm afraid.' He perched on the edge of the sofa.

'Oh.'

He twisted his mouth regretfully. 'I know – it's a real pity. Where was it? Ah, here we go. Have a look.'

Dear Jake,

Thank you for getting back to me. Georgia, Sophie and I are delighted that the Christian Fellowship would like to be involved in this ecumenical event. Like you, we are keen for all Christian students at Stancester to be able to work together to proclaim the Good News on campus.

It is for this reason that we must regretfully decline to accept the stipulation you propose. The organisers are unwilling to sign the Christian Fellowship's Statement of Belief, as it is our view that this would be likely to needlessly exclude fellow Christians such as our Quaker and Orthodox colleagues.

I do hope that you and your team will be able to reconsider this requirement – it would be absolutely fantastic to have Fellowship involved. Even if you feel that it is not possible for your group to have an official part in the proceedings, you and any other Fellowship members would of course be very welcome to participate on an unofficial basis, and to attend the event when it does come to pass.

We will be holding an initial planning meeting at 12.30 on Wednesday in the Chaplaincy Centre.

I trust that you will feel able to assist us with publicising it and further Christian mission in this city.

With grateful thanks, and in Christ,
Peter Nathan
Vice-President and Ecumenical Representative
Anglican, Methodist and United Reformed Church Society

'We can't, of course,' Jake said, shaking his head sadly.
'Can't what?'
'Publicise it.'
Lydia did not much care whether Fellowship publicised it or not; what she wanted was to be involved in the event itself. But she said, 'Why not?'

He smiled patiently. 'Because supporting it by publicising it is just the same as supporting it in any other way. People will get really confused if we say one thing and do another.'

'So you're saying that Fellowship shouldn't have any involvement at all?'

Jake opened his mouth, and then shut it again. 'Essentially, yes,' he said.

'I think that's a real pity,' Lydia said. She was not sure – dared not consider – why she was so disappointed.

'Well, of course, if you feel that God is leading you to do something else...' Jake said, in tones that suggested he thought it unlikely.

'I'm not sure what God's leading me to do,' Lydia said. 'I shall pray about it.'

Which was perfectly true; all the same, she could not help being rather pleased that there was nothing Jake could say to contradict it.

Chapter 4

The Chaplaincy at Stancester University is based on the ground floor of Markham Grange. Here you can find the Chaplaincy Office, Roman Catholic chapel, and the prayer and common rooms. (The Anglican chapel is down the hill.) The full-time Chaplain is Rev. Tanya Darcy (Church of England). The rest of the Chaplaincy Team is made up of ministers from other denominations who are based at churches across the city – you can find more information here.

For more information about the Chaplaincy please contact Tanya (t.darcy@stan.ac.uk) or Nat Plunkett, Chaplaincy Assistant (chaplaincy@stan.ac.uk) by email.

www.stan.ac.uk/chaplaincy

It took Lydia some time to find the Chaplaincy Centre. She knew it was in Markham Grange with the university's administrative functions, but the perfect Enlightenment symmetry meant that every corridor looked the same. She missed the sign to the Chaplain's Office and Roman Catholic Chapel, and ended up somewhere in the Academic Registry before a woman in a dog-collar pointed her in the right direction.

Lydia knew that Ellie disapproved of the Chaplain, but could not remember why. She considered the matter as she retraced her steps. Rory objected to the Chaplain's being a woman – not, he was always keen to stress, on any personal account, but just because it was not very inclusive to have a woman in the role when some people sincerely believed that women shouldn't teach or be in a position of authority, and it meant that those people would miss out... Lydia knew that she herself was fortunate that nobody in her hall group had voiced any concerns about being taught by a woman. Fellowship would have been within their rights to replace her on those grounds alone. Not to mention the things they didn't know about her...

At any rate, she thought, she could not fault the Chaplain's directional skills. It was, as promised, simply a case of finding the Catholic Chapel; the rest was across the corridor.

A quiet hum of conversation emanated from the common room. It was only twenty past twelve, so, not examining her motives too closely, Lydia slipped into the Catholic chapel, and found it empty. She was surprised how beautiful it was, a snug jewel-box of a space, even if the gilt and stained glass were not precisely to her taste. She breathed deeply, almost enjoying the lingering hint of incense in the air, shutting her eyes to avoid seeing the crucifix above the altar or the icon of Mary on the left hand wall. 'God is everywhere,' she reminded herself. He couldn't be less here than He was outside, and so there was no reason to feel guilty about the way that the peace of the room calmed her. It was ridiculous that she needed calming in the first place. These were only students, after all: how scary could they be? And what could – for instance – Jake do to her for going?

She prayed: *please God, show me if I'm doing the right thing*; opened her eyes, nodded politely and walked out.

In the common room she found a scene of comfortable mayhem. Two girls were attempting to repair a collapsed bookshelf on the far wall. In the corner to her right, a little knot of people was debating the opposing merits of two different hymnbooks. In an armchair under the window she was relieved to recognise Georgia, a third-year Music student who seemed to have taken it upon herself to adopt all her department's Freshers. These included Lydia's next-door neighbour in Richmond, Gabe Hammond. Now Lydia remembered that Georgia had been waiting outside the Union in Freshers' Week as well: a short, plump girl with glossy dark hair, who, though she was sitting still, conveyed the impression that she had energy coiled inside her, as if someone only needed to give her a gentle push to send her clattering around in circles.

Georgia was talking to a blond man propped on the windowsill. Her friend, the black Anglican whom Lydia had not quite met in Freshers' Week, was sprawled over two beanbags doing the crossword on the back of some newspaper. An older woman, who could either have been a mature student or a member of staff, was testing a jar of ancient felt-tip pens in the margins of another newspaper. On her left, the Chaplaincy Assistant, identified as such by the white lettering on his navy-blue hoodie, was tending to the kettle.

'Lydia!' Georgia exclaimed. 'Hello! I didn't realise you would be here.'

The newspaper was cast aside. 'Ah, *you're* Lydia-from-Fellowship. I'm Peter. You emailed me...?'

'I did,' Lydia admitted.

Peter wriggled up into a sitting position. 'Excellent. Very nice to have you here.'

'Have a seat,' one of the bookshelf girls suggested.

'Thank you.' Lydia sat down on the edge of a low stool and waited to see what would happen next.

Georgia said, 'Do you know anyone else here?'

Lydia shook her head. 'Only you.'

'OK. Starting from the door, then.' Georgia drew a theatrical breath. 'Stuart Ashwin, Bella Shepherd. Stuart is a Fresher, and Bella is from Kingdom Come! Me. You. On the windowsill, Tim Benton, grand old man of Cathsoc, he's been here through a Bachelors, a Masters, and he's now writing up his PhD.'

Tim smiled at her; on Georgia's evidence he must have been at least twenty-five, but looked younger, a plump man with twinkly eyes, who put Lydia in mind of a friendly potato. 'Good to meet you. I'm really glad we've got someone from Fellowship.'

Georgia took another deep breath and continued. 'Peter on the floor, the AngthMURC Vice-Pres – but you know that, if you've been emailing. That's Cathsoc, fighting that bookshelf and the laws of gravity. Kasia Sedzimir on the left, she's the Vice-President, and Sophie Rawlings is the President. Anna Blackie, sorting out the stationery there, is the AngthMURC treasurer. She calls herself an immature student. Nat is the Chaplaincy Assistant; he's actually paid to be here. Making the tea counts as pastoral support, or so I'm told. We're also expecting some more of Cathsoc, apparently, Kingdom Come!, and some Quakers. You won't remember any names. Don't worry about it.'

'Becky can't come,' Peter said; 'she's in Birmingham.'

'What does she want to go there for?' Anna asked. 'Well, apart from the boyfriend and everything?'

'Giving the motorbike some exercise,' said Georgia.

The Cathsoc pair gave up on the bookshelf, and resorted to stacking the books on the floor. Anna said, 'Should we start?'

'Give it another five minutes,' Georgia said, though it was already twenty-five to one.

Peter read out, '*Ersatz mystic menace due. Oi, noisy spuds!* It's obviously an anagram...'

'Pseudo Dionysius,' Kasia said.

'Of course. Fake Dennis. Durrr.' Peter started to write it in. 'How do you spell Dionysius?'

Kasia spelt it, very fast. Four or five more people piled through the door. Encouraged, Georgia stood up, took a step towards the middle of the room, tripped over a stool, and said, 'Shit! Sorry! That wasn't a good start... Er... welcome, everybody, to this planning meeting thing!

'So, for those who don't know me, I'm Georgia, I'm the President of the Anglican, Methodist and United Reformed Church Society, and I thought it was a good idea to revive the prayer vigil that used to happen on campus a few years ago.'

She glanced at the scrap of paper in her hand. 'All the Christian societies on campus do fantastic work, we know that, and it's amazing to see God's grace flowing among us; but we very rarely work together. AngthMURC and Cathsoc have fun together – don't worry, we will give you a chance to get us back for your drubbing at bowling last week – but we don't pray together, and that is very sad.

'I've spoken to Tanya – the Anglican chaplain – and she can wangle us into being allowed to stay here all night. She will entrust us with the secret code that opens the back door, and we can use these rooms, the kitchen and the chapel.'

She cleared her throat, and continued: 'In terms of timing, we thought that it might be appropriate to do this the weekend of Remembrance Sunday. It's the Cathsoc retreat the weekend after, chapel choir are doing the Fauré Requiem the weekend before, the weekend before *that* is the Fellowship Away Day and there's no way they'd be back from Weston-super-Mare in time. Working backwards brings us to this weekend coming. Any later, it starts getting mixed up with Advent and Christmas.' Georgia glanced around the room, daring anyone to disagree with her. When no one did, she continued, 'Good. Now, does anyone have any good ideas for a theme?'

'Unity,' Bella said. 'Reconciliation.'

'Peace,' said Peter, 'given the date.'

'Ooh, controversial. Have we got any Quakers here yet?' It seemed to be a rhetorical question; at least, nobody admitted to being a Quaker.

'Faith?' Kasia suggested. 'Wisdom?'

Sophie said, 'I don't think we want to be doing anything too intellectual. Not if we're staying up all night to do it.'

Georgia nodded. 'It is about prayer, after all. Not theology.'

'It would be nice,' Stuart said, 'to celebrate all our different traditions, if we can manage that without mortally offending anyone.'

Lydia remembered what Jake had said about Catholic prayer. It looked as though she had been right: nobody was setting out to upset or exclude anybody else. Was Jake being a little paranoid about this? She supposed he had to be, in his position, but it was a pity.

'Excellent,' Georgia said. 'So far we have: unity, reconciliation, peace, wisdom, prayer.'

Anna quoted, 'Love, joy, peace, patience, kindness, gentleness...'

'Good one!' Sophie exclaimed. 'We could do a Fruit of the Spirit per hour!'

Georgia scribbled a timetable on yellow sugar paper and outlined the structure of the event. 'Twelve hours, eight p.m. to eight a.m., broken up roughly into one-hour slots. We need volunteers for each of the slots. You don't have to be a super confident teacher or anything, you'd just need to lead it.'

Lydia wondered how on earth one would lead something – complete strangers, at that – *without* being a confident teacher. She was only just beginning to feel that she had something to offer her hall group.

Georgia nudged her. 'You're not up for leading one?'

Lydia jumped. 'Maybe next time,' she said. 'I really only came along to see if I could be useful, and it looks like everything's covered.' She pointed to the timetable, which was filling up fast with names and ideas. Even 'Patience', in the four a.m. slot, had been claimed – by Kingdom Come!, she thought, though she was finding it difficult to match names to faces to affiliations.

'Well,' Georgia said, 'nobody seems to have volunteered to feed anyone.'

Lydia was grateful. 'I can do that. I may be one of only eight second-years still living in catered halls, but I haven't completely forgotten how to cook.'

'That's the spirit! Martha this year, Mary next!' Georgia took a pen from someone who looked as if they had almost finished with it, and wrote LYDIA – CATERING at the top of the sheet.

Peter glanced up at her. 'Oh, excellent. That's two. At least, Colette said she'd rather cook than have to speak to large groups of strangers, so I think she counts as a volunteer.'

'Colette?' Lydia asked, bewildered.

'Colette Russell. Chemistry. My housemate. Methodist. AngthMURC secretary,' Peter explained. 'Terrifyingly clever. You'll love her –' And stopped, as if it had suddenly occurred to him that the feeling might not be mutual.

Nat-the-Chaplaincy-Assistant said, 'I'll do breakfast. That means that if you two want to stay up all night – which I have no intention of doing myself – you won't then burn the place down in the morning. Fatigue does strange things.'

'Brilliant,' Georgia said, and added COLETTE AND NAT to the timetable. 'OK, then!' she screamed. 'It's one o'clock and I promised we'd finish! Everyone know what they're doing?'

A chorus of 'Yes!' 'Sort of!' 'I will do!' Lydia seemed to be the only one who was still confused. To her relief Peter stopped her as she was standing up to go. 'I need to put you in touch with Colette,' he said, 'so you can plan this epic task, you poor innocents.'

'I'm sure it won't be as bad as all that,' she said.

'Well, maybe,' he agreed equably. 'Do you mind if I give her your number?'

'No, of course.' She wrote it down for him. 'Where do you guys live?'

'Alma Road, just off York Street, except we're at the end nearest the railway bridge.'

'Alma Road,' she said. 'That rings a bell. I'm sure I know someone else who lives there.'

'Quite likely. It's very studenty.'

She frowned. Then she remembered. 'Oh, yes. You don't live with Posh Will, do you?'

'Well,' Peter said, 'we live with *a* Will. And he's certainly posh. And he does go to Fellowship. He could be your Posh Will.'

'Random!' She smiled. Her last lingering doubts dissolved – after all, if Will was happy to hang around with these people, it must surely be all right for her to do the same, whatever Ellie or Jake might insinuate about them. And, as today had made abundantly clear, they *were* Christians.

Chapter 5

The main task of the Vice-President is to keep the President sane. Georgia likes dark chocolate. Other Presidents may vary.

Being Ecumenical Rep ought to be easy. AngthMURC is, by its very nature, ecumenical; not only do we have Anglicans, Methodists and the URC, we have all sorts of rag tag and bobtail who identify as Christian but don't feel they fit in with any of the other societies.

Most of the time, being Ecumenical Rep *is* easy. Campus Quakers are lovely, Kingdom Come! will work with anybody on justice issues, and Cathsoc are fine so long as you're sensible about the question of receiving mass. If you look at the membership lists, you'll find that most AngthMURC regulars also belong to Cathsoc (and vice versa) because bumping up the numbers is in our mutual interest. Where things get difficult is the Christian Fellowship.

AngthMURC, as a body, does not have a problem with Fellowship. As individuals, we may well have problems around complementarity, Biblical literalism, the way they market themselves as the only Christian society on campus, and verse 2 of *In Christ Alone*, but as AngthMURC we would be happy to work with them. They won't work with us. Or, rather, they won't work with anyone who won't sign their Statement of Belief – which they like to present as a summary of basic facts that all Christians can agree on, but which is actually nothing of the sort – and that usually means 'at least half of the AngthMURC committee'.

How to run AngthMURC, Peter Nathan

Alma Road was a terrace of Victorian three-storey redbrick houses, half way between campus and the city centre. As Peter had said, it was a quarter largely inhabited by students; the atmosphere was pleasantly scruffy. Lydia checked her phone, and checked it again, as if the text message might have magically changed in the last fifteen seconds. No: still number 27, still the house on the end with the red door. The door was indeed, she saw as she got closer, properly scarlet, a real fire station colour. A collection of herbs straggled in faded plastic pots in the front garden. Posters in the front window exhorted her to Save The Riverside Centre and use People Power Against Trident.

Lydia paused a moment on the path, glancing in the glass to check her reflection. She looked reasonably tidy, she thought, tucking a strand of hair back behind her ear – then the net curtain swished back, and Peter's face appeared, grinning, hardly clearer than her own – which, as the curtain drew further across the window, became superimposed on another – a girl – woman – an oval face – a wary smile. That must be Colette.

Peter had disappeared. The front door opened almost immediately.

'Hi, Lydia, lovely to see you again, come in, come in, this is Colette; Colette, this is Lydia, your new partner in crime, oh, drat, I must get the albs out of the washing machine, excuse me...' He strode away towards the back of the house.

Lydia, coming from the autumnal brightness of the street, could see at first only that Colette was taller than she had thought, almost as tall as Peter. Blinking, she made out grey eyes, fine wavy brown hair, and again that reserved smile – which broadened slightly when Lydia said, 'Hello. Albs?'

'White robes. Peter is in charge of all the chapel laundry,' Colette said. 'And hi. Come upstairs. Would you like a cup of tea or anything?'

'That would be lovely.' Lydia followed her past a couple of obvious bedrooms, up narrow stairs and into a wide, airy kitchen.

'I don't know who thought it would be a good idea to put the kitchen on the first floor,' Colette chattered over her shoulder as she filled the kettle. 'I mean, it would stop the people on the ground floor getting burned to death if someone set the oven on fire, but it's a real nuisance with getting shopping upstairs, and the bins downstairs, and everything.'

'Odd,' Lydia agreed politely.

34

'So,' Colette continued in the same tone, 'it would be all very well for Becky – I don't think you've met her, she's my housemate; she's a Quaker and is also hoping to be involved in this prayer event – or Peter, and Georgia might just get out – but the rest of us would be stuffed. In this hypothetical fire, I mean. Was it tea? Or coffee? We'd have to hope the rest of us were in the sitting room.'

'Tea, thanks. As it comes. No sugar.'

'No problem.' She mashed the teabags against the insides of their mugs, then flipped them accurately at the bin. 'Rats, that's going to be too strong.'

'Looks fine to me,' Lydia said. It did.

Colette smiled ruefully. 'I drink it really weak. Oh, well. I'll add a bit more sugar, that'll sort it. Here's yours. Help yourself to milk. I've got all my AngthMURC stuff upstairs – sorry, another climb, I know...'

Colette's room looked out over the back garden, down towards the railway and across the town. The terraces ran in neat russet lines down the hill; on the other side of the river, the beech trees in the park were vivid amber, and the yellow-grey stone of the old town glowed gold in the October light.

'Wow,' Lydia said, 'you get a lovely view of the cathedral from here.'

'I know; I'm very lucky. It's my reward for having the smallest bedroom.'

The window was open, a cool breeze stirring the yellow curtains. Down in the garden they could hear Peter bellowing, '*Fa-ac me-e te-e-cu-um plangere!*' as he put his laundry up on the clothesline.

'Don't mind him,' Colette said. 'It turns out to be a lot less obscene than it sounds when you realise it's actually in Latin. These High Church types, eh? Though I think that's actually something they were doing in Choral Soc, rather than a Chapel thing. Dvořák, or someone like that. He doesn't do so much singing in Chapel – too busy organising everything else. Peter, I mean, not Dvořák.'

Lydia was looking at Colette's photographs, some of which lined the back of her desk like sentries, and some of which were blu-tacked to the wardrobe. 'Sorry,' she said, when she saw Colette had noticed. 'I love looking at people's photos. Trying to work out who everyone is...'

Colette took two steps from the window to the desk to join her. 'That's my mum and dad – me and my best friends from school – my cousin – my church youth group – family picnic on the Malverns – whole family group at my brother Chris' wedding – my ex-girlfriend – that one's Hannah, my sister-in-law, with Olivia – Great-Aunt Nico – the people I lived with last year (that's Becky on the far left, in fact) – and on the end is my other brother Richie, with our dog Badger.'

Lydia's gaze had snagged on the picture of Colette's ex-girlfriend – a bold-eyed, dark-haired girl, radiating confidence even through the murky, overexposed snapshot. 'Oh. I didn't realise you were –'

'Bisexual, actually.' Colette's eyes narrowed, but she left it at that.

Lydia said, 'You've kept her photo?'

Colette looked minutely less defensive. 'Yes,' she said. 'I don't believe in pretending that things didn't happen – and I don't regret any of it. We parted on good terms; we only split up because we were going to different universities.'

Lydia wanted desperately to ask how Colette reconciled her faith with that, but she did not quite have the nerve either to ask the question or to hear the answer. Somewhere at the edge of her vision a whole new world was shimmering, trying to force itself into being. She could not let it. She could not risk thinking that it was possible to choose both.

She turned away from the photographs and said, as lightly as she could, 'So, how did you get lumbered with the catering for this?'

'Oh,' Colette grinned, 'that's what you get if you don't show up to the planning meeting. I said I'd do food if not enough people volunteered.'

'They didn't, and so you're stuck with me,' Lydia said, as if it were a joke. 'Well, the chaplaincy assistant guy – Nat, isn't it? – said he'd cook breakfast, but I think he's counting on most people not making it through the night.'

Colette nodded. 'That's excellent news. He makes a good bacon sandwich.'

'That's probably the sort of level we want to aim at,' Lydia mused. 'What kind of facilities do we have?'

'You'll have to fill me in on anything I missed at the meeting,' Colette warned. 'Oh, sorry, have a seat, if we're talking business. I assume we *are* using the Chaplaincy Centre? And that sorting out access to Markham Grange in the middle of the night isn't our problem?' She arranged herself primly at the end of the bed.

Lydia sat down gingerly on the rickety computer chair, turning it so that she was facing Colette, and away from the photographs. 'Correct on both counts.'

'Good – that means we've got a stove to play with. Hob, oven – also microwave and kettle.'

Lydia was relieved. 'So it doesn't have to be seventeen sorts of salad, and too much quiche.'

Unexpectedly, Colette looked straight at her and laughed. 'You've been doing Christian stuff too long, haven't you?'

Lydia said with calculated irreverence, 'And now these three remain: bread, quiche and salad, but the greatest of these is salad.'

'No, no, the greatest is quiche!'

With relief, Lydia felt the tension dissipate. Now, she thought, they could get on with the important work of sharing God's love – even if it did come in the form of quiche. 'You know,' she said, 'I'm tempted to do baked potatoes. Nuke them, crisp the skins in the oven, and let people help themselves to toppings.'

'I like the sound of that,' Colette said. 'I was worrying about allergies. Vegetarians, vegans, coeliacs, diabetics, soy intolerances... I've heard some horror stories, believe me. Living with a Quaker, you hear about some very weird food requirements. It's the whole ecology thing. But I've never heard of anyone not being able to eat potato.'

'Oh, I see. Yes.' It was not something that Lydia had really thought about.

'Let's think,' Colette said. 'Tuna. Cheese. We can heat some baked beans on the hob. Chilli? We could make that beforehand and warm it up. I don't suppose you have a decent kitchen in halls?'

'Unfortunately not – as we're catered, they give us a kitchenette with a mini-fridge and a microwave and that's it.'

Colette nodded. 'Not to worry. We have a perfectly good kitchen here; it'll just be a pain carting all the stuff up the hill.'

'I'm happy to come down and help,' Lydia said, eager to please.

'Great. Though Georgia may be able to twist Olly's arm and get him to drive me.'

The door slammed shut, caught in a sudden draught from the open window. Someone yelled from downstairs, '*Colette!*'

She screamed back, '*What?*' Then, turning back to Lydia, said, 'Sorry.'

'That's all right,' Lydia said.

Thumping footsteps followed the voice up the stairs, finishing with a crash on the top landing. 'Are you decent?' the voice asked, rather more quietly. At close range, it manifested a northern accent.

'Am I decent! What a question!' Colette rolled her eyes in what Lydia hoped was not a flirtatious manner. She opened the door. 'I've got company. But come in! This is Becky,' she explained to Lydia. 'Becky, this is Lydia.'

'Nice to meet you.' Becky nodded at her, and smiled. Somehow, Lydia had expected her to be taller; she was, at a guess, five foot three, with a fizzing shock of red hair that reclaimed six inches. She wore a pair of leather motorcycle breeches held up with braces over a bright green T-shirt that read *Justice and Solidarity*.

'Nice to meet you too. Becky-the-Quaker?'

'That's me. Sorry about the general sweatiness. I didn't realise Colette had anyone interesting here.' Becky looked very inquisitive. Lydia tried not to notice.

'She doesn't care whether or not I mind her being sweaty,' Colette observed. She told Becky, 'Lydia's been press-ganged into doing food for this ecumenical prayer thingy. I think it was Georgia.'

'Ah, I see,' Becky said. She looked at Lydia with a different interest. 'We hadn't met, had we? You're not Quaker or Kingdom Come! or AngthMURC. So you must be either Cathsoc or Christian Fellowship.'

'Fellowship,' Lydia admitted.

'Aha, yes. Good to have you involved.' She chuckled. 'She says. I haven't actually managed to get involved myself, yet.'

'You will,' Colette said, darkly. 'Did you just get in? I didn't hear the bike.'

'Five minutes ago, maybe? You were obviously distracted. *Anyway,*' she said, 'since you do have actual polite company here, I'll go and have a shower and come back.' She disappeared again, leaving Lydia feeling faintly exhausted.

'So,' Colette said, 'the food...'

They had managed to put together a convincing meal plan by the time Becky came back, this time in jeans and a different T-shirt, and with wet hair. 'Hello again,' she said. 'I saw Peter. Apparently I'm on Peace, with the rest of the Friends. That was predictable.'

'Ah, well,' Colette said. 'It's easy for you: all you have to do is make everyone sit in silence for an hour. Lydia and I are feeding the five thousand.'

'Yeah, yeah,' Becky said, without heat. 'Anyway – Lydia, lovely to meet you. Can I interest you in a three hour road-crossing protest next Saturday?'

'Rebecca Mary,' Colette groaned. 'Really?'

'What's all this?' Lydia asked, intrigued.

Becky looked pleasantly surprised by her interest. 'Do you know All Saints Primary, just off Western Road? Just on the left after the road to the sports park?'

Lydia frowned, trying to visualise the walk into town; she summoned a memory of bright-painted railings and hopscotch grids. 'Ah, yes.'

Becky sat down cross-legged on the bed next to Colette. 'We're campaigning to get a proper pelican crossing put in. It's ridiculous that there isn't one already, and the poor kids who live on the town side of Western Road are risking life and limb.'

'So what are you going to do?'

Becky grinned. 'We cross the road.'

'*You cross the road*?' Lydia wondered if she was missing something.

'We cross the road *a lot*. Like, a chain of sixty, a hundred, people or more, crossing the road continuously.'

'The idea,' Colette explained, 'is to hold up everybody coming into town to do their shopping on Saturday, cause a massive tailback, and thereby generate sympathy for the campaign. Or something. I'm going, apparently, and praying I don't get arrested.'

'Don't stress – it's perfectly legal,' Becky said. 'I checked with Will. He's not coming – he'll be at the Fellowship Away Weekend – but he is ninety nine per cent sure that at the worst it'd be breach of the peace.'

'I like the idea,' Lydia said. 'But why aren't you doing it in November, after the Christmas lights have gone up and you'll have a much bigger crop of shoppers to annoy?'

Becky and Colette looked at each other, impressed.

'Unfortunately,' Becky said, 'it's been planned for weeks and I don't think it can be changed now. But I like your point. I like it very much indeed. Fancy joining us? Or are you going to be in Weston-super-Mare, too?'

'Not at a hundred and fifty quid I'm not,' Lydia said. 'I don't know. Maybe I'll come and wave the flag with you.'

Chapter 6

The harshest critic would struggle to fault the setting of Stancester cathedral. Built on the site of a Saxon minster, presiding over the crossing of two Roman roads, it dominates the north side of the city. Its honey-gold hamstone is echoed all around the old town, and, should one be fortunate enough to visit on a sunny afternoon, the overall effect is charming.

The buildings that compose the University of Stancester cluster around Markham Grange, a frigidly elegant Queen Anne mansion. Once upon a time, the Grange sat solitary on top of Markham Hill, looking across the river to the cathedral, aloof from the Roman road and its workaday traffic. Then the railway came to Stancester, the lines coming in from north and east and joining just outside the main station to run down towards Exeter. The city crept southwards, across the river, up the hill. In the fifties and sixties the university buildings billowed out around the Grange like a starched petticoat. A few formal lawns and venerable trees remain between the concrete blocks and the repurposed Victorian villas, and the campus is a pleasant place to walk or study.

Exploring Stancester, R. V. Foyall, 1988

The tailback stretched all the way up Markham Hill, a long string of red lights gleaming through the drizzle. Lydia risked a glance at each driver as she passed; their expressions ranged from the resigned to the furious. Looking at them, her law-abiding heart quivered. *Blessed are you*, she quoted to herself, *when men revile and persecute you for my sake.* Was this for Jesus' sake? The Bible did not have much to say on the subject of pedestrian crossings. Perhaps it would come under the general heading of *Let the little children come to me* – but then the idea behind getting a crossing installed was that the little children didn't go to Jesus quite so soon as all that. She giggled, guiltily amused, and pulled the hood of her waterproof further down over her face.

The noise hit her long before the protesters came into view. From a distance it was an indistinct rumble, but as she made her way downhill she could make out whistles and airhorns rising above a base of steady chanting. The words crystallised as she approached: *Speed greed! Kids' loss! Give us a safe place to cross!* Undeterred by the weather, the crowd was already four deep all the way across the road; no wonder the traffic was going nowhere. Most of the drivers had switched their engines off, but they kept up an indignant chorus on their horns, which, Lydia thought, rather added to the atmosphere.

Some of the marchers carried flags, cardboard replicas of traffic lights, or placards. *'Kill your speed!' 'Crossing now!' 'Keep our children safe!'* There was even a pantomime horse – or, rather, a pantomime zebra – and a giant pelican. Becky was there, looking simultaneously official and anarchic with newly-dyed blue hair and a hi-vis jacket. Peter and Colette, too, the pair of them made distinctive by their height.

Becky noticed her, and waved. This was it, then. She was committed; she would have to join in now. Lydia glanced around. A couple of bemused police officers hovered at the edges of the crowd. She swallowed. She had never been involved in any sort of civil disobedience before. What if she got arrested? Becky's probably right, she told herself. It's probably not really *illegal*. There's no law against crossing the road.

The noise enveloped her, and as soon as she stepped into the swarm she felt better. She was no longer the timid girl on the pavement; she was part of a cause, a movement. She saw, now that she was absorbed into it, that the apparently random motion of the crowd had in fact been choreographed. She had thought that people were simply walking back and forth across the road, but it was more complex than that: they formed a long snake, looping around and around in four zig-zagging lines and then threading around the top to get back to the beginning again.

'Lydia! Hello!' It was Peter and Colette, in the next line to her and moving in the opposite direction. She had just time to scream, 'Hello!' before they were on one pavement and she was on the other. They met again on the next pass. 'You came!' Colette said.

'Yes!' Lydia admitted. 'Having fun?'

'Yes! Peter wanted to be a pelican, but couldn't be bothered with all the papier maché...'

'Shame – he'd look good in the beak,' Lydia shouted, as they moved apart again. This time she met Becky at the side of the road.

'You made it! Well done!' Becky handed her a black-and-white striped flag.

To her surprise, Lydia found herself smiling. 'It's more fun than I was expecting!'

Becky grinned at her and stepped into the road to help an old gentleman out of the crowd and into a folding chair at the side. 'All right, Gordon?' Lydia just heard her say as she was swept away.

The press appeared, bearing expensive-looking cameras and spiral-bound notebooks. Lydia recognised the severe black bob and thick-rimmed spectacles of Emma Greer, one of the higher-achieving English undergraduates in her year and the star reporter of the University's student newspaper. The long-haired, wispy-bearded, photographer also looked as if he was there on behalf of the *STANdard*. The other press representatives were older. They must be the real thing, Lydia thought, if one could call the *Stancester Comet* the real thing. She kept half an eye on them all, not sure whether she was secretly hoping to get into the papers, or secretly hoping not to. She wondered what her parents would make of it – and if it was a good idea to tell them.

The rain kept up all morning. So did the march, which seemed to surprise the protesters. 'I'd have thought they'd have broken us up by now,' she heard Gordon say, a little while later, as he rejoined the snake. Lydia was glad that she had worn walking boots: virtue and adrenaline could only carry her so far and her feet were beginning to ache. A couple more police officers appeared. They talked to the organisers, shrugged their shoulders, and retired to a safe distance.

At half past eleven, with no warning that Lydia could see, Becky blew a whistle and one of the other organisers shrieked through a megaphone, 'OK, everyone, we're done! Thank you very much.' The train immediately disintegrated into a mass, which parted, in the manner of the Red Sea, and swept towards the two pavements. The queue of traffic moved off with derisive honking.

Lydia was lingering at the side of the road, wondering what to do next, when she felt a tap on her shoulder. She swung around. 'Colette!'

Colette smiled at her. 'That wasn't nearly as bad as I expected. Fancy going on into town for a coffee?'

She wondered what the Fellowship gang were up to, and pictured Mel, Rose, Jake and Will, tramping in wellington boots across the beach at Weston-super-Mare. It would be a horrible anti-climax to return to hall, alone and bored. 'Yes,' she said. 'Why not?'

Peter was just behind Colette. 'I'm off home,' he said. 'Essay crisis. Or it will be, if I don't do something today. Have fun, you two.' He sauntered off down the road.

'I suppose we'd better hang around for five minutes and make sure Becky doesn't get arrested,' Colette said.

'I suppose so,' Lydia agreed, suddenly shy. It was just as well, she thought, that they had the fascinating subject of jacket potatoes as a potential topic for conversation.

Becky was talking (amicably, it seemed) to one of the police officers. 'I think,' Colette said to Lydia, 'that she's got a debrief meeting now, so I'm not proposing to wait for her unless there's some sort of a problem. Which –' as Becky nodded, smiled, and walked off – 'there doesn't appear to be. Good. Do you like Café Brasilia?'

'On Exeter Road? Yes. But –' it had just occurred to her – 'I came out without my handbag...'

'Oh, don't worry about that,' Colette said. 'You can get me one another day.'

That seemed reasonable enough, and Lydia, as awkward as she felt, liked the implication that there would be other visits to other cafés.

They pounced on a recently vacated table just inside the door of Café Brasilia.

'Do you think it'll make any difference?' Lydia asked when Colette got back with the drinks.

Colette shrugged her shoulders. 'It might. It's a popular cause. After all, "we're killing children" is not exactly a message that the council would want to convey, and it should be comparatively cheap to install a crossing.'

Lydia sat down and shuffled her chair up close to the wall, out of the way of the queue. She bashed her elbow on the rococo frame of a huge mirror, and winced. Absently, she noticed the way it reflected the gradient of the street outside and sent it straight back up the way it had come, giving the impression that they and the café were suspended in a giant hammock. She saw her own face, flushed in the sudden warmth, and Colette twice over, a wisp of hair escaping across her forehead, and grey eyes dancing in bashful enjoyment.

'It was fun, anyway,' Lydia said. 'I wasn't really expecting to enjoy it.'

'Same.' Colette said. 'I'm not usually this actively political. In fact, I'm rarely political at all. The nearest I get...'

'Yes?'

Her hand shook as she added milk to her tea. 'I was going to say, signing the odd petition that comes round the LGBT mailing list.'

'Ah, right,' Lydia said, interested. 'I didn't realise you were in LGBT Soc as well as AngthMURC. What are they like?'

'LGBT? They're OK, by and large. Some of them are a bit biphobic. Most of them can't get their heads around the fact that I'm queer and also a practising Christian.'

Lydia laughed awkwardly. 'Interesting to hear it from the other side. But –' She stopped.

Colette sighed. 'Go on,' she said. 'Ask the question.'

Lydia stiffened. 'How did you know there was going to be a question?' she asked, knowing she was fooling nobody.

'There's always a question,' Colette said, staring at the cup. 'It's either, how can you, as a bisexual woman, collude with a patriarchal institution that systematically oppresses you and erases your identity, or how can you, as a Christian, continue to follow a sinful lifestyle?'

Lydia fidgeted with the sugar sachets. 'It wasn't going to be quite that,' she said.

'Am I close, though?'

She settled for, 'Fairly.' Then, defensive, 'What would the answer be, then?'

Colette frowned. 'To which?'

Lydia thought about that. 'Isn't it the same question?'

Colette looked up, slowly, looked at her as if she were seeing her for the first time. 'Yes,' she said. 'Effectively, it is.'

'So?' Excitement bubbled in Lydia.

Colette's tone was very measured. 'OK. Ask it the way you would want to ask it, if you could, and you didn't think I'd mind.'

'Well, then,' Lydia said, 'how *do* you reconcile those apparently incompatible aspects of your identity?' She realised as she spoke that she had not quite managed the emphasis that she had intended. Perhaps that was just as well. She added, for good measure, 'And you've obviously been asked the question often enough: doesn't that drive you mad?'

A bitter laugh. 'It does. I deal with it using a mixture of cynicism, rudeness, and reminding myself that I have, of necessity, thought about it far more than anyone who is giving me grief about it.'

Lydia, who thought about it a lot herself, found that she was gripping the handle of her coffee cup absurdly tightly. 'That makes sense. Go on?'

Colette spoke rapidly. 'I'm both bisexual and Christian, and I don't do well if I pretend that I'm *not* bisexual, or, if it comes to that, Christian. I don't find they're incompatible at all. They're just two facts about me that happen to be true. It's like saying, I have a clean driving license, and also I like cheese on toast. There are drivers who don't like cheese on toast, there are people who like cheese on toast who don't drive, but there are also people who can drive and who don't find that stops them eating cheese on toast. I conduct my private life with as much integrity as I can manage, regardless of which gender my partner happens to be. Anyway, I don't have one at the moment. But, you know. Thank you for not being *completely* obnoxious about it.'

'That's all right,' said Lydia, refusing to take offence, though she felt she didn't quite deserve that, and it stung. 'Perhaps we should talk about baked potatoes, instead.'

'That,' Colette said, 'is a very good idea. Let's.'

The second official planning meeting was little more than a check-in, confirming that all those who had assumed responsibility had things in hand. The event developed a name – at least, someone called it a vigil, and suddenly it was the Vigil. ('I thought that was one of the Thunderbirds,' Lydia muttered to Georgia, who laughed; but it stuck.) Posters were displayed on the official noticeboards of all the societies involved. Flyers were distributed amongst all the organisers, for circulation as far and as wide as was feasible. Lydia was not audacious enough to hand them out to the Christian Fellowship under the noses of Jake and Ellie, but she took a handful and, when her hall group gathered in her bedroom for that week's Bible study, passed them. After all, she told herself, that was no different from a member promoting an event that was happening at their own church. She was making it very clear that the Christian Fellowship had no official involvement. None of her group seemed to mind, anyway.

'Oh, I've got one, thanks,' Zoe said airily. 'From AngthMURC.' She had settled into a compromise whereby she attended AngthMURC, hall group, and the University Chapel. Lydia thought this odd, but goodness knew she could not afford to turn people away, and it seemed to work for Zoe.

'There you go, then,' Lydia said. 'If anyone asks, Zoe was really keen to encourage you all to attend. It's not a Fellowship thing. It's a *Christian* thing.' She was joking. At least, she was joking about passing it off as Zoe's idea, but she was still conscious of an uneasiness. Was disobedience too strong a word? Yes: she had not been forbidden. Of abusing her position, then? No. She was here to teach and to encourage her group to learn. She knew that they would learn from the Vigil. Think of what she had herself learned already, simply from being involved in the planning and talking to Colette!

Thinking of Colette, she frowned. That clear-eyed truthfulness, that courageous self-acceptance, seemed against all logic to come from a confident faith way beyond Lydia's reach; she felt small and confused in comparison. In theory, it was impossible. Yet Colette managed it. How? How, without hypocrisy, could she be simultaneously bisexual and Christian?

There was nothing hypocritical in Colette. Even her occasional surliness, Lydia thought, came from honesty. She admitted, quite freely, to being who she was.

So much was reasonable, if, for Lydia, unattainable; but Colette went further. Lydia made herself think about that. Colette claimed to be happy as she was, to have no desire to change. She didn't even seem to care whether or not her next partner was male – and why shouldn't they be, Lydia thought miserably. Why didn't Colette, who had been given the choice, free herself of this whole excruciating question? Didn't she know she danced on the edge of damnation? Lydia scrabbled for mitigating circumstances. Colette ignored one tiny verse, that was all it was, but it didn't matter *which* verse it was. Lydia dared not even let herself start thinking like that. Take one block away, and the whole tower would fall down. The world seemed to tremble before her eyes.

Shuddering, she wondered if she had been wrong after all. Should she pull out of the Vigil? Of course not, she told herself. It was hardly as if Colette was going to be preaching on sexuality. She was not going to be preaching at all. She was just going to be there, being herself, and she was – Lydia believed, in defiance of everything she had ever been taught – already being herself in the most Christian way she could.

Then could Colette possibly be *right*? What she told Lydia was contrary to all other teaching on that particular subject – and yet Lydia wished desperately that it could be true. Colette was single, she told herself. It was not as if she was actually engaging in sexual immorality. Surely there was nothing to worry about. And yet... *if anyone causes any of these little ones to stumble, it would be better for them to have a large millstone hung around their neck and to be drowned in the depths of the sea.* She was responsible for these Freshers and their spiritual welfare, and she could not afford to forget that.

She looked at them all: Kris, a foot and a half taller than she was, and years more sophisticated; pious Simon; independent Zoe; sardonic Ed; clever Michaela; thoughtful Vicki; quiet Fiona. She laughed to herself. Fiona was the only one she could worry about, at least in terms of her own influence; the others would make up their own minds whatever she told them or did not tell them to do.

They were all staring at her, waiting for her to begin. 'Right!' she said. 'Sorry – I was miles away. Michaela – would you mind reading today's scripture passage for us? Let's make a start.'

Chapter 7

11pm GENTLENESS – a prayer walk around campus and a chance to think about our stewardship of God's creation

12am KINDNESS – we'll greet the crowds coming out of the Venue with sweets and a smile

1am LOVE – Peter will explore 1 Corinthians 13, the great Hymn of Love. It's Bible study, Jim, but not as we know it.

2am JOY – break out the glitter and the marker pens and explore spirituality through playful creativity. No artistic talent necessary!

3am PEACE – worship Quaker style

4am PATIENCE – as the night watch waits for the morning... we think about waiting for God

The Vigil: programme for the night (extract)

Colette's cheese-on-toast analogy should have been the end of the conversation, but through the following weeks Lydia kept returning to it, worrying at it, asking the questions in her imagination that she had not dared to address in real life. ('Isn't it more like drink-driving?') Perhaps she should not have been surprised when the two of them were left alone in the tiny Chaplaincy kitchen on the night of the Vigil, and she found herself asking, 'Was your ex-girlfriend a Christian, as well?'

Colette almost dropped the pan of baked beans, but she answered calmly enough, 'Jess? No – at least, not when we were together. I doubt she's converted since, but you never know. She was always a bit of a law unto herself. Why do you ask?'

Lydia jabbed a fork violently into a potato. 'Idle curiosity, I'm afraid.'

'Oh?'

A volley of laughter seeped through the wall. Next door, Becky was leading the group in raucous ice-breaker games. Here, Lydia was silent, considering how best to proceed. 'I've been – thinking,' she said. 'I was wondering what it was like to be you, to have to be constantly fighting people who want you to be one thing or the other. Whether I could ever be brave enough.'

Colette laughed awkwardly. 'Oh, I'm not brave. If I were brave I'd be next door playing British Bulldog and talking to people I don't know. I'm just – who I am.'

'I'd call that brave,' Lydia said. 'And you're talking to me.' She jerked the oven door open and swapped in a new batch of potatoes.

'That's true,' Colette said. 'You're different.'

'Why?' She hoped she had not sounded defensive.

Colette passed her the cheese grater and a large hunk of cheddar. 'Here. Make a start on this and I'll take over potatoes. You're different because – well. You remember that question you didn't quite ask me the other week?'

'Vividly.' She peeled back the wrapper from the cheese.

'You're the only person I've ever met who actually seemed interested in the answer.'

Lydia nodded, relieved. 'Thank you. I am interested.'

Colette turned away and opened three tins of tuna without speaking. 'Right, then,' she said when she had finished. 'I suppose I'd better tell you. Yes. Oh, God, you Evangelicals have no idea how hard it is, if you're not the sort of person who usually talks seriously about God... Well. I did have trouble, when I first got together with Jess, working it out in my own head. It really wasn't something I could talk to *her* about. My minister was great, though.'

'Really?'

'Yes. He just gave me a cup of tea and suggested that maybe God loves Colette, just the way she is, just as – well, just as God loves Lydia,

52

just the way you are. Deeper than that. God loves the parts of you that you are scared even to acknowledge to yourself. You don't often hear that, even in church. I was lucky.'

'You knew, then,' Lydia said, refusing to chase the implications of this, 'that it *was* who you were.'

'Yes,' Colette said. 'I do wonder, sometimes, how much of that was Jess. She had an amazingly strong personality; I don't think anyone could *not* fancy her. She was so bright and funny and clever, not to mention sexy as hell. But there have been other people, since, that I've been attracted to. Male and female.' A faint smile played across her lips. Lydia tried not to wonder who it honoured.

'What about the Biblical instructions?' That was the important point, surely.

Colette winced. 'You have to remember that I'm a woolly Methodist, who sees the Bible as a record of one particular group's relationship with God, rather than as a rulebook to be followed to the letter. Nevertheless –'

'Yes?' Lydia was intrigued, and faintly scandalised.

Colette began ticking the verses off on her fingers. 'Leviticus. You shall not lie with a man as with a woman – it's part of the purity code; why do we enforce the bit about homosexuality and ignore the parts about eating shellfish and wearing blended textiles? Genesis. Marriage. A man leaves his father and mother, et cetera, et cetera; well, it's *a* Biblical model of marriage, but it's hardly the only one, and in the New Testament we're not even sure that marriage is a good thing. Romans – the only one that mentions women at all, if you want to be pedantic – doesn't actually refer to same-sex relationships as a sin to be punished; it's the other way round. Corinthians. Homosexuals will not enter the Kingdom of Heaven – but nobody's even sure what Paul means by the word that's usually translated as "homosexual". Any more?'

Lydia could not think of any. 'But isn't it better to be safe than sorry?' she ventured.

'The thing that I find,' Colette said, 'is that it would be very easy for me to pretend to be straight, but it would not be anything like the truth. And the Bible has an awful lot more to say on *that*.'

'But you can't just ignore what the Bible says!' Lydia protested, cowed but not convinced by the glib demolition of the commandments that made the very fabric of her life.

Colette sighed. 'I'm afraid that you're just going to have to trust me when I say, I don't; it's just led me to a rather different conclusion than the one I assume it's led you to. Anyway,' she said, abruptly, 'it's all on the internet. You can always Google it. I suppose we'd better feed these people, hadn't we?'

Dinner passed off successfully. Nat-the-Chaplaincy-Assistant and Tanya-the-Chaplain swept up all the plates and refused to accept any help with the washing-up. A scratch band led a lively worship session in the Catholic chapel. Kingdom Come! was next up, showing an informative presentation on the topic of Fair Trade, and then passing round a batch of petitions for signing. At eleven o'clock, Sophie took them out into the chilly night, leading them on a prayer walk all the way around the campus, culminating in the distribution of sweets to the revellers emerging from the Venue as midnight struck.

It was a significantly smaller group that returned to the Chaplaincy Centre. All but the very keenest had taken the opportunity to go home. Lydia felt rather superior. (*Could you not watch with me one hour?*) Colette looked exhausted, but she came back to Markham Grange and withdrew to the common room for a nap. Lydia, meanwhile, followed the rest of the group into the chapel, where Peter was preparing to lead the next session.

'I got landed with *Love*,' he said. 'I don't think I have much to say about love that hasn't already been said, and even if I did, it's not something that you can put across in words. So I thought we'd look at what the Bible says about it. And I thought we'd look very closely indeed, using a technique called *lectio divina* – literally, "divine reading".'

Lydia, suspicious of the Latin, sat up, but resolved to keep an open mind. Peter passed out felt-tipped pens, index cards, and photocopies. Looking at hers, Lydia saw it was 1 Corinthians 13, repeated several times in different translations.

Peter spoke deliberately slowly. 'I want you to forget everything you know about this passage: who it was written for, what it was about, who even wrote it. I want you to clear your mind. Before you even look at it, I want you to just sit quietly for three minutes. Even longer, if you want to. Open your mind to God.

'Then I want you to read this passage, several times. You can stick to the same translation or move between the different ones on the sheet. Read at your own pace, or a bit slower than your own pace. You may find that there's a word, or a phrase, that really jumps out at you. And, as I said, forget everything you think you know about this. Just trust that God has something to say to you now, through this scripture, and that the Spirit will reveal it to you.'

He stopped talking, and the chapel was flooded with silence. Lydia shifted in her chair to sit up very straight. She was *nervous*, she realised, and felt irritated with herself. Silence. She tried to clear her mind, as instructed, and the thoughts rushed back in to fill the space. Google it, Colette had said. She would, tomorrow...

Guiltily, she glanced at the printed sheet in front of her. She loved this chapter, though it was hard to think of it out of the context of weddings. Come on. Corinthians. The Church at Corinth – but this was just what Peter had said *not* to do. Lydia gathered her errant thoughts and twined them into a prayer. *Dear God, I'm not very good at this. Please help me be silent and hear your Word.* She breathed in, deeply, through her nose, and felt calmer.

'If you're ready,' Peter said, 'begin to read.'

That was never three minutes – or perhaps it was – perhaps she had spent all that time thinking about rubbish... anyway, she didn't have to move on to reading now if she didn't feel ready. Did she feel ready? No. But would she ever? People around her were beginning to read. She gave it another thirty seconds, trying hard not to count them out in her head, and began.

Though I speak with the tongues of men and of angels, and have not charity, I am become as sounding brass, or a tinkling cymbal.

Too fast. And the traditional language felt uncomfortable. She skipped down the page until she found the New International Version. That was better: she could concentrate on the meaning without being distracted by the words. She began to read, very slowly, very deliberately, repeating every word to herself in her head.

If I have the gift of prophecy and can fathom all mysteries and all knowledge, and if I have a faith that can move mountains, but have not love, I am nothing.

She could not help but be a little disappointed when nothing spectacular happened. Not that it usually did, but she had hoped that, reading the Bible a different way, she would discover something new, and exciting. She yawned – and as she looked back down, a line further down the page caught her eye.

rejoices with the truth

She made herself go back to the beginning. *If I speak in the tongues of men and of angels...* She made herself read all the way to the end. *Now we see but a poor reflection as in a mirror; then we shall see face to face. Now I know in part; then I shall know fully, even as I am fully known. And now these three remain: faith, hope and love. But the greatest of these is love.* All the while she was racing, she knew, to get back to that verse.

Love is patient, love is kind. It does not envy, it does not boast, it is not proud. It is not rude, it is not self-seeking, it is not easily angered, it keeps no record of wrongs. Love does not delight in evil but rejoices with the truth.

It wasn't even a verse, just those four words: *rejoices with the truth*. How had she never noticed it before? She hugged it to herself. Was this what she was meant to be looking out for? She didn't care. It seemed meant for her, meant for her now.

'Write it down,' Peter said. 'Write down whatever it is you've come across that has that energy for you. If nothing jumped out, you can just pick something you like the look of; that's fine, too. Write it down, and keep it.'

She wrote it down, red pen on beige card. *Rejoices with the truth*.

'Now,' Peter said, and his speech was still slow and calm, 'meditate on those words. Try to discern what relevance they might have for your life today. Again, don't worry if it doesn't show up straight away. It might not show up at all today. Doing this in the middle of the night won't work for everyone. We're all tired. Just sit, and wait. If something does come to you, think about turning that into a prayer. But really, the important thing is to be quiet, and listen. You can take as long as you like, and there's no right answer.'

The words hung in her mind. *Rejoices with the truth*. She was too tired to make them mean anything in particular at the moment, but she let them stay there, glowing, until they dissolved into the dark silence.

Afterwards, they moved back into the common room, dislodging a couple of sleepers from the chairs and beanbags.

'You can go into the prayer room if you want to keep sleeping,' Sophie said heartlessly.

Colette sat up and stretched, blinking like an affronted owl. 'Might there be tea?' she asked, yawning.

'I'll put the kettle on,' Tim said.

'The rest of us,' Georgia said to the room in general, 'will get the art supplies out of the box in the corner, and have an hour or so making a mess. The theme for this hour is *joy*, but you don't have to be joyful if you don't want to. Just have a play, really. We're thinking about prayer through play, prayer through creativity. The only thing is to be mindful of the fact that there *are* people trying to get to sleep next door, so don't be too noisy.'

She began to unpack the art box, strewing paints and papers, sequins, glitter tubes, and feathers from one end of the table to the other. 'There's clay if anyone wants it, beads here, nice pens... Go wild!'

Lydia could not think what to do. She got up and helped Tim make the drinks, and came back with her own, still considering. She thought for a moment that Colette had gone back to sleep, curled in an armchair, but when Lydia put a cup down in front of her she opened her eyes, smiled, and unclenched her fist, to reveal a large, purple, glass bead.

'That's gorgeous,' Lydia said, rather annoyed that she had not spotted it herself. 'What are you going to do with it?'

'I'm not sure, yet.' Colette shut her eyes again.

Struck by a thought, Lydia put her hand in her pocket and felt the card that she had written her verse on. *That* would do as well as anything: the card was already getting dog-eared, and it was worth remembering properly. She selected a piece of stiff, cream-coloured cardboard and a packet of fine-line felt-tip pens, and set to work.

Colette seemed to come to a decision; she reached for a reel of gold-coloured wire, threaded the end through her purple bead, and twisted it securely. Lydia glanced up, intrigued, but Colette was clearly concentrating, and she did not want to distract her. She turned back to her text. *Love rejoices in the truth.* Properly, it should have had an ellipsis between *love* and *rejoices*, but it would have spoiled the look of it, and it was not as if the missing words changed the meaning. She added a border of generic leaves and flowers.

'Drat,' she said, after twenty minutes of work, 'that's gone really twee.'

Colette glanced over. 'Oh, it's not as bad as all that. You've not put any teddy bears or kittens in.'

Lydia laughed. 'I suppose not. May I see yours?'

'Of course.' Colette showed her: she had made a delicate cross, three inches high, from the twisted wire, with the bead caught at the intersection.

'That's beautiful,' Lydia said, impressed.

'Thank you.' Colette looked up and down the room. 'Is there a pair of scissors anywhere, that nobody minds my ruining?'

'Here.' Zoe stood to pass them. 'Wow, good work!'

'Thanks.' Colette reeled out a little more wire, laid it at the hinge of the open scissors, and squeezed them hard. They did not sever it completely, but made a nick deep enough that she could, by bending it back and forth, break it. She wound the tail a couple of times around the neck of the cross, and used the points of the scissors as pliers to turn the sharp end in. 'There.'

Nestled in her hand, the cross caught the light of the candle that stood on the shelf behind her, and the bead at the centre gleamed with calm fire.

The sun rose at last on an intimate, bleary-eyed congregation. They walked out onto the lawn, watched the sky turn a solemn red over the hills to the east. Peter had prepared a brief prayer for this morning hour, Lydia knew, but he remained silent, and indeed there was no need for words. It was only when, tired, awed and chilly, they turned to go back in that Lydia felt the gentle pressure of a hand laid upon her arm.

'I wanted,' Colette said, 'to give you this.'

Lydia put her hand out obediently, not knowing quite what to expect. Colette laid hers over it, and Lydia felt the sudden warmth, and something equally warm, but smooth, hard and angular, within it. She looked: the little wire cross that Colette had been making in the darkest hour of the night. The purple bead was almost opaque in the grey light.

'To remember a very successful meal. And to apologise for being a grumpy cow at too many points of the preparation.'

Lydia ran a finger down its trunk. 'Oh, Colette – really? It's lovely. Are you sure you don't want to keep it yourself?'

'I'm sure,' Colette said, smiling.

Impulsively, Lydia hugged her. 'In that case I had better reciprocate.' She scrabbled in her coat picket and found a pen, then drew out the card she had drawn at the same session. *Love rejoices in the truth*. 'It's very you, actually.' She turned it over, and wrote on the back: *Colette – love Lydia x*

'Thank you,' Colette said gravely. She took the card and laid it with care between two pages of her Bible. Then, her mood changing like quicksilver, 'Come on inside. We've got a Taizé morning service, and then it's bacon o'clock.'

Chapter 8

So much for the cathedral and churches of Stancester city. The energetic visitor may, however, care to walk up to the University and examine its two chapels. The Roman Catholic chapel is a hidden gem in the back of Markham Grange, an extension added by a peculiarly devout Curzon in the late nineteenth century, which has been maintained in its original purpose since the house became the base for the university in 1955. Within: a riot of gilt and colour. The reredos in particular rewards a closer look.

The Anglican chapel, by contrast, is a well-proportioned but somewhat austere hall in red brick and concrete, the first building one passes on the way onto the campus. The interior is unadorned brick, but the stained glass is glorious. Do not attempt to visit during July, as the University's graduation ceremonies take place here and access is by ticket only.

The Churches of Stancester, Henry Hodder, 1997

Lydia was surprised how flat she felt after the Vigil; floundering through the next week in a fog of fatigue and anticlimax, she jumped at the chance to attend the debrief meeting.

'Talk about how it went,' Georgia instructed them.

'My circadian rhythm still hasn't got back to normal,' Colette complained. 'I'd have slept until lunch if I hadn't had to get up for Inorganic Three.'

'Yes,' Sophie said, 'that sounds like exactly the sort of thing that one might go to specifically in order to catch up on some sleep, but apart from that?'

'Oh, apart from that it was great,' Colette admitted. 'It's really good to do something together once in a while – to remind ourselves we're more similar than we are different.'

A murmur of agreement.

'Speaking of which,' Tim Benton said, suddenly serious, 'I'd like to place it on record how disappointed I am that the Christian Fellowship chose to play no part in this event.'

'No *official* part,' Colette said, glancing at Lydia.

'Actually,' Lydia said, quelling a sense of disloyalty 'I'm disappointed too. Though I think I'd rather that wasn't placed on record.'

'Of course,' said Kasia, who was taking the minutes. 'I wouldn't worry: I doubt anyone's going to read these, unless they're the committee planning the next round. To be honest, Tim, you'd be better off writing to the *STANdard*.'

'I might do that,' Tim said, thoughtfully. 'Yes, I might.'

It occurred to Lydia as the meeting broke up that perhaps it was not the event that she had been missing so much as the people. She would have liked, for example, to go for coffee again with Colette, but they had no excuse now there were no more meals to plan, and she was not quite brave enough to text her and suggest it as if on a whim. Should she go to an AngthMURC meeting? No – if that ever got back to Ellie (and it would; she had worked out now that Ellie and Peter shared several lectures, and she could hardly ask Peter not to mention her attendance) she would never hear the end of it. The Vigil was one thing – she could attend that legitimately as a common-or-garden Christian, but Ellie was very suspicious of AngthMURC ('they've had *Muslim* speakers, you know...')

She could, however, go to the chapel service before AngthMURC. As a Christian member of the university she was, she told herself, perfectly entitled to attend the university's chapel. If the Christian Fellowship insisted you shouldn't set foot in the place they'd never be able to graduate.

The service was called Choral Evensong, and consisted mainly of singing, with two scripture readings sandwiched between. Lydia, feeling small and chilly in the great dark building, made up exactly one half of the congregation; to her great relief, the other half seemed to know what he was doing, and she was able to follow his lead in the standing up and the sitting down. The choir, thirteen strong (she supposed she ought not have been surprised they included Georgia) and flapping around in black academic gowns like a flock of untidy rooks, sat in two rows, facing each other across the central aisle. Peter, looking official in a long black robe that buttoned down the front, led in the Chaplain, who was wearing something similar, but with her dog collar showing under it, and a flimsy white garment and an academic hood over the top.

Well, Lydia thought, the Christian Fellowship had no need to worry about hundreds of eager young souls being led astray, not if the attendance at this service was any indication.

She was a little surprised, having got to the end of the text on the printed card, to find that she had still to sit through the anthem and prayers before at last everyone could say the Grace and the choir walked out, with Peter and the Chaplain behind them.

Well, she said to herself, *that* was a new experience, anyway. She had thought this sort of thing only happened on *Carols From King's.*

Peter was back almost immediately. 'Nice to see you, Lydia,' he said, meaning it. 'I don't know if you're aware, but we do a bring-and-share supper now, in the Chaplaincy Centre, if you'd like to come? And then AngthMURC starts at half past seven.'

She felt a tug of wistfulness. 'I didn't know,' she said ruefully, 'and so I haven't brought anything. And I can't stay for AngthMURC.'

'That's all right – the rest of us will share! Follow the choir – or you can wait for me, but I'll be a minute or so. I've got a couple of things to put away before I lock up...' He waved vaguely at the altar.

She laughed. 'It's OK – I know the way by now.'

'Excellent. See you up there.'

The choir was well ahead of her, stampeding up the hill as if it had never eaten in its life. Lydia dawdled. She got to the Chaplaincy Centre just as everyone had settled down and found seats, and when she came in they all looked up and stared at her. She was pathetically grateful for the presence of Georgia, who said, 'Come and sit next me, Lydia, and tell me what you're doing at Choral Evensong.'

'Oh, you know,' Lydia said. 'The arms get tired after a while, all that happy-clapping.'

Georgia smiled at the feeble self-deprecation. 'Will you come back again?'

'I might. Why not?'

'That's the spirit! We'll have you genuflecting next.'

'What's genuflecting?' It sounded very esoteric.

'She's teasing,' Peter said from the doorway, an unlikely quantity of white cloth over his arm. 'I'm probably the only person in this room who even knows how to. Has someone put the kettle on?'

'Yes.' Tanya-the-Chaplain emerged from the kitchen carrying a plate stacked high with bread rolls. The company added a motley selection of snacks and oddments.

'Bloody cheeky psalm,' Peter said, peeling a satsuma. 'Don't think I didn't notice that *We shall not be moved* riff in whichever verse it was.'

'Wordpainting, innit,' said the organist. 'It's all about the tree standing by the waterside. Couldn't resist.'

'Evidently. I won't ask what lectionary you were using. I didn't think it was even possible to sing Psalm 1 at Evensong.'

The organist swallowed a mouthful of flapjack and said, indistinctly, 'Don't ask me. I just work here. I thought we did what you told us?'

Peter snorted. 'I doubt there's a church in England where the musicians do what the clergy tell them, let alone the lowly sacristan.' He turned to Lydia. 'What's it like lower down the candle?'

Interpreting this as an inquiry as to how things worked at her own church, she said, 'It's just the same. The band runs everything. I think that's why so many of our ministers play guitar, actually, so they can keep an eye on what's going on.'

'That's not a bad wheeze,' Peter said, thoughtfully.

'Are you going to join the choir, then?' Georgia asked him. 'We could do with another tenor.'

He grinned at her. 'Nah, haven't time. I can't see anybody else volunteering to take on all the laundry.'

Georgia tore another roll open and layered ham and crisps in it. 'Someone will have to, next year. Or are you going to do a PhD and stay around forever, like Tim?'

'Good Lord, no. I have Plans,' Peter said, mysteriously.

She paused in the act of shaking the crumbs out of the crisp packet. 'Ooh. Plans?'

'Well, *a* Plan. Specifically, an interview.' He was affecting nonchalance, without any degree of success.

'When did you hear? Why didn't you say?'

'This morning, and you were out.'

One of the other singers looked up. 'An interview? Exciting! What for?'

'A job as a pastoral assistant at a church in Cambridge.'

'What, like Nat, you mean?' The organist looked at him sharply. 'Well, we all know where *that* leads.'

Lydia did not know anything of the sort, but would have felt silly asking.

'Not necessarily,' Peter said, rather shiftily. 'It doesn't all depend on me, you know.'

'Maybe not,' Georgia said. 'I could see you in a dog collar, though.'

Lydia glanced at Peter with new interest, and ventured to ask, 'Is this a recognised career path, then?'

Peter turned to her with what might have been relief. 'Of sorts. I suppose it would be fairer to say that you're encouraged to Get Some Experience In A Parish, and See More Of Life, which a job like this might help you with if you're lucky. The way the sharp end works is that when you've Seen Life you get interrogated by some gorgons, and then if they turn out to like you, you get to go to theological college and do another three years of study. Then you get ordained deacon, and *then* they send you to get some experience in a parish. It's a never-ending circle. I don't know why I actually want to do it.' But his eyes were shining with excitement.

'Well,' Lydia said, 'good luck.'

He nodded. 'Thank you.'

Across the room, somebody was saying, 'no, but it turned out to be the other sort of dog collar. You know. Leather, with inch-long steel spikes!'

Bawdy laughter drowned all hope of making out the context for this.

'Well,' Georgia called, 'he'd have been fine if it had been a Vicars and Tarts party, wouldn't he? That'll teach him to order stuff off the internet.'

Lydia wondered who this unfortunate online shopper was. Perhaps, she thought, it was just as well that she didn't know. The whole evening had left her feeling bewildered and daringly transgressive.

'Sounds like a bargain,' Peter said.

Georgia swallowed the end of her roll. 'Oh, Lydia, I was going to email you. Would you like to come and have dinner with us? Are you free next Thursday?'

Lydia felt an excuse darting to the front of her mind. In her head, her mother said, *Who are these people, darling? Are you sure...?* She shot back, *They're all Christians, Mum. It's fine.*

She *was* free, and, more, she *would* like to come for dinner. 'Thank you,' she said, 'I'd love to.'

And then, feeling that she might as well be hanged for a sheep as for a lamb, she sent a text to Colette as she walked home. *Fancy a coffee tomorrow? L.*

Chapter 9

Dear Editor,

As a long-serving student and longer-serving Catholic, I write as a result of six years of increasing frustration with the Christian Fellowship's deliberate and systematic exclusion of – oh, delicious irony! – the majority of Christian students at this university. This issue was brought home to me forcibly last week, when representatives of the Catholic Society, the Anglican, Methodist and United Reformed Church Society, Campus Quakers and Kingdom Come! joined to celebrate their shared heritage and vision of divine love directed to all humanity – a true fellowship of Christians. The Society which calls itself "Stancester University Christian Fellowship" declined to be involved in this event, claiming that its policy is not to endorse Christian teaching unless all speakers and leaders sign its "Statement of Belief". A number of Christians involved in the planning – myself included – declined to so do; consequently the "Christian Fellowship" refused to be involved in this open and outward-looking event.

Contrary to what the "Christian Fellowship" would have us believe, this "Statement of Belief" is not common to all Christians. In its insistence on Biblical literalism, in its puritanical interpretation of Christian teaching, and in making a message of unconditional love conditional upon the unquestioning acceptance of these small-minded stipulations, it is in fact running in a completely contrary direction from the good news of Jesus Christ as many – may I say, most? – Christians understand it. As such, the sheer effrontery of the "Christian Fellowship" in laying exclusive claim to that name is abhorrent. If its leadership possessed any integrity it would move towards changing the society's name as soon as possible. The simple addition of the word "Evangelical" as a descriptive prefix would suit very well.

I remain, a Christian, and a non-member of the "Christian Fellowship",

Tim Benton

Letters, *STANdard*, 23 November

Lydia went to Balton Street the next week for lunch with Ellie, and found her in an incandescent rage. 'Look at this. I mean. Just *look* at it.'

Lydia tried, but Ellie's hand was shaking too much to make it easy. 'The *STANdard*. What about it?' She did not usually read it, but had sought out a copy after Emma Greer turned up at the Western Road protest, and had found the resulting article surprisingly accurate. The accompanying photograph was less impressive, but she had been able to make out Peter and the back of Colette's head.

Ellie thrust it closer to her face. '*Look*. The letters. Who is this Tim Benton, anyway?'

'Oh.' Lydia remembered. 'Cathsoc.'

'Well, yes, I can *see* that.' Ellie rolled her eyes to show how patient she was being.

Lydia took the paper and, now that it was staying still, could see that the Letters page featured, in pride of place, Tim's thoughts on Christian dialogue as practised at the University of Stancester.

'Well,' Lydia said, when she had read it under Ellie's close supervision, 'he has a point, but he's being very obnoxious about it.'

'You don't *agree* with him?' Ellie crumpled the offending page and threw it furiously at the recycling bin.

'We *are* Evangelical – why not admit that?'

Ellie's eyebrows went up in disbelief. 'Because it won't help our mission. The word "Evangelical" puts people off – come on, you know it does – and we're not going to be able to reach out to them the way we can as the plain Christian Fellowship.'

Lydia bit her lip. 'Isn't that rather dishonest?'

Ellie was affronted. 'Of course not. It's not as if the other groups are teaching true, Biblical, Christianity.'

'How do you know that, though?' Lydia asked.

'Just think about it logically,' Ellie said. 'If they were teaching sound doctrine then they wouldn't object to signing our Statement of Belief, would they? I don't know why we're even arguing about this – this

Tim Benton's a Catholic, isn't he, and nobody seriously tries to claim that Catholics are really Christian. I mean, they pray to Mary, that's idolatry for a start...'

Lydia wanted to say that nobody was praying to Mary at the Vigil, but judged it best not to draw attention to her own attendance. Instead, she ventured, 'I'm beginning to wonder, actually – whether any of us actually have the right to claim that somebody isn't a Christian when they say they are...'

Ellie sent the surviving portion of the *STANdard* the same way as the Letters page. 'Don't be ridiculous. It's perfectly obvious with some people, isn't it? No, Lydia, the Devil is at work on campus. This isn't the only sign of it. Jake told me last week that you hall officers won't be allowed to live-in next year. It's all very worrying. I think we should pray about this.'

'We what?' Lydia exclaimed in horror.

Ellie, intent on praying, did not answer. Instead, she shifted her chair so that she sat directly opposite Lydia and grabbed both her hands painfully tightly. 'Father God,' she intoned, 'we see Your people under attack, we know that the Enemy is moving on this campus, we pray, Lord, we just pray for Your help and guidance today.' Squeeze, squeeze. 'We know that You are in control of all things and we ask that You would show Your power here today, Lord, we ask that You would reveal Your truth, that You would convince those who are doubting,' squeeze, this time with nails digging in, 'that You would complete Your great work at this university, so that every student here will know that You are Lord. Lord, we just ask this today. Lord, You said that whoever is not for You is against You. We ask You to protect us all against these attacks from Satan, by these people who claim to speak in Your name but who are working to undo the great things You have already done here. Amen, Lord, Amen!'

A chilly November fog hung over Stancester that evening, but the house at Alma Road was snug. The kitchen table was just about big enough for six. To fit Lydia in as well, Becky had squeezed onto a bench with Colette and Peter. Will and Lydia had a chair each on the opposite side, leaving Georgia at the head and Olly, the only housemate she had not previously met, at the foot.

'Nice to meet you,' Olly said grudgingly. 'Just in case nobody's told you, I'm an atheist, and we don't do grace here.'

'Don't mind Olly,' Peter said, 'he's only on the defensive because you're on Will's side.'

'But I'm not – ' Lydia began, and then remembered that technically she was.

Colette raised her eyebrows. 'Grace may be *thought* by anyone who cares to do so,' she said.

'Personally,' Becky said, 'I am going to give thanks. To Georgia, for making all this.'

'You're welcome. And stop squabbling.' Georgia hefted a huge saucepan across from the stove and dished spaghetti bolognese out onto seven mismatched plates. The smell was delicious. Lydia, remembering that the menu for tonight at Richmond had included the worryingly non-specific 'breaded fish' and all-too-familiar 'mixed vegetables', decided it had been worth going out in the dark.

'So, Lydia,' Peter said, 'other than olives, tomato, onion, *meat,* or peppers, about which Georgia had us all correspond at length, is there anything in here you can't eat?'

Georgia said, 'Shut up. Just because you tried to feed Adam parmesan cheese...'

Becky explained, 'My boyfriend. Who is very strictly veggie.'

Lydia could not resist saying, 'You forgot gluten.' And then, 'But it's fine – I don't have any allergies. I would have said. And this is fantastic.'

'Thank you.' Georgia cleared her throat. 'Thank you for coming, Lydia.'

Which seemed an odd thing to say, with the meal only just begun. 'Thank you for having me,' Lydia responded.

'We wanted,' Georgia said, 'to ask you something.'

Colette smiled suddenly, mysteriously.

Georgia continued. 'Next year, I'm staying on to do my PGCE, but Olly and Peter will be moving out. Olly's going to move to London and look for jobs. Peter's got that one he applied for in Cambridge.'

Lydia nodded congratulations to him; he responded in kind.

Will said, 'And obviously hall officers are getting kicked out of halls next year, which is ridiculous if you ask me.'

She wondered how it was that he knew already. 'Indeed we are,' she admitted. 'There's going to be a record intake of Freshers, apparently.'

'First they came for the hall officers...' Will murmured.

'Oh, good *God*!' Peter exclaimed.

Becky glowered at Will. 'That's not funny,' she said. 'And if you're going to claim it was serious then I'm even less impressed. If you're worried, you could do something about it.'

'Like what?' Will challenged.

She began counting possibilities off on her fingers. 'Join whatever committee it is that organises the hall officers –'

'Teaching and Study,' Lydia said.

'Teaching and Study, thank you. You can lobby the administration to keep the hall officers in halls, or, if that fails – and you have to remember that having officers in-house is a privilege that nobody else has, and Accommodation have a perfect right to stop it at any time – you can work towards a way of helping the existing officers do their job without being on the premises.'

'Fair point,' Will said. 'Lyds, how would you feel about my joining Teaching and Study?'

'You'd be very welcome, of course,' Lydia said politely.

Georgia banged her spoon on the side of the saucepan. '*So,*' she said, 'we wanted to ask if you would like to move in with us.'

'If you don't want to run away screaming after that little scene, anyway,' Peter added. 'I'd like to say it was an aberration, but it's pretty typical.'

Colette said, 'You have to know that Will and Becky are the best of friends, really.' She looked absurdly worried, as if she thought Lydia might turn them down flat. 'That's why they're so vile to each other. And Pe – Ol – that is, other things will be easier next year.'

'Who else are you asking?' Lydia asked. Then, realising how that sounded, 'I mean, yes please, I'd love to, I'm just curious.'

'Stuart Ashwin,' Georgia told her. 'I think you might have met him? AngthMURC Fresher. Curly hair. Glasses.'

'Oh, yes,' Lydia said. Her head was buzzing with elation. Her problem had been solved before she had so much as summoned up the courage to look it in the face. She had been dreading entering the housing market a year after everyone else, getting her head around the baffling world of damage deposits and tenancy agreements, and here was a Christian household (for Olly would be tidying himself off to London) opening its door to her. Every obstacle had been cleared away, and efficient Georgia was ready to deal with all the technical parts. An answer to prayer, before she had even prayed it.

Chapter 10

According to the Union rules one is not allowed to discriminate against potential committee members on any grounds whatsoever – which insofar as it applies to AngthMURC means that you can't stop anyone standing, or, should they be elected, from joining the committee, just because they don't happen to belong to the Anglican, Methodist, or United Reformed Churches. In practice, this is only sketchily enforced, though I am sure that one of these days the Union will get around to looking at Fellowship's interpretation of this particular rule. Personally I think it's verging on the paranoid to suggest that the committees of Christian societies are being infiltrated by godless heathens who will subvert our Christian values. In practice, anyone who is as firmly opposed as all that to AngthMURC's beliefs and values is unlikely to be standing, and very unlikely indeed to get elected. Trust in the Lord, and He will keep the society on its feet for the next year or so.

How to run AngthMURC, Peter Nathan

Since Lydia's first tentative text message, she and Colette had fallen into the habit of meeting up in the Students' Union coffee bar on a Thursday afternoon, in the hour between their respective lectures and seminars. As the term rolled on towards Christmas, Lydia had found herself looking forward to Thursdays more and more. Colette was refreshing: a different perspective, a link to the world outside the Christian Fellowship.

It had been all right last year, when Mel and Rose lived in Richmond and they could hang around together. These days, she saw Rose in lectures (and they only shared one module, this semester), and Mel only at Fellowship and church. They were very busy, Lydia supposed; no doubt Ellie had them folding programmes for the Fellowship carol service or something like that. However it had happened, she was round at Colette's house more than she visited her best friends these days. And she was so very conscious of the special nature of her relationship with her hall group. She couldn't be friends with them, not when she was, effectively, their teacher.

Lydia checked her thoughts as she cut around the back of the Grange and walked carefully up the steps into the Union Building. Colette was already in the Coffee House; Lydia, unwinding her scarf, saw with satisfaction that she had managed to grab one of the window tables. She was scribbling away at something, her head bent over a ruled pad. As she wrote, her arm brushed one of the tinsel garlands, sending silver light shimmering up her sleeve.

She looked up from her notes, smiling, as Lydia approached. 'I got you a coffee,' she said. 'That mob from Accounting came in just after me, so I thought I'd get yours while I was there, rather than you having to wait while they sort themselves out.' She gestured at the queue, and her pencil flew out of her hand. 'Drat!'

Lydia scrambled for it. 'Here you go. Thank you – that was sweet of you. How much do I owe you?'

'Don't worry about it,' Colette said. 'Honestly. I'm in such a bad mood that I'd pay for someone to rant at.'

'What's up?' Lydia asked, sitting down.

Colette sighed deeply. 'I had a run-in with one of the people on my course, during the group work. You wouldn't think, would you, that a Chemistry student would be a creationist?'

'Um...' Lydia said, instantly wary. She glanced at the cardboard Santa Claus on the counter as if he could tell her the right answer.

'You would?' Colette's voice was sharp. 'Oh, Lord, you're not one, are you?'

'No, but...' She was not a creationist, but she knew plenty of them, and, if she was honest, rather admired the dedicated stubbornness of their faith. She took a swig of the coffee to cover her consternation, and burned her tongue. 'I don't know. I suppose I've not really thought about it.'

'How can you *not* think about it?' It came out as a screech.

74

Heads turned. Lydia sat up very straight. 'Well, it's not as if I'm a scientist, is it? It doesn't make much difference what I think; it doesn't change anything.'

'I suppose not,' Colette said, more quietly, but not much mollified. 'But it's just so ridiculous – how can you believe it? You of all people – no, that's not fair, why should I expect that just because I think you...? Never mind. Ignore me. But it really is stupid.'

'It's in the Bible,' Lydia protested, knowing that was a feeble argument, and praying that Colette would not pursue it. Again she saw the towering edifice of her faith tremble before her eyes, and would have begged her friend to stop, if she could only have found the words.

'I just can't understand how anyone with a brain can subscribe to this bollocks,' Colette said. Her voice dropped. 'It's stupid, and they just come up with even more stupid things to explain away the things they can't deny. Were there dinosaurs on the Ark? Why would you even need to invent that?'

She was gazing at some invisible point on the other side of the room; it seemed to Lydia that she was no longer talking to her, but replaying an argument that she had rehearsed over and over again and perfected long ago. 'It's cowardly. It dishonours faith and science together. Someone who can't trust God to hold the universe together according to the reality God has revealed is someone who doesn't deserve to know God. How can they have so little faith – how can they be so idolatrous as to put a human story above God's reality? Is it so difficult to say, that is how they understood the way the world worked then, and this is how we understand it now? When it's so beautiful the way it really is?'

Colette turned suddenly back at Lydia, who started backwards, scared by the disappointment and intensity in her eyes (the angel, turning her out of Paradise with the flaming sword). 'You. You're an English student, for God's sake. Why can't you just let the Creation be a wonderful story?'

'Because,' Lydia said at last, and not meaning the Creation, 'if I lose that, I lose everything.'

They left it at that, and Lydia thought of several witty and incontrovertible answers over the Christmas holidays.

Lent Term

Chapter 1

A very happy new year to you all, and a special welcome to our student congregation returning after the Christmas break. Today is our Covenant service, when we recommit ourselves and our lives to God. 'No longer my own but yours': to call that a challenge is putting it mildly! We'll be exploring that further throughout today's service.

News Sheet, Wardle Street Methodist Church

Doctrinal differences aside, the chief drawback of being a Christian student was having to get up earlier on a Sunday than on any other day of the week. Every weekday Lydia could get out of bed at ten and still be in good time for her first lecture; it was hardly surprising that rising before eight on a Sunday morning to gulp down breakfast in an empty dining room and then walk down Markham Hill, across the city, and up Mount Pleasant to St Mark's, was an unattractive prospect. She had lived in Stancester for fifteen months now and it never got any easier.

On the first Sunday after the Christmas break she did not manage it at all. Either she had failed to set her alarm clock following the journey back to university, or she had slept through it, or she had managed to turn it off in her sleep. She woke with a jolt at half past nine, swore, and had most of her clothes on before realising that, even if she started walking now, she would only get to church in time for the post-service coffee.

She thought about undressing again and getting back into bed, but she was wide awake now. What, then, to do with the morning? She dragged on a jumper, wrestled with the catch of the window until it sprang open, and leaned out to breathe in the chilly, damp air. She looked down: the sickly lawn, deserted but for a couple of bedraggled rooks; the bare chestnut trees at the end of the drive; the glimmer of wet rooftops of the city beyond. Stancester seemed dead, but she was bubbling with energy. Coming abruptly to a decision, she yanked the window shut again, pulled on a pair of boots, and stuffed her keys into the pocket of her jeans. She would go out.

The sleety rain swept in from the west, and Lydia buttoned her coat up to the neck as she strode down the hill from campus. She pulled her hat down over her forehead, wound her scarf securely around her neck, and walked on.

Then she heard the bells of All Saints', pealing insistently across the hibernating city. Her heart leapt. After all, there was more to life than St Mark's. She could go to church after all.

But could she? Granted, she had been to the chapel last term, but All Saints' was a completely different matter. All Saints' had a reputation. Incense. Mary. Processions. More Catholic than the Catholics. The congregation was notoriously small; as a newcomer, she would be conspicuous. If news of her attendance got back to anyone at Fellowship – well, she could write the lecture herself. *Position of responsibility. Sound Biblical teaching. Idolatry.* In which case, she thought, feeling rebellious, she might as well go today, before anybody she knew got back to Stancester.

She regretted it from the moment that she stepped into the dank grey church. It was far colder inside than out; the clouds in the air were condensing breath rather than the infamous incense, and there would hardly be sufficient body heat rising from the congregation to compensate. Such attendees as were present had gathered into little clumps and looked distinctly unwelcoming. Except for Peter. He looked deep in conversation with an old lady, but he waved to Lydia, smiled, and nodded towards a pew. His own. Gratefully, she sat in it, hoping sincerely that no one else she knew would turn up.

She followed Peter's lead through the first half of the service, which felt choreographed and artificial. Standing up. Sitting down. Turning round to face the other direction. And singing the Gospel reading: what was the point of that? It made it impossible to understand the words. It was just as well that she already knew that the theme of today's service was the Baptism of Jesus, because this was emblazoned across the top of the church newsletter; and she remembered the Bible story, more or less.

Anyway, the really important bit formed the text for the sermon. The minister hauled himself up the pulpit steps, fiddled with the radio microphone, and began, '*This is my beloved Son, in whom I am well pleased.*

He let the echoes die, and continued, 'This is the moment where Jesus comes out.'

Lydia jumped as if an electric current had surged through her.

'This is the moment when Jesus acknowledges to His cousin, to His people, to His Father, and to Himself, who He really is. He's thirty years old at this point; up until now His devotion, His special connection to God, has been something that's been private – but now God wants him to do more...'

Lydia tried desperately to listen to every word that followed, but her mind was racing away on its own track. Had he really said that? Did he mean it like that? She realised guiltily that she had lost the thread completely; the preacher was talking now about grace.

'Most of us won't remember our own baptisms,' he was saying.

I do, Lydia thought, and tried to hold on to that – the drenching, the awe, being submerged in water as in the love of God: and how, for someone who had never been quite brave enough to jump into the swimming pool, it had been both terrifying and liberating: the certain knowledge that, in that mighty flood, her sins were washed away.

Where had it gone, that certainty? *O God*, she prayed, not knowing quite what she was asking. *O God...*

And suddenly the sermon was over. Around her, people were shuffling to their feet.

She felt increasingly uncomfortable as the service moved towards Communion. Such a *fuss*! She felt it should be much more simple than this, the way that Jesus had done it all, just himself and his friends, sharing a meal together. The jangle of the bell and the rattle of the censer chain were raucous distractions; the fog of incense obscured the meaning as well as the fact. What had they to do with anything Jesus had said or done?

It worked for Peter, however awkward she felt herself. Standing serenely next her, he seemed completely at home, never even having to look in the service book to see what to say or sing next. She wondered, worried, whether she ought to go up for Communion. Whether anybody here would mind. Whether God would mind. What her Christian friends would think about it. Whether they believed at this church that the bread and wine were literally the body and blood of Jesus. Whether she even wanted to. Peter would go, of course, and given that she had been shadowing his every move up to this point, she would need to make up her mind quickly.

She let him go without her. He raised his eyebrows in invitation, but smiled when she shook her head. It was just as well that they had the pew to themselves. She would not have enjoyed having a whole row of people climb over her. Actually, she told herself, it was rather nice just to be able to sit there, and watch, and listen.

'You could have gone up if you'd wanted,' Peter said afterwards. 'Father Steven wouldn't mind; and anyway, it's not as if we're *Roman* Catholics.' He took her empty coffee cup and stacked on top of his own.

She hesitated. 'I don't think I did want to,' she said at last. 'I'm not convinced it's for me...'

He laughed. 'Fair enough. So, what are your plans for the rest of the day?'

She buried her hands in her coat pockets. 'I don't know. I was going to go to St Mark's, and not getting there has thrown my whole schedule. I'll nip into town and get something for lunch, I suppose.'

'Come back with me?' he offered. 'I can give you beans on toast.'

'That would be lovely – thank you.' Then, remembering, 'Where's the rest of your house?'

'Oh, Georgia and Colette have gone to the Covenant service at Wardle Street – G's Methodist when she's not singing – Will's not back until later, nor is Becky – she was staying in Brum last night, coming down on the bike this evening – and Olly's still in bed, or at least, he was when I left.' He held the door open for her, and they stepped out into the drizzle.

'I didn't think you'd be here,' Lydia said, gesturing at All Saints' Victorian Gothic spire. 'I thought you'd be at the chapel.'

He shook his head. 'There isn't a service there this morning, though we are doing Compline tonight. Do you know what, though, it's very nice not to have to *do* anything in church for a change... I spent the last two weeks of term running around like a headless chicken organising the chapel Christmas services, and then I went home and got dragged straight back into the choir.'

'You're not in the chapel choir, though – or are you?'

'Only when they're really desperate,' he said.

'No, I suppose you can't do everything,' she said, too quickly. She took a deep breath. 'So do you do all that – you know, with the candles, and the cross – do you usually do that at the chapel? And is that an every-week thing, or a special-occasions-only thing?' She had a definite idea of where she was taking this line of conversation; she didn't want to ask about the sermon in the middle of the street and out of nowhere. The only thing was not to get distracted.

'Oh, the servers?' Peter said. 'We try. It's a question of manpower – well, womanpower, mostly. About eighty per cent of my team are women.'

Lydia knew about the typical attendance at the chapel. 'And by eighty per cent you mean, four out of five?'

'Something like that. That's my loyal, dedicated, core. Otherwise, it depends whose arm I can twist into doing it. Even Becky helps sometimes, for really big services, though of course she doesn't really *approve*. And in answer to your other question, yes, we do try to have a crucifer and acolytes – cross and candles – at all the communion services.'

'What about the incense? Do you have that at chapel, too?'

Peter laughed. 'That's only for special occasions – only your friend Zoe and I know how to do it – though I'm teaching Stuart.'

'Zoe does incense? She's never admitted it to me.' Lydia wondered if she ought to raise this at Teaching and Study Committee.

'She does, but, as I say, only on special occasions. All Saints have it every week though.'

They turned the corner into Alma Road. Lydia nodded. 'I can see why you do it,' she said, reluctantly. 'Well, not the incense, though of course that's scriptural, isn't it? They did use it in the Temple. But coming out –' she hadn't meant to say it like that, but there was no sense drawing attention to it now, and Peter might not have noticed '– with the cross and the candles, it does make it obvious, doesn't it, that this is about to be an important bit.'

'Well, yes,' Peter said, 'that's the idea. The Gospel is important.' His eyes twinkled wickedly. 'As, of course, is the Eucharist.'

Lydia refused to be baited. 'Communion. The Lord's Supper. Indeed.'

He scrabbled in his pocket for his keys. 'Here we go. After you.'

'Thanks.' She went in; she knew now to head straight up the stairs, and looked over her shoulder to say, 'Oh, yes. I was going to say: at *my* church, if we were to have candles and all that, we'd probably get them out around the preaching, as well. Because, you know, the teaching is really important, too.'

'That's true,' Peter said politely. He hung his coat over the back of a chair and opened a cupboard labelled with his name in Georgia's neat handwriting. 'Bugger, I was sure I had another tin of beans – ah, here we go.'

'But is the preaching like that at the chapel?' She removed her own coat.

'Like what? I would say that Tanya is a better preacher than Father Steven, but actually he was on very good form today.'

'Do you think –' Lydia started, then found she had to take a deep breath, 'do you think he – I mean, when he talked about Jesus "coming out",' (she made inverted commas with her fingers in the air) 'do you think that was deliberate? Is he aware of, you know, the popular meaning of that phrase?'

'Oh, almost certainly,' Peter said cheerfully. 'One slice of toast, or two?'

'Two, please, so long as I'm not eating your last piece of bread. So you think it was deliberate?'

He put four slices of bread into the toaster. 'I would have thought so. That is, I don't think that was the only thing that he was trying to say, but it will have occurred to him that the gay meaning exists, and he'll have made the decision to say it anyway. I don't know. You're the English student.'

'You're the theologian.' She smiled, but she did not quite see the relevance of her studies to this. 'So you reckon he's not saying Jesus was gay?'

'No – though I suppose he might have been. We wouldn't know.' Peter looked severe. 'But there are parallels there, I think. Yes. Actually, what about when Jesus uses the phrase? After all, he says "Lazarus, come out!", doesn't he?'

'You're not going to suggest that *Jesus* was going to use an expression that didn't even exist...?'

'No, of course not.' He stirred the beans, his expression thoughtful. 'I just think that it could speak to somebody who did happen to be in the closet, which – well, I don't know from personal experience, but I dare say one could compare it to being dead. And then of course baptism is a symbolic death, isn't it? Dying to sin and rising to new life in Christ Jesus. I bet Father Steven had that in mind...'

Certainly it had spoken to Lydia. Again, the shifting sands, the shuddering tower.

Downstairs, the front door creaked. Peter looked up. 'Georgia and Colette, I expect.' He compiled the two plates of beans on toast, put them on the table, pushed one towards Lydia, and fished knives and forks from the draining rack. 'Here you go. Enjoy!'

'Thank you.' She laughed shakily. 'So – what's Compline, then?'

'It's a service. Like Evensong, but later in the day, and shorter. No choir, usually.'

'Do you have to have a choir for Evensong?'

'No, not at all – though the choir would disagree, of course.' He sawed at his toast, then looked up with a conspiratorial grin. 'Did you know, by the way, that Will knows his way around the Book of Common Prayer? He keeps it quiet, but he used to be a cathedral chorister.'

'No! No, I didn't.' Lydia was almost gleefully shocked. 'Why doesn't he do that kind of stuff now?'

Peter shrugged his shoulders. 'I guess it just doesn't do it for him. I'm sure God doesn't mind, though from the sordid worldly point of view it's a shocking waste of a good baritone.'

Will put his head around the kitchen door. 'My ears are burning. Oh, hi Lyds. How goes?'

Feeling herself blushing, she cut up her own toast. 'Good, thanks. You?'

Unabashed, Peter laughed. 'Hello, Will. I've been telling Lydia all about your secret past. Good journey?'

'Very, thanks. Hardly any traffic at all. Fortunately, you don't know everything about my secret past, and I intend to keep it that way.'

'Oh,' Peter said lightly, 'that's all right. I'll just ask Olly.' He turned to Lydia. 'Those two went to school together, would you believe? Proper cathedral school, Latin and ruffs and everything. I only found out last term.'

'Trust me,' Will said, 'you didn't miss much.'

Someone called from downstairs, 'Whose is all this crap in the hall?'

Will called back, 'Mine! Sorry, Georgia!' He withdrew from the room, leaving Lydia and Peter to exchange awkward smiles. They heard him clumping down the stairs, and someone else coming up.

In that instant, Lydia would have said that she was half-prepared. There had been enough false alarms, after all, and she would not have accepted Peter's invitation to lunch if she had not thought that she was willing to see Colette. But she was not prepared at all.

It was not that Colette was still the avenging-angel-scientist. Quite the reverse, in fact: she looked hesitant, unsure of herself. Her hair was loose under a soft grey beret starred with raindrops, her duffel coat open, revealing a sage-green jumper over faded jeans. She said nothing; her eyes widened a little, and she simply looked at Lydia, long and silent.

'Hi, Colette,' Lydia said, and her own voice seemed very far away.

'Lydia.' Colette looked up to the ceiling, down to the floor, and finally settled on her own hands; she removed her gloves finger by finger, with intense concentration. And then, apparently able to think of nothing else to say, she laid them on the table, and left the room.

Chapter 2

Motion to Stancester University Students' Union General Meeting, 25th January

This meeting notes that the Christian Fellowship at the University of Stancester is affiliated to the Federation of Student Christian Societies (FSCS), an organisation which explicitly identifies itself as 'Evangelical', and that the Christian Fellowship is required by the FSCS to adhere to a "Statement of Belief". This meeting further notes that the Christian Fellowship excludes any person from membership of its committee and sub-committees who does not sign this "Statement of Belief" and also prohibits any person from speaking at its meetings who does not sign this "Statement of Belief".

This meeting believes that the "Statement of Belief" sets out a distinctively Evangelical interpretation of the Christian faith, to the exclusion of Christians from the Roman Catholic, Orthodox, Methodist, some Anglican Churches, and others. The requirement that committee members and speakers sign the "Statement of Belief" effectively excludes Christians who do not identify as Evangelical from full participation in the Christian Fellowship, and the name "Christian Fellowship" implies a group where Christians of all backgrounds and expressions of churchmanship can meet on an equal footing. Therefore, as matters currently stand, the name "Christian Fellowship" is misleading.

This meeting instructs:

- that the Christian Fellowship be formally renamed "Evangelical Christian Fellowship" with effect from the first day of the Trinity term;

- that all publicity, documentation, and other materials, whether printed or electronic, and whether produced or distributed by the Christian Fellowship, the Students' Union, or any other associated body, use the new name "Evangelical Christian Fellowship".

Proposed: Timothy Benton

Seconded: Oliver Sennick

Lydia was trying to estimate the size of the meeting. The Venue was full, but not to bursting. If a Fellowship meeting usually drew a hundred and twenty, there must have been twice that number here. The porters had put out extra rows of seats, and it looked as if they would all be filled.

She jumped when someone touched her shoulder. 'Lydia!'

'Peter! Hi!'

'You're at a Students' Union General Meeting? On your birthday?' Peter shook his head.

'I know,' Lydia sighed. 'I have no life. At least, I have, but my life is apparently revolving around the Christian Fellowship name-change motion at the moment. I wouldn't have come, but my friends are all here and it was less depressing than spending the evening watching the telly on my own in hall.'

'They abandon you for a Union meeting, make you wear a flashing badge saying *20 Today*, and you call them friends?' Peter was joking, but Lydia wished he wouldn't. He accosted Ellie: 'What's all this about poor Lydia not getting a birthday party?'

'I never said that,' Lydia said. Although, she supposed, Ellie must be well used to Peter by now.

'We *all* have to make some sacrifices,' Ellie said, hideously understanding, 'when the important things are at stake.'

'Oh, indeed,' Peter said lightly, 'depending on how you define "important". Personally, I'm here from sheer vulgar curiosity.'

'Really,' Lydia said.

'Well, it's possibly a duty in my capacity as Ecumenical Rep for AngthMURC,' he suggested, then, apparently finding that idea unexciting, 'or perhaps one could think of it as a piece of Church history in the making. Be there or be quadrilateral.'

'At any rate,' Ellie reproached him, 'you're not taking it seriously.'

'That's because I don't think it's particularly serious,' he said,. 'I mean, look at my own group. We have the stupidest name in the book, and we bumble along quite happily. I wouldn't have thought that the mere addition of "Evangelical" in front of "Christian Fellowship" would damage the society.'

'You chose to become AngthMURC, though, didn't you?' Lydia said. 'Nobody imposed the change on you. That's what makes the difference.'

'There is that,' Peter agreed happily. 'It had its pros and cons, of course. Pro: you come in first in the student handbook, before Archery and Astrosoc. Con: nobody knows what the hell it is you actually do.'

Ellie seemed not to have thought about this aspect of it; Lydia could almost see the wheels turning in her mind. It wouldn't work in Fellowship's favour. 'Ellie and I disagree about this one,' she told him. 'I probably won't vote.'

'Fair enough,' he said. 'Anyway, I was going to drop this off with the porters at Richmond, but since you're here, I'll give it to you now.' He extracted an envelope from the sheaf of papers under his arm. 'Not from me, but happy birthday anyway.'

Lydia recognised Colette's writing, with surprise and a sudden unclassifiable pang. 'Thank her for me,' she said.

Peter was waving at someone across the hall. 'I will. Enjoy the debate!' He turned to leave.

'Peter!' she called after him.

He looked back. 'Yes?'

'What *is* it that AngthMURC actually does?'

He grinned. 'Come along some time, and you'll find out!'

The chilly waft of Ellie's wordless disapproval stung like an Arctic gale.

'It passed. I can't believe it passed.' Ellie hurried off at speed, muttering to herself. Lydia, texting Rose to say where was she, and did they want to meet at Curzons for a quick drink, did not immediately register the absence; she looked up to find that Ellie was half-way across the floor.

Evangelical Christian Fellowship. Lydia murmured the words a couple of times, to see how they felt. A mouthful, but a mellifluous mouthful; not as off-putting as all that. Not worth getting upset about. Lydia Hawkins, Hall Officer, Evangelical Christian Fellowship. Sighing, she went to find Ellie.

She was with Jake and Rory; they made a tight, angry knot in front of the podium. Lydia hesitated at the edge, feeling conspicuously alone, but too conscious of her lowly status to interrupt. This was executive committee stuff. The 20 today! badge flashed its irritating little red lights, just on the edge of her vision. *Our lifeguard walks on water*, said Rory's T-shirt. She hovered. It was not as if they were worried about people listening to their conversation. She could hear every word, and blushed for it.

'I can't believe it,' Rory was saying, 'I literally cannot believe it.'

'Then I suggest you try harder,' Ellie snapped. 'This is ridiculous, but true.'

Jake, more cautious, murmured, 'Faith as small as a mustard seed... We prayed.'

'We'd better pray more,' Ellie said, becoming practical. 'I would get the Worship and Prayer committee onto it if I were you, Jake. See if we can't pull something together for Monday. And talk to Max at the Bath office. This must have happened elsewhere: there should be guidance.'

What about the hall groups, Lydia wanted to ask. There were resources there that had barely been tapped: small but prayerful gatherings (two or three, in His name), thoughtful, engaged, surely as powerful, cumulatively, as the main meeting. But she said nothing. She did not relish the task of selling the idea to her godly, intelligent charges, and anyway – here was Will Seton.

'Well,' he said, 'that was the Devil at work, wasn't it?'

And Rory and Ellie moved to make space for him in the circle.

Chapter 3

From: l.hawkins2@stan.ac.uk

To: n.r.russell@stan.ac.uk

9 February, 00:23

Dear Colette,

How are you? It feels as if I haven't seen you since before Christmas. I am very sorry if I offended you when we last had coffee. If so, I would like to apologise in person. Are you free at all next week?

Love,

Lydia.

From: n.r.russell@stan.ac.uk

To: l.hawkins2@stan.ac.uk

11 February, 11:03

Lydia – I thought it was the other way round. Can do Monday, 3pm, at the Coffee House if you think it's really a good idea. Best, Colette.

Lydia arrived half an hour early. Bought a mug of hot chocolate and sat and watched it cool. Looked out of the window at the trampled crocuses on the lawn. Watched the staff taking down the Valentine's Day decorations. Listened to the music that was seeping in from the radio in the kitchen: a woman's voice, rich, sad, aching. The song had been doing the rounds lately, but Lydia did not know its name. Nor could she make out many of the lyrics; only the tone of longing regret. Best not to listen too closely. She laid her hand on the edge of the table, and lifted her fingers one by one, until her hand hovered an inch in the air. Then she laid it down again and started over.

It was as much as she could do to stay there. The only way to stop herself standing up and walking out was to not think about what was going to happen, to concentrate instead on raising the fingers of her left hand, one, two, three, four, thumb, and then her right hand, thumb, one, two, three, four.

Colette despised her: that much was clear from her email. Reluctance oozed from every grudging word of it. Lydia had hoped that the birthday card was an invitation to return to their previous carefree friendship, but there had been no reply to her text message of thanks, and no contact since. Now she regretted pushing to meet again. All that she would gain from meeting Colette in person was confirmation of her leaden certainty. And, oh God, they were going to have to live with each other next year.

(The song ended, and the DJ began to babble inaudibly.)

She dared not start believing that Colette was right.

She did not believe that Colette was *wrong*, exactly. Of course Lydia was not a creationist – but she had been under attack, and the natural reaction was to retreat to safety, no matter how uncomfortable, and pull up the drawbridge.

How the hell was she going to explain that?

(One, two, three, four, thumb. Thumb, four, three, two, one.)

The hot chocolate had grown a skin. Wrinkles stretched in starbursts across the top. She hadn't wanted it in the first place.

A shadow fell across her. Lydia caught Colette's blurred reflection in the steel-panelled wall. 'Hello,' she said, and turned.

'Hi.' Colette's face was set like concrete.

'Thank you for coming. I was afraid you might not.'

'I almost didn't.' Colette slid onto the bench, frowning as the hem of her coat caught on the end.

Lydia nodded. 'Thank you,' she said again.

The conversation shrivelled and died. At last Colette said, 'Go on, then. Why did you want to meet me?'

'I wanted to ask if I'd offended you, and to apologise if I had. I know I said some stupid stuff the last time we met up for coffee, before Christmas. And if that's why you've been avoiding me – I'm sorry.' Lydia shook her head. She allowed herself to admit, 'You're so strong in the faith, you don't understand what it's like. I envy you so much, being able to love God without being afraid. I've acted like a spoilt child, and I'm so sorry, and I want to be your friend.'

Colette looked incredulous. 'I'm the one who should apologise. I was rude beyond all belief.' Then, picking up a different thread, 'Why I've been avoiding you.'

'Yes.' Lydia made herself look at her: the delicate fingers, tightly interlaced, the bitten nails. The shapeless cowl-necked jumper, swamping the torso in muddy folds. The dark shadow below the eyes. The fine lines between the eyebrows.

'You really want to know.' Hope twitched at the corner of her mouth.

'Yes. And –' blinking back tears, surprised by how much it hurt now she was letting herself think about it, '– I'm confused. We had that argument. Then it was Christmas. Then you sent me a birthday card. Then nothing at all, for weeks. I just want to know why...'

'You really don't.' She sounded as if she meant it.

'Try me.' Anything, surely, would be better than this.

'OK, then.' Colette propped her chin on her hands and looked hard at Lydia. 'I have a massive, embarrassing, hopeless crush on you.'

Lydia froze. Of all the things that she had thought Colette might say to her, this had not so much as crossed her mind, and she crumpled like tissue paper in the face of the challenge. 'Oh,' was all she could say. 'Oh.'

Colette's gaze dropped; she stared down at the tabletop and babbled, 'You see? I knew you'd be horrified, I didn't want to tell you, I was hoping I'd get over it and you'd never have to know, but I was worried that if I kept seeing you I'd give myself away...' She looked up at Lydia with anguished appeal in her grey eyes.

'It's OK,' Lydia said, searching desperately for the approved response. 'I understand. I know. If that's the way you are, you can't help it.'

It was so far from what she would have said, given time to formulate a reply, that she had to suppress a bitter laugh. Even so, Colette looked devastated. Lydia, cursing herself for her clumsy words, could hardly blame her. She stood up, tried desperately to mend matters. 'Thank you for telling me. But this – I've never – this is difficult for me. I'm sorry.'

And, having made things immeasurably worse, she turned and scuttled out. She could think of nothing else to do.

Chapter 4

How to run an AngthMURC election? You begin half-way through the Lent term by sending out an email to the society at large, including the members that have not been seen since they signed up in Freshers' Week, announcing that Elections Will Shortly Be Upon Us, and would prospective candidates please see a member of the current committee. They never do. They are timid little things, and they have to be cajoled and persuaded into running for a post. So you take one of these callow youths aside and say, (let's say Zoe) 'Zoe, have you thought about running for the AngthMURC committee? We think you'd make rather a good President. You've got the right combination of tact and enthusiasm, you know?'

She will equivocate. 'Oh, do you think so? I don't know... I'll think about it, if you like...'

You assure her vehemently that you would like. You suggest that she talk to Georgia (or whoever the current President may be) about it, so she gets some idea of the responsibilities. She says, OK, yes, she'll do that, and she'll think about it.

Eventually you will have got a potential committee together. About half of it will be Freshers recruited under the scheme outlined above; the other half will be the current committee, rejigged slightly to allow for leavers leaving and potential post-grads not having a clue what they'll be doing next year. It will all come together. Trust me.

How to run AngthMURC, Peter Nathan

'What are you doing this afternoon?' Gabe asked over breakfast the next day.

Lydia finished buttering her toast. She thought about saying, *avoiding Colette.* 'Not much. Taking a couple of books back to the library, and that's about it. Why?'

He smiled ingratiatingly. 'Want to come to a concert?'

'Are you in it?'

'Briefly.' Taking her question as assent, he said, 'In the Anglican chapel, two o'clock. It's the usual Music department mid-term. All of us who haven't done enough for our performance module digging up the thing we are least worst at and playing it. I've some Mozart in the first half and some jazz in the second.'

'That sounds good,' Lydia said cautiously. 'Is there any discordant modern stuff you're not telling me about?'

'Oh, almost certainly,' Gabe said, pushing his hair back behind his ears. 'I don't know who, or what, though. If you're lucky there might be a programme given out at the door.'

'You're really selling this to me,' Lydia said.

He spread his hands wide. 'There's nothing to sell. Entry is absolutely free.'

'There's my valuable time,' she protested, amused.

She went, though; she knew she needed to socialise more outside Fellowship and Alma Road. It was just a pity it had to be at the chapel.

The musicians had set up on the wide steps that led up to the altar; they stood around in little groups, muttering things like, 'But you *are* going to play the bassoon cue, aren't you, Tamsin?' Somebody was in the organ loft; they shouted down, 'Heather, I can't see you!'

A tall black girl turned around and called back, 'Can you move the mirror?'

'Hang on a sec... No, not far enough! You're going to have to come forward...'

Some other performers turned around to watch; among them, Lydia saw, were Gabe and Georgia. She smiled, not wishing to distract them while they were preparing. No fear of that: Gabe grinned and waved vigorously. 'Look, G! An actual audience!'

Georgia dashed across to her. 'Hi, Lydia,' she said. 'I'm glad you're here. I wanted to invite you to my birthday party. Twenty-sixth of April, at Angelo's.'

'Wow,' Lydia said, unable to think of an excuse, 'that would be lovely. Are you in this, too?' she asked, running her eyes down the programme. 'Oh – twice!'

'Yes – both on trumpet. I'd have liked to sing, but it's very vocal-heavy already; anyway, I need the credits in trumpet.' She turned around as a door opened behind her. 'Hey, it's Peter! More audience!'

'Don't you believe it,' he said. 'I'm just here to make sure you don't destroy my chapel.'

Georgia turned to Gabe. '*His* chapel – you hear that?'

Peter pretended to ignore her. He surveyed the arrangements with a proprietorial air. 'Just don't go messing around with my veiling and my Stations. Mind if I sit next to you, Lydia?'

'Of course you may.' She shuffled a little way along the pew, wondering if either of them *knew*. If they did, they showed no sign of it.

'Actually,' Peter confided to her as he sat down, 'I came to support Georgia and the rest of the chapel choir bods; but you can't *say* that – they're big-headed enough as it is.' He began to read the programme.

Lydia glanced around the chapel. The rest of the audience seemed to be other Music students, with a few stray lecturers. Much like Evensong, those there to produce the music outnumbered by some measure those who were there simply to listen. Georgia, wandering over to talk to Peter and Lydia just before the concert started, seemed resigned. 'That's what happens if you don't advertise,' she said. 'And they never do. Bloody elitists. Bloody *lazy* elitists.'

Lydia was not really listening; still hoping that a bigger audience might show for them, she had her eye on the main door – and so she was looking at it at the moment that Colette walked in.

Colette looked as if she had hardly slept. Her eyes were hollow; her hair straggled in elf-locks down her back. Flustered, Lydia whipped her head back to face straight ahead, and stared at the brickwork on the opposite wall while she worked out how she should react. She needed to apologise to Colette – but not here, not with Peter and Georgia looking on. She could hardly pretend that nothing had happened –

But Colette was walking straight past them all. She said, 'Hello, Peter. Hello, Georgia,' and passed without stopping into the row behind them. Georgia looked sharply after her, but said nothing.

Lydia ducked her head, avoiding Colette in her turn. She became conscious of Georgia's eyes upon her, concerned, questioning. If Peter had noticed anything amiss he gave no sign of it; he was fidgeting with a large bunch of keys. Would he think it was strange that Colette was not sitting with them? Georgia looked as if she was about to say something, but just then a snub-nosed, dark-haired man strode to the front with violin in hand, to a pattering of applause from the opposite side, and she scuttled back to join the other musicians.

Lydia barely heard any of the early pieces, her thoughts a whirl. There was no reason why Colette should not come to support her friends. She had as much right to be there as Lydia. But it was awkward, and Lydia could not shake the consciousness of Colette's presence from her head. Oh, God: why this, why now? Arne, Prokofiev, Ligeti, Mozart – everything sounded the same. Only when Georgia stood up could Lydia begin to pay attention to the music. She glanced at the programme. *The Trumpet Shall Sound (The Messiah)* – G. F. Handel. Yes, she supposed, it would be a shame to do that *without* a trumpet. Lydia recognised the singer from the chapel choir. She sat up straighter and listened. Georgia stood there, almost lazy, waiting for the singer and organist to be ready, and then raised her trumpet to her lips, and blew.

It was a fanfare, a long, full, soaring cry of hope and triumph. Lydia was enthralled. Compared to the holy vision that Handel had framed in music, her own mind seemed diabolically curdled. She could not bear it; the purity of the sound was such that she feared she might crack like a wineglass.

It was easier when the singer started; his voice was like garnets but he was at least human, and the words gave her something to hang on to, unattainable as they seemed. *The trumpet shall sound, and the dead shall be raised, be raised incorruptible.* The trumpet called back to him, urging him onwards, upwards. *For this corruptible must put on incorruption. And this mortal must put on immortality.* How? This was *perfection*, all over again. Handel dodged the question: he went straight back to *the trumpet shall sound.* The end seemed almost an anti-climax. *And we shall be changed.* As if it were simply not possible to make a satisfactory conclusion.

Peter touched her shoulder. 'You all right?'

She nodded, sniffed, fumbled for a tissue. 'Yes. It was just – so beautiful.'

Which was not what she meant at all.

She listened hard to the last two pieces in the first half, but the miracle had gone. A polite drawing-room piano trio; a showy but soulless violin solo; and it was over. Peter got up to do something to the lights. She could have tried to speak then; she turned around – but Colette was ostentatiously reading *Framley Parsonage.* Lydia had no idea what she wanted to say to her, beyond the fact that she was sorry. She did not try to come between her and Trollope.

She did not even know what she might apologise for. Her beliefs? They had not changed, and would not. Her unwillingness to contemplate Colette as a potential romantic partner? If anything were needed to make this situation more awkward, it was bringing that up. The tactless way she had explained herself? Yes, of course, but she could not make amends without touching on her reasons for so doing. Could she not apologise without causing further offence, or contradicting herself? Apparently not. Fine: best to leave it, then.

This seemed a cowardly option. She glanced behind her, seeking affirmation. Colette looked up as she turned, caught her eye for a fraction of a second, and looked down again. There was mute suffering in her face. *For God's sake leave me alone.* Lydia let herself turn back to face the front, and sat in tormented silence until Peter returned.

The second half of the concert was much more frivolous; most of it seemed almost blasphemously shallow. Lydia enjoyed Gabe's Gershwin and an insubstantial string quartet, but it was an ill-suited soundtrack to the turmoil in her soul. Then Georgia stepped out again. With Gabe on clarinet, one of the pianists from earlier, three singers, a double-bassist and a drummer, she had dragged together a jazz band. There was a little bit of fussing around and a scraping of furniture. Then, complete stillness. A few seconds – perhaps more – and the insistent *tss-tss-tss-tss* of the snare drum. The three singers and Lucy picked up the beat, stamping their feet. Two bars, and the piano entered, tinkling in the treble, a mere suggestion of the tune to come. The two women sang, pianissimo, '*Joshua fought the battle of Jericho, Jericho, Jericho…*' Then the man, brash and confident, '*Joshua fought the battle of Jericho, and the walls came tumbling down.*'

The pianist crashed out three mighty, accelerating chords, tumbling down the scale. This was Georgia's moment. She raised the bell of her trumpet so that it pointed up towards the great dark ceiling, and played with all her heart. The pianist had only to supply the background for the wide brazen stream of music that was pouring forth. His right hand was embellishing the tune of its own volition; with his left hand he was producing indecent, offbeat chords that propelled the music onwards. Lydia was enraptured.

Then Georgia stopped playing. The singers began again. '*Joshua fought the battle of Jericho, Jericho, Jericho. Joshua fought the battle of Jericho, and the walls came tumbling down.*' Then they stopped singing, and all that was left was the drum, sharp, on the beat, like marching footsteps.

The trumpet cut in again, in another energetic, aching solo. Then –
silence. They stood still; the trumpet, the piano, the drums cut out.
Very quietly, more whispering than singing, they breathed, '*Joshua
fought the battle of Jericho, Jericho, Jericho... Joshua fought the battle of
Jericho, and the walls came tumbling down.*' They sang again, louder, and
again, louder still. The trumpet joined them on the melody; the
pianist's hands flickered in ecstatic elaboration. The singers huddled in
a crowded clump; they were almost shouting. The music was slowing
up now, in one long luxurious rallentando. '*Joshua fought the battle of
Jericho... and the walls... came... tumb... ling... down!*' Two final, decisive
chords from the piano, and it was over.

Lydia was clapping frantically. A shape blundered out from behind
her, crashed through her vision, and was gone.

Chapter 5

Welcome to the AngthMURC committee! Let me guess: you've just been elected to help with the running of this society, you haven't yet quite managed to meet up with your predecessor in order for them to hand over the bumf, you were handed a copy of this handbook straight after the election, and now you're flicking through it and wondering what you've let yourself in for.

It's a daunting prospect, and rightly so. Running AngthMURC is no picnic, but I can assure you that if done correctly the amount of stress is more than compensated for by the amount of fun and sense of achievement. It's also a lot less daunting if you take it one step at a time. Your first step should be in the direction of the pub.

How to run AngthMURC, Peter Nathan

It was a long Lent. Lydia's reading had never been so assiduous; her preparation for hall group meetings had never been so thorough. For three weeks running she got through every book, every article, on the assigned list, and almost managed to believe that she would remember it. She dragged herself through the rest of the term and did her best not to think about what came after Easter. She did not hear from Colette again, and this time did not dare to make contact herself.

Peter came round to Richmond to ask Lydia what was wrong with Colette. 'She's not herself,' he said. 'She's dyed her hair black, and she's barely eating, and, um, acting really weird, and she won't talk, even to Becky, and none of us can work out what's up with her. So Georgia said I should come and see if you know anything...?'

'Why should I know anything?' Lydia demanded.

Peter looked awkward; he was clearly hating this as much as she was. 'Oh, no reason. Just, you're her friend; she might have talked to you. But then she's not talking to any of us, and it's not as if you're any different.'

'No,' Lydia said. 'No, she hasn't been talking to me.'

Which was not at all the same thing as, *No, she hasn't told me anything*.

It was easier at home. In Hastings she had her own predestined path, worn smooth by years of treading. In Hastings everybody did and was what was expected of them. Her mother, dedicated and brightly cheerful. Her father, stern and loving. Rachel – well, Rachel was fifteen, after all. And Lydia herself. Here there were no unexpected lines, no awkward declarations, no graceless responses. Denial was easy here; years-old secrets could be kept safe out of sheer habit. Their parts were as familiar and unquestioned as the script of the passion play, and though Lydia now played a Woman of Jerusalem rather than a Child With Palm Branches, the world still turned as it was meant to.

Only Lydia did not, as she would usually have done, spend her Easter Monday walking out over the Downs, rejoicing in the fierce fresh breeze, the new world, the life renewed. She was afraid of what she would see, when the wind and the sun had stripped her soul of inessentials; she was afraid that under the guilt and injury and revulsion there was nothing left of her to find.

Trinity Term

Chapter 1

From: commsofficer@stancester-su.org.uk

To: j.j.warner@stan.ac.uk

2 April, 11:39

Dear Jake,

Thank you for your email last week. I regret to inform you that the Students' Union Executive is unlikely to approve the proposed logo for the Evangelical Christian Fellowship. I would expect the Exec to rule that, while adhering to the letter of the resolution passed at the General Meeting in January, it makes no effort to abide by the spirit. My advice would be that the word "Evangelical" should occupy at least as much page space as the word "Christian". Ideally, the same font size should be used. I am sure your designer will be able to work within these specifications to produce an equally impressive logo.

I need not remind you that the name "Christian Fellowship" must not be used after the last day of the Easter vacation, and that any material using the old name or logo should be destroyed by this date.

Yours sincerely,

Harriet Haymes

Communications Officer, Stancester University Students' Union

The Christian Fellowship became the Evangelical Christian Fellowship. Little else changed. Lydia tried not to think about it, but it was the only thing that any Fellowship member was talking about. It was a relief to meet up with her study group and discuss *Dracula* instead.

In first year, study groups had rotated around the bedrooms of those in the most spacious – and central – halls. Now, Lydia was the only one who still lived on campus, and they met in the bar at the Venue. Their meetings, which had once been perky morning affairs with earnest discussion over strong coffee, had slipped later and later; often they were lunch and study together, books, pints and MegaBaguetz all jostling for space on the table; sometimes they stretched long and beerily into the afternoons, and some people never seemed to leave the bar at all. Today's was one of this sort. It was already quarter past two and Jenn was on her third Strongbow. Nisha had finally managed to get Keira to shut up about Aspen. Nobody had so much as mentioned yesterday's lecture on The Gothic.

Lydia glanced around the table. She liked her group well enough, though she was intimidated by the effortless way that Keira got her head around the theory, and she resisted the Freudian angle that India applied to everything. Mike, Jenn, Susie, Nisha – they all seemed so much cleverer than her, so much less inhibited. She always felt like an outsider, suspected that the rest of them held themselves back in her presence. That was nothing new. School had been just the same, and it was always implied that this was part of the cost of following Christ, that one would always be that little bit different. Set apart. It was lonely. Particularly when she must always be different at church, too... No. She must not think like that. It was hardly church's fault...

She looked up at the sound of a familiar name in an unfamiliar context. 'For all his faults,' Susie was saying, 'C. S. Lewis is very good on that.'

Lydia looked at her, lost. 'On what?'

'The medieval worldview,' Susie said. 'I was talking about my other module. Have you read *The Discarded Image?*'

'Oh, right,' Lydia said. 'I'm a huge fan of his Christian books, but I haven't read any of his academic work.'

'Ah,' Susie said.

Lydia, who was not in the mood for a fight, would have left that, but Mike said, 'What do you mean, *Ah*?'

Susie glanced at Lydia, half-apologetic, half-challenging. 'Well, for fuck's sake, the man was a massive hypocrite...'

'Oh?' Lydia said, mentally arming herself for the conflict, and doing her best to project an air of reasonable Christian love and forgiveness. Just in time, she had recognised this beer-fuelled conversation as a God-given opportunity to witness to her classmates. Her heart glowed. It was worth it, then, this degree and all the angst and self-doubt it had thrown at her; it was worth it, because she could help to bring these people to Jesus.

'He was a hypocrite,' Susie said. 'The man was a professor of English Literature. And – I will give him this – he wrote the most amazing book. It helped me get inside the heads of people who lived centuries ago, it gave me a tool to *understand* the way that those people thought, to read what they wrote and to appreciate the subtleties, the nuances within that writing. I always *knew* that people in medieval times didn't see things the way we do, didn't write things the way that people write things today, but – I don't know. Lewis made it a reality, that's all. And then I read *Mere Christianity*.'

'And?' Lydia couldn't help asking, though she knew it was a tactical mistake.

Susie turned on her. 'And? And it's a massive disappointment. You must know. The arguments are simplistic. It's sexist and dated. The worst thing, though, is that he's basing his central argument on an outrageous lie. He wants you to believe that everything in the Bible is literally true. He's asking you to believe that *he* isn't aware of the existence of metaphor, of exaggeration for dramatic effect, of the fact that people wrote things differently two thousand years ago. And he thinks he can get away with it because you're too dim to have read his real books for real men.'

'Wow,' Lydia said, shaken.

'Having said that,' Susie added after a pause, 'he's also pretty good on Milton.'

They laughed uneasily. Mike fished out his copy of *Dracula*, and the study group began at last to study. Lydia found it hard to concentrate. Susie's rant buzzed in her head. She tried telling herself not to take it personally, but she had a fearful suspicion that Susie was right. (And if she was, what then? Truth like a battering ram, and the walls were shivering.) She made some half-hearted notes *(Jonathan + Dracula; what about Lucy? Mina – damnation – monster nature – she can't fight it off by willpower alone)* and threw in a couple of comments that she hoped were intelligent. As soon as the discussion veered away from the business of the day she mumbled something about needing to get something out of the library and slunk off.

Having made that excuse, she felt obliged to at least visit the building, and hope to remember some book or other that she might want to borrow. In fact, she told herself, defiantly open-minded, she could go down to the English Literature section and browse the Medieval shelves, on the off-chance that this Lewis book would be there, and she would remember its title when she saw it. She liked the idea of a cosy evening with a good book. The twenty-first century was proving difficult; why not step back seven hundred years or so?

That plan came to nothing. She was barely fifty yards into the library before she caught sight of Colette, absently turning over book after book on the Returns shelf. Horrified, Lydia retreated between the stacks. It was a trick of the light, surely, or a product of Lydia's own troubled imagination: all the colour seemed to have been bleached out of Colette, all the life; she was like a walking effigy of herself. Lydia was tempted to step out and stare after her, but she did not want to be seen. She looked, instead, at the cadaverous reflection in the long windows, and watched her walk away.

Then, perturbed almost beyond endurance, she turned around and trudged back to Richmond.

She sat down on her bed and stared, unseeing, out of the window. She had not expected to see Colette. Nor had she expected the sight of Colette to affect her so.

It was not just the hair. The hair was a shock; it looked so wrong, so stark and cold and unlike Colette. A dull black that was no colour at all. She was thinner, too, or perhaps it was only – only! – that she had lost something. *Bounce,* Lydia thought, and immediately rejected the word. Colette was never bouncy; but there had been some indefinable quality about her, and suddenly it was gone.

(Suddenly? It could have been any time in the last two months, and Lydia would not have known. And Peter had tried to tell her, and she had refused to hear. Oh, God, she thought, what kind of friend am I? To leave someone to deal with that alone, when I *knew,* and yet –)

She could not bear to follow that thought, and sought a distraction. She thought about writing up her notes from the *Dracula* lecture, but all she could hear was Susie castigating C. S. Lewis. She knew that she should pray, but she was scared to look herself in the face, let alone God. She picked up the notes from her other module, but they were on Donne's *Holy Sonnets,* and almost as hard to countenance. The knock on her door was a welcome interruption.

'Lydia, you can spell, yeah?' Rory said, as soon as she had opened it. (*Jesus loves the hell out of you,* said his T-shirt.) 'I need your help. I have to submit this motion by six, or it won't make the deadline for the next Union meeting.'

It did not occur to her to resent his assumption that she had nothing better to do. The better things were too daunting to contemplate. She checked her watch. 'Two hours. Yeah, I'll have a look at it.'

'Really? Fantastic! Here you go.'

This union deplores the discriminatiory attitude of this union towards the Christian faith and commands all Christians to deounce this outrage and reverse the actions of the last meeting.

Automatically, Lydia reached for a pencil and underlined *discriminatiory* and *deounce*, before skimming the rest of the page with increasing dismay. 'Do you have a copy of the Rules?' she asked. For she knew that there were Rules about this, and she was certain that this motion must be breaking several of them.

Rory looked shamefaced. 'I guess they're online?' He moved as if towards her computer.

'*Don't –*' she squeaked, remembering what her browser history might reveal. 'I mean, I don't think there's time to rewrite the whole thing from scratch, and neither of us is an expert...'

'It's got to get through, Lydia,' Rory said. 'I don't think you realise how serious this is.'

If he knew how little she cared! She could not refuse to help, and if she helped and the thing was rejected it would not be seen as Rory's failure. Therefore she must get it through. 'Do you have a copy of the first motion?' she asked. 'We know that got through. And –' seeing his face – 'we know that the Union will be looking for any excuse not to debate your motion. I mean –' she crossed the fingers of the hand that didn't hold the pencil – 'there's nothing wrong with it, it's great, but maybe it would work better as a speech...'

'I suppose that makes sense.' Rory was trying to sound reluctant, but he was clearly picturing his impending rhetorical triumph. 'Yes, we need to keep the motion as simple as possible, and leave the difficult bits for the speeches.'

'Indeed,' Lydia said, gritting her teeth. 'Right, you need to capitalise Statement of Belief, where you're actually talking about the thing, otherwise it's a bit confusing... What do you mean by this bit?'

He peered over her shoulder. 'Oh – that you don't actually have to be Evangelical to join the Christian Fellowship, you just have to be able to sign your name to the, you know, the sentence that goes "I accept Jesus Christ as my Saviour, my Lord, and my God, and the word of God as revealed in the Bible..."'

'I see. So: *This Union notes: that membership of the Evangelical Christian Fellowship* open brackets *ECF* close brackets *is open to any student who signs to give assent to the following sentence* – and quote it – *and is therefore not specifically restricted to those who identify as Evangelical.*'

'Yes,' Rory said happily. 'That's exactly what I want. But it should be the Christian Fellowship.'

Lydia shook her head. 'You're going to have to live with the "Evangelical" until this gets passed, or your motion won't actually mean anything. They'll just say there's no such thing as the plain Christian Fellowship, and dismiss it.'

He made as if to protest, but she looked meaningfully at her watch, and he desisted.

'Then you have all the stuff about the Statement... OK, how about this? *This Union further notes that the ECF is required by its own constitution to adhere to a Statement of Belief that summarises fundamental Biblical Christian beliefs.*'

'I don't like "fundamental",' Rory objected.

'Really? No, perhaps better not,' Lydia agreed, while some detached part of her mind wondered how she could sit here so calmly and disassemble the text, while the centre of her being screamed in distress. 'I'll say "core Biblical Christian beliefs". And you're saying here that committee members and speakers don't have to identify as Evangelical, they just have to sign the Statement?'

'Yes.'

'Right.' Lydia scribbled again. 'The middle bit is fine as it stands. You're saying that calling it the "Evangelical Christian Fellowship" is actually *exclusive*. And that other societies have the right to call themselves what they like. That's all clear. And then the final section is pretty much the reverse of the original motion. Everything that was changed to "Evangelical Christian Fellowship" goes back to "Christian Fellowship", implementation date as soon as possible. You're done.'

'Awesome! You're a legend! Um...' Rory frowned at the paper. 'Your writing's a bit difficult to read. Is there any chance you could type this up and email it to me? Then I can get down to the library and submit it online.'

Lydia rolled her eyes, but doing it herself was preferable to having Rory look at her computer, and it would ward off the guilt for another ten minutes. 'Of course,' she said. 'Bet I email it to you before you get to the library.'

'You're on,' Rory said cheerfully, and left, letting the door bang shut behind him.

Left alone, she rather regretted saying that. She could have stretched it out until 5.55, put off Donne and prayer a little further.

'Pathetic,' she said out loud. 'Scared of yourself, Lydia?'

She was.

Best not to think about it. She typed up the motion, emailed it off to Rory. Half past five. She glanced out of the window. Outside, the clouds were retreating, begrudgingly; the tentative April sun was touching the cedar with watery gold. A couple of lads were sloping up the path; they might as well have been aliens. Lydia had no desire at all to interact with any other human being.

Any human being.

(If talking to yourself was the first sign of madness, what was not wanting to talk to yourself?)

Lydia felt, superstitiously, that she must not leave the building until she had finished – whatever this was. She could not face the prospect of hall dinner – but, she remembered, she had a prawn sandwich in the fridge in the kitchenette, meant for lunch today and never eaten. She went to retrieve it, and made a cup of coffee to take back to her room.

'Now,' she said, out loud. She locked the door; then she laid everything out on the desk in an orderly line from left to right. The notes on 1 Corinthians 13 for the next hall group meeting. Her Bible. Donne's *Complete English Poems*. The sandwich. The annotated first draft of the motion. The coffee cup. Finally she placed Colette's twisted wire cross at the end.

'Right, then,' she said.

They sat there like an interview panel.

'But I'm not there,' she said.

She found a blusher compact with a mirror in the lid, and propped it up, open, between the Donne and the sandwich.

'I really have gone crazy,' she said.

None of them replied.

She sat down.

'Well,' she said, waiting for the courage to confront the festering mess at the centre of her soul.

She bit her lip and, suddenly brave, darted a hand out and grabbed the Donne. She read the sonnet almost surreptitiously (*Like an usurp'd town*) as if it might itself turn on her if it noticed her reading it. (*Reason your viceroy in me, me should defend, But is captived, and proves weak or untrue.*)

'Seriously,' she said, 'I'm losing it.' She put the book back, gingerly, and reached for the coffee. Much safer. Her hand was shaking. She sipped tentatively and replaced the cup where it had been.

What now?

She put out a hand towards the Bible and the teaching notes, but drew it back again. Not yet. She could not look that pure, divine, declaration of love in the eye, not with her poor besieged heart. (No:

that was the wrong way round. She squinted at the tiny mirror, trying to see her whole face at once, as if that would help.)

Very well. Immediately in front of her lay Rory's motion to the Union, her own pencilled corrections overlaying his printed assertions. That at least was simple.

But was it? She had disagreed with the text even when writing it. She had made a good job of it, but even art was not above morality, and this was hardly art. She made herself re-read it, first Rory's bluster alone, and then her own elegant translation. She had coated the pill with sugar, but the pill was poison.

No: that was melodramatic. She did not care whether or not the Christian Fellowship kept its "Evangelical" prefix. It would make little difference in years to come, and if this cleared the dispute up then perhaps they could all move on to something that mattered.

She could not ignore, however, the logical foul that stared up at her from the first section, an omission more glaring, to her guilty eyes, than any lie could be.

One did not have to call oneself an Evangelical, he – they – *she* had argued, to influence or speak at the Christian Fellowship. One merely had to assent to the Statement of Belief.

But they had deliberately refrained from pointing out the fact that one could not, in good conscience, sign the Statement of Belief without also being the sort of Christian that would normally be described as "Evangelical".

She had signed the thing herself, but then she was an Evangelical. Add x to both sides of the equation. No: the motion was a monstrous piece of sophistry and she was ashamed to have colluded in its composition. And there was nothing to be done about it now: it was well past six, and the thing was submitted.

Outside, the sky was streaked with angry purple and flame. She thought about tearing the motion up, setting fire to it, even; but that would make no difference. It existed now. She laid it back on the desk and picked up Colette's little wire cross.

It was not a particularly delicate piece of work – Colette would have needed pliers to do something really skilled – but it had an endearingly human wonkiness to it, and Lydia liked the swirls and bubbles of the purple bead at the centre. She laid it against her forehead and felt the coolness of the glass and her hand hot behind it.

Colette. What about Colette, then? How did she do it? How had she managed to be who she was? Lydia dared not even articulate it, and Colette lived it.

Still grasping the cross, Lydia let her hand fall and leaned back in the chair. Her world was, for the moment, perfectly quiet. She could feel the tide of guilt and panic ebbing away. She had still to consider Colette as she had been today, but that was too hard. She shut her eyes tight, tried to think of nothing but the feel of metal and glass in her hand, and almost succeeded. Somewhere, somewhere very far away, there was peace and stillness.

When she opened her eyes again, she saw that the sun had fallen behind the other side of campus, and the warmth was draining out of the light to leave impersonal, deepening blueness. She was tempted to let it; there was much that she did not want illuminated. But she stood up, laid the cross down reverently, and switched on the lamp. When she sat down again she reached for the hall group notes.

'One verse,' she told herself. 'Just one verse.' She shut her eyes and jabbed at the text with a finger.

She opened her eyes and read, *Love does not delight in evil but rejoices in the truth.* She laid the sheet down again. That was the Vigil, and Colette again, extolling the wonder of reality. She skipped further down the page. *For we know in part, and we prophesy in part, but when perfection comes, the imperfect disappears.*

(Not that anybody behaved as if they knew only in part, said something nasty in the back of her mind. Rory, for example...)

'Now you're just being bitchy,' she said. Her eyes fell upon the sandwich. She was, she realised, incongruously hungry. She peeled its plastic casing away and began to eat.

That reminded her of something. Rather to her surprise, she found that she was brave enough to look at the Bible. She opened it at the back, looking for the lists of useful verses intended to succour the confused. *Hardship and Suffering. The Holy Spirit. Homosexuality.* Leviticus 18:22. She did not bother looking it up. That was the one next to the one about shellfish. She knew it by heart, and it was hardly applicable to this particular case. Genesis. Sodom and Gomorrah; but that was supposed to be about the abuse of hospitality. She was surprised how well she knew the counter-arguments. *See also* Genesis 2:24: a man will leave his father and mother... The Biblical model of marriage, except it wasn't. Solomon. The New Testament. Temple prostitutes. Oh, God, she was tired. None of it seemed at all convincing, either for or against. She had heard it all before, Googled it to death. None of it felt like it had anything to do with her, or her friends.

She felt the battlements tremble again. The entire foundation of her faith was shifting. (*Batter my heart, three-personed God* – no.) Hurriedly, she laid the Bible down again. She took a draught of the coffee; it had long since gone cold. Should she get up and make another? No. No. She had to finish this. (*Break, blow, burn.*) The motion? There was nothing more there. She picked up the notes again, and turned to the commentary on the other side.

This chapter is often read at weddings – but why not take a moment to imagine God addressing it directly to you? This is divine love; this is how God loves you.

She remembered Colette saying, *God loves Colette, just as God loves Lydia.* That hardly seemed to mean anything at the moment. She inverted it. *God loves Lydia, just as God loves Colette.*

Feverishly, she turned back again.

116

Love is patient, love is kind. It does not envy, it does not boast, it is not proud. It is not rude, it is not self-seeking, it is not easily angered, it keeps no record of wrongs.

What had she done to Colette?

That was the worst thing. That was the thing she could not face. Yet it was true. She had to face it, or know her faith to be false forever.

Whatever wound it was that Colette was bearing, it was Lydia who had struck the blow. Whatever quality it was that Colette had lost, it was Lydia who had robbed her of it. Very slowly, very deliberately, she made herself remember Colette as she had seen her that afternoon: the toneless dyed hair, the eyes that gazed straight ahead and looked at nothing, the face sunk to an angular caricature, the unnatural pallor.

It was Lydia's doing. She had bullied the confession out of Colette and then run away, leaving her to sweep up the mess alone. Leaving her to think she hated her, despised her, thought her an abomination.

How could she ever atone for that? Lydia reached for the flimsy wire cross and clutched it tight though she feared it might burn her. The mirror caught her convulsive movement, and for one mad moment she thought it was Colette's face she saw, not her own.

That seemed the wrong way round, too. Had she seen her own face in Colette's? No. No. She could not think that. She dared not think that, and she could not remember why.

O'erthrow me. Romans 1:26. If there was one stone left standing upon another, that was it, the only one that mentioned women. *Because of this, God gave them over to unnatural lusts.*

Because of what? She turned back to the previous page. *They exchanged the truth of God for a lie* – and there was Colette again, scorning her for being too cowardly to see God's creation. *Even their women exchanged natural relations for unnatural ones.* Unnatural. Colette, with her dyed hair, starved to a skeleton, suddenly half a human; but that made no sense, because that was *afterwards.*

There were tears streaming down her face. *Then we shall know fully, even as we are fully known.* She snatched the mirror up, afraid that she might somehow have disappeared. *Poor reflections.*

I am only a resounding gong, or a clanging cymbal. A sounding brass. The trumpet shall sound.

Trumpet. Joshua. Jericho.

And the walls came tumbling down.

Not a stone left standing upon another. Nothing. There was not even rubble.

She realised with wondering gratefulness that it had never been there at all.

The little cross was still nestled in her hand. *These three remain. These three remain: faith, hope and love.*

And the greatest of these?

Chapter 2

From: g.robinson2@stan.ac.uk

To: p.m.nathan@stan.ac.uk; o.sennick@stan.ac.uk; n.r.russell@stan.ac.uk; r.m.seymour@stan.ac.uk; w.h.f.seton@stan.ac.uk; g.l.hammond@stan.ac.uk; b.z.marsden@stan.ac.uk; l.hawkins2@stan.ac.uk; [+ 8 more]

20 April, 17:25

Hey guys,

Just a reminder that my birthday party is this Thursday, 26th April, at Angelo's. (Gabe, Peter, I still need your menu choices! Will, I assume you're away with the sailing club, but please confirm.) I have been asked about what we're wearing – I really don't mind, but let's say smart casual.

See you all there,

Georgia xxx

From: r.a.barnes@stan.ac.uk

To: [Christian Fellowship – Executive]; [Christian Fellowship – Teaching and Study]; [Christian Fellowship – Hall Officers]; [Christian Fellowship – Prayer and Worship]; [Christian Fellowship – Social]

21 April, 08:29

Guys,

Just a reminder that there is a Students' Union meeting this Thursday lunchtime, starting at 12.30 – in the Sports Centre, not the Union itself this time. As we sadly know from last term, it is really important that there is a good turnout from Christian Fellowship so that we can make sure that our views are represented and God's great work can continue on campus. Praise Him!

Rory Barnes

Lydia made herself go to the Union meeting, to hear her motion (no! Rory's motion!) moved, debated, and passed. She felt like a stereotypically tortured detective attending the execution of the criminal their brilliance had brought to justice. Or, in this case, injustice. As if the detective had realised, all too late, that the defendant was innocent, or that the crime was not a crime at all – and that some masterful embracery had filled the jury box with a single-minded mob bent on conviction.

The mob was very meek and well-behaved, as befitted a congregation of Christians. That was unnerving enough in itself. Surveying the crowd gathered in the sports hall that lunchtime, she was struck first by its relatively small size, at least compared to the evening meeting on her birthday, when that first motion had been passed, and next by the number of faces she knew within it. Rory, of course, and Ellie – but there were Simon, Mel, Fiona, too. Every other person was a member of the Evangelical Christian Fellowship.

Rory had been more clever than she had thought: lunchtime meetings, scheduled for the benefit of those who lived off campus or had other commitments in the evenings, were never well-attended, and this one was hampered by its venue. Nobody would traipse all the way up here unless they really cared; and it seemed that only the Evangelical Christian Fellowship really cared. Someone had cared enough to make sure that this particular motion went to this particular meeting. Someone had cared enough to mobilise the whole membership, to ensure the presence of a convincing majority. Someone had cared enough to enlist her to make sure that the motion was technically competent.

And she had played along. She would have to watch the motion go through, knowing all the while that it was morally a falsehood, and that it was her fault. Perhaps, Lydia thought miserably, the corrupt prosecuting lawyer was a more fitting role for her. The arrogant silk, well aware of the defendant's innocence, but pulling out a brilliant argument for her own pride's sake. Not that she spoke, of course. She imagined being brave enough to stand up and dispute the assertions that she had herself set down, phrased, polished, perfected.

My fellow students, she would say, *the words you have before you are mine. I disown them.*

She would never do it, of course. They would throw her out of Fellowship. They would expel her if they so much as dreamed what she had been thinking recently, what she was contemplating even now. And so she remained seated, spoke neither for or against, and the democratic process was followed and the motion was passed, and once again the Evangelical Christian Fellowship was the Christian Fellowship, pure and simple.

The cloudburst that caught and drenched her on her way back to hall seemed no more than just punishment. The bolt of lightning that tore the sky in two might have been an expression of divine displeasure. And the power cut that plunged half the city into darkness really felt rather heavy-handed, symbolically speaking. Storm clouds aside, it was not even very convincing darkness, it being only half-past two.

It rained all the rest of the afternoon, and the power never came back on, and Lydia had the presence of mind to dress for Georgia's birthday party well before daylight faded. She was not really in the mood for a party; she felt guilty, cowardly, and snappy. But she believed – she had to believe – that she had the courage to do one thing right, at least, and so she put on her newest dress, slipped a note under Gabe's door, and went to see Colette.

The house was in darkness. The whole of Alma Road was dark, and beneath the heavy storm clouds the spring twilight was fading fast. Lydia shivered. Twice she walked up to the front door, lifted her hand to the bell, and let it drop again. Twice she turned and crossed back to the street before at last she mustered the courage to stand and ring the bell.

Peter came to the door, which surprised her. Somehow she had forgotten that other people lived in the house.

'Hi,' she said. 'I came to see Colette.'

A frown settled on Peter's face, but he only said, 'She's in her room, I think.' Lydia wondered how much he knew. And, for that matter, how much there was to know. 'Here –' he said, pressing something into her hand '– you'd better take this.' A small electric torch. 'The power's completely gone. Georgia's put candles on the landings, but there's not much to be done about the stairs.'

'Thanks.' She smiled, wanting, absurdly, to apologise to him. But he disappeared.

It seemed inconceivable that she would be living here next year. The house felt alien in the candlelight, its angles exaggerated and its shadows deepened. The two flights of stairs and the cramped little landings seemed to go on for ever like a mountain in a nightmare, and only in the bright white circle of the torchlight could she make out the familiar – the pattern of the carpet, the Christ the Redeemer poster on Georgia's bedroom door, the tentacle cord of the telephone. Even those seemed stark and hostile. The house had closed itself against her, protecting its own; it knew that she had hurt Colette.

Telling herself not to be so silly, Lydia reached the top landing and tapped, hesitantly, on Colette's door.

'C'min!' Colette said. Then, when she saw Lydia, 'Oh.' She was sitting at her desk, upon which she had propped a mirror to improvise a dressing-table. A flickering candle flame lit the glass; Colette sat with her hair streaming around her shoulders, a half-eaten apple in one

122

hand and two bottles of nail varnish in the other. She said, in a clumsy attempt at everyday conversation, 'What colour would you say *Aurora* would be, and would it go better with this dress than *Nectarine*?'

Lydia saw herself reflected in the mirror, a weird sprite over Colette's left shoulder. 'I suppose a sort of orangey-pink,' she said. 'I don't think I've ever seen you wear that dress before, though, and it's difficult to tell in candlelight.' She took the bottles and squinted at them. 'I didn't realise you even *wore* nail varnish.'

'Didn't have me pegged as a girly girl, eh?' Colette said brusquely.

Lydia flinched. 'No, I...' Deciding too late that there was no good answer, she settled for, 'I'd go for *Nectarine*.'

Colette took them back with a bad grace. 'I don't think I'm even going to have time to paint my nails, by the time I've finished my apple and done my hair. And I have to do it in that order, for obvious reasons.'

Lydia said, too fast, 'I can do your hair, if you like.'

Colette eyed her suspiciously, then said, 'I suppose so. I mean, you've had my heart and my dignity; I might as well let you loose on my hair.'

That stung, but Lydia knew she deserved it. 'No problem,' she said, her heart beating fast. 'Why are you eating, anyway? Will dinner be so late?'

A world-weary sigh. 'That was what I said, but Georgia made me. She thinks I'm not eating enough.'

Lydia privately agreed, but she only said, 'What do you want to do with your hair?'

'Anything.' Colette shook her head. 'If you could manage to make my hideous amateur dye job a little less obvious, that would be a bonus, but at this point I'd settle for "tidy".' She turned away from Lydia to face the mirror.

'I can do that.' She picked up the comb.

'Perhaps,' Colette said, with an edge of steel to her voice, 'you could also tell me why you're here, while you're doing that?'

Lydia drew a breath. Suddenly they were back on the script that she had prepared, but she could not find her place, and had to start from the beginning. 'Well, I was going to say that I'd come to see if I could walk down to Georgia's party with you guys. And then I was going to explain that I really came to apologise for everything I said. You know, that day in the Coffee House. I know exactly how it must have sounded, and I am so, so, sorry.' She separated out three strands of hair and began to make a French plait. She was glad that it took concentration.

'It doesn't matter,' Colette said.

'It does. May I explain?'

In the mirror, she could see Colette's face tighten. 'I guess?'

There was a frantic fluttering at the base of her ribs. She caught her breath. Her throat was constricted and she feared she might weep. The confession that for half her life she had confined unspoken even to herself trembled now on the tip of her tongue, ready to jump back down her gorge. Yet she said it, and it was almost casual.

'I'm gay.'

Then, 'Don't move: I'm going to have to do that whole bit again now. There.'

'Why on earth,' Colette asked, 'didn't you say so before?'

She sounded half-disbelieving, half-angry. Lydia did not care. She had said it, and the sky had not fallen. 'I panicked. Why else do you think?'

A grudging chuckle. 'I suppose that makes sense.'

'Everything makes sense if you begin by assuming that I'm a huge wuss.' Then, moving the comb to the other hand, 'I've known for years, but I was always praying that it would turn out not to be true, that God would somehow make me fall in love with some miracle boy.'

'Go on.' Grim.

124

Lydia combed out another soft strand of hair. 'You know what it's like, being gay and Christian – I mean, I know you're bi, not gay, but it comes to the same thing, doesn't it – can you hold this? Thanks – and eventually I thought, right, I can't change this. Maybe God can, but I can't. I'm just going to have to get on with life. Because what's the worst that could happen? I could be single forever. Well, I thought, I can deal with that, and maybe God will miraculously make me fall in love with a bloke one day. I mean, He's omnipotent, He could do that, right?'

'I don't know,' Colette said.

'Anyway, He hasn't. What He has done is given me a friend who is both actively queer and a devout Christian, He's given her a crush on me, and – well, put me square in the line of temptation.' She felt Colette's shoulders stiffen, and she ploughed on. 'I have wanted to be with you ever since – oh, God, I don't know. Before Christmas. Maybe when you gave me that little cross at the Vigil. I want to be with you now.'

'Temptation?' Colette was frowning.

'I know. I'm still not sure if it's right. But I've seen you trying to pretend it isn't happening, and you're becoming more and more unhappy and less and less like yourself – and – I don't know. I can't see God in that. I could in who you were before.' The strands of hair were soft and light between her fingers. She caught, twisted, wove, and let herself enjoy it. 'And if that's what I look like, what I've looked like ever since I found I had something to hide...'

'Go on,' Colette said.

'Pass me the comb? Thanks. So I thought, right, this is ridiculous, I'm going back to the Bible. *That* bit.'

'Romans.' Colette sounded a little warmer. They were allies now.

'Exactly. And I sat down, and I read it, and I read it again, and all I could see was that it was saying how terrible it is when people try to be something that they aren't.' She gathered up the last few wisps of hair and made a long plait down Colette's back. 'Pass me an elastic. I swear it didn't used to say that.'

'How long was it since you'd last read it?' Colette asked.

Lydia flinched. 'Longer than I'd like to admit. It does rub it in. At least, I thought it did.'

'I know.'

'I need three hairgrips – thanks – and so, I thought that the least I could do was come and apologise for running out on you, and letting you think I meant – whatever you thought I meant.'

'I didn't think it was flattering,' Colette said drily.

'No. I can imagine.'

Their eyes met in the mirror.

'Apology accepted,' Colette said, slowly.

So much for the past. 'Do you – still feel the same way?'

'The last ten minutes,' Colette said, 'have been torture. Amazing. But torture. I do.'

'I don't think I'd have been brave enough to come if I didn't.' Lydia laughed nervously. 'Do you have any hairspray?'

'Only glittery stuff – on the bookcase.'

Lydia reached for it. 'That'll do – it'll make your roots look less obvious. Will you go to Georgia's party with me?'

Colette was looking at her as if she were an angel or an alien, but she said, 'I'd love to. Are you sure?'

'About the glitter?' Lydia joked feebly. 'Or about going with you? Either way, yes, absolutely.'

Finally, mercifully, a smile broke across Colette's face. 'Let's try it, then.'

'So,' Colette said, as they walked, fifty yards behind Peter, Becky, Olly and Georgia, 'what are *you* playing at?'

'Playing at?' Lydia was confused. The words were aggressive; the tone was not, and the emphasis made it, apparently, a genuine question.

Colette had thrust both hands deep in her pockets; now she withdrew one of them to point ahead of them. 'Everyone's playing at something, particularly at university. Look at my housemates. Georgia's playing at being Mummy – eat up your fruit and veg and make sure you get an early night, darling. Peter pretends he's a vicar – he has the whole chapel to play in. Becky's playing politics. Olly's playing brave new world that has no religion in it. Will's playing at being a good Christian and feeding the poor.'

'Why is any of that playing?' Lydia tried to look surreptitiously at Colette's face.

'It might not be, when it comes to the sticking point. But university is a good place to play – because nobody knows you, and even if they do they're not really surprised when you do something a bit off the wall. Because it's only three years, and so there's a natural break if it doesn't work out for you. Because you don't have to be committed.'

'Oh.' Lydia had not thought of it like that. 'What are *you* playing at, then?'

The hands went back into the pockets; the shoulders hunched. 'Hmm. Up until about an hour ago, I was playing at being straight. Not a fun game. I don't know what I'm playing now. Anyway, I asked first.'

'So you did.' This was important, Lydia knew. 'I'm not playing any more. I've never been more serious in my life. I mean this.'

'Oh, you have to be serious,' Colette said. 'That's the most important rule of the game.' But she sounded at least a little reassured.

They walked in silence a little while, and then Colette laughed. 'What's so funny?'

'I was just thinking: my gaydar is evidently buggered. Even if I'd thought about it, I would have put good money on your being straight.

Quite apart from our disastrous expedition to the Coffee House, there was the last time you dropped round the house.'

'Wow,' Lydia said. 'I can't even remember when that was.'

'Oh, way back at the beginning of last term. You were having lunch with Peter. I thought –'

It took Lydia a few seconds to work out what Colette meant. She dropped her voice. 'You thought *Peter* and I...? No! I mean, he's lovely, but not my type. Obviously.'

'Not for very long,' Colette said. 'About five seconds at most. But it was quite long enough.'

'Long enough for what?'

'To walk in, see him having lunch with you, think, thank God, he's got over me at last – and then realise that this was actually no consolation, because I'd fallen for you like a ton of bricks.'

Lydia laughed in confusion. 'What made you think I was going out with him? Peter and *you*, I could see...'

Colette shook her head. 'He did ask me once, last year; but I wasn't over Jess. Then last term I wasn't over you, and he could see that. But he was very sweet about it. Anyway, imagine me a vicar's wife! You and him, now... It seemed a fairly logical conclusion. I didn't think you knew each other that well, so I had to assume that if you were spending time together, it was because you really wanted to spend time together. In fact – why *were* you having lunch with him?'

'I went to All Saints', and ran into him there.'

Colette whistled. 'You went to *All Saints*'? Good grief. And you weren't struck down by fire from heaven?'

'It was a mistake,' Lydia explained, inadequately. 'Well, not really a mistake, but a bit of a spur-of-the-moment thing.'

'Right.' Her sudden smile was exhilarating. 'Don't ever stop surprising me.'

Georgia had seated Lydia and Colette a tactful distance apart, with assorted members of AngthMURC and the Music department between them. Lydia, knowing that she ought to be walking on eggshells, feeling as if she was walking on air, acknowledged reluctantly that this was just as well. She talked almost exclusively to her left-hand neighbour, a charming floppy-haired flautist, not for his scintillating conversation, but because if she was looking that way she had half a chance of catching a glimpse of Colette. She had no idea what she said or ate that evening; she drank a single glass of wine and found herself intoxicated.

The mains were cleared. The flautist popped to the lavatory. Georgia plumped herself down at his place and murmured in Lydia's ear, 'Sorry. Didn't realise you'd made up until after I'd done the seating plan.'

'I couldn't have given you much warning,' Lydia said. 'We've only – it's only been since about six o'clock.' Tonight she did not care who knew, or how. Tomorrow she would start worrying.

Georgia laughed affectionately. 'Fair play. Well, the original plan was that the pissheads would go back up to Alma Road and continue the party there, and you are very welcome to join us.'

'Thank you,' Lydia said. She hesitated a moment, then said, 'Georgia?'

'Yes?'

'Would you – would you mind not telling Will? Or Gabe, come to that. If he hasn't noticed, I mean – don't say anything that's not true – but I don't think I'm quite ready to explain to my hall group yet.'

Georgia patted her hand. 'Of course. If he does say anything to me, I'll ask him to keep it quiet. He'll understand. Just – look after her, OK? She's had a rough time of it.'

Lydia, touched profoundly by the implicit trust and forgiveness, could only say, 'I will.'

Georgia might have claimed to be kicking herself, but her social skills proved more than equal to the task of mending any omission. She manoeuvred her own neighbours into a little group at the far end of the table, summoned the charming flautist to talk to her while the bill was sorted and the coffee went round, and moved Colette into the seat next to Lydia, arranging them like so many chessmen on a board and all the while managing to make it look as though it had been the pieces' own idea. Lydia felt like Cinderella, tended to by a very efficient Fairy Godmother.

Colette nodded in Georgia's direction. 'She approves,' she said. 'I'm glad.'

'She's amazing,' Lydia said.

'That's what they call *people skills*.' The sweet sharpness – like raspberries, Lydia thought, confusedly – in Colette's voice was something to cling to, made her a human being after all. Then, politely, 'How was your meal?'

'Lovely,' Lydia said. She had no idea. And, with similar formality, 'Yours?'

'Yes, lovely.' Colette smiled, ruefully. She lowered her voice; Georgia's other guests were milling around. 'I'm not sure that this was a terrific idea for a first date, you know. This place is a bit crowded!'

Feeling deeply transgressive, Lydia slipped a hand under the table, and found Colette's. 'I know. It's not ideal. The thing is, I don't think I'd have been brave enough ever to ask you on a real date.'

Fluttering fingers in her own. Nervous, or reassuring? Colette's face gave no clue; she continued in the same flippant tone. 'That Georgia, eh? Such a meddler! Who does she think she is, having a birthday, and inviting us to it? I certainly wouldn't have asked *you*.'

Lydia could hear the wariness behind the mocking, discern the second meaning of the light-hearted insult. She could not quite match the tone herself. 'I know.'

The hand became still. 'It's been a long time since I went on a date with anyone.'

Lydia confessed: 'You're my first.'

'The first you asked?'

'Asked or accepted. I'm picky.' She had it at last, that veneer of sophistication that smoothed the heartwood beneath and made it glow. She had stripped herself bare, earlier; she could see, now, that she could not expect Colette to do the same, not again. Not yet.

Georgia touched her shoulder, making her jump. 'Girls? We're off. You know the way.'

They were the only two still seated; the rest of the party was heading for the door.

'We'll follow you,' Colette said. She let go of Lydia's hand and stood up.

Lydia picked her coat up. 'Back to yours?' she asked.

'I think so. No hurry, though, unless you want to hurry. They'll be up all night.'

'I don't want to hurry,' Lydia said. Contented, fascinated, she watched Colette as she wound her scarf around her neck, dragged her jacket on, slung her bag over her shoulder.

'Let's amble, then. Goodnight!' Colette said to the barman and the waitresses. Lydia echoed, 'Goodnight!'

They came out into the night. The thunderclouds had cleared, though the pavements still glistened damp under the streetlights. The street was practically empty. The others must have already got a long way ahead. Colette looked at Lydia, raised an eyebrow, offered her an arm.

Ah, Lydia thought, *that's* how you do it. She smiled, nodded, accepted. A clever way around it, allowing you to walk so close together, and look so innocent. It was a little awkward, at first; Colette's stride was longer than her own, and Lydia could feel her holding back, slowing down to her speed.

'What happens next?' Lydia asked.

'Whatever you like.'

'Seriously. I have no idea what to do next.' The closeness of Colette was intoxicating.

'It'll be very much like it was before,' Colette said, 'before you ran away and I went crazy, I mean. Getting to know each other again. The same path, but not so many "no entry" signs.'

'Telling the truth, this time round.' Lydia felt the impulsive pressure of Colette's elbow against her arm. 'What?'

'I was thinking what I'd have done if I'd known. Been a whole lot nicer, probably.'

'That would just have been weird.' By no stretch of the imagination, Lydia thought, could Colette have been described as "nice". It was too feeble a word for her. Kind, generous, forgiving, by all means, burningly honest where she could be, and civilised enough to keep silence where she could not, but never merely *nice*.

Colette smiled. 'Perhaps it would. We're not there, anyway; we can't get back there, and it might not have made things any easier. I mean, all this seething resentment, unfounded jealousy, and unrequited love. Who'd be without that? It's certainly made the past six months memorable.'

'Love?' Lydia said, half alarmed and half delighted.

And Colette was immediately on her guard again. 'Maybe. We'll see. I only met you three hours ago.'

Lydia winced. Colette, repentant, said, 'Actually, probably, yes. I think so. It's just difficult to tell – I've hardly seen you since January, and neither of us has been herself since. Could you take it on account, borrowed from some future version of ourselves who have got all this sorted out?'

Lydia inclined her head. Colette's courtesy was hard for her to accept. Once before she had been offered this heart, and she had broken it – no, had snatched it, thrown it to the floor and trampled it –

and here was Colette giving it to her again, trusting her to mend it. She asked, 'How will we get there from here?'

'"I said to the man who stood at the gate of the year,"' Colette quoted, '"Give me a light, that I might tread safely into the unknown." I don't know that there's a map for this. I think we just start walking.'

They were leaving the old town now, heading down the hill. The river was a black satin ribbon, streaked with orange where the light from the streetlamps fell upon it. Ahead of them there was darkness.

Lydia said, experimentally, 'We can find a time to go for coffee together again. I'll come to AngthMURC with you, or Folksoc. Lunch. Shopping. You could come out walking with me...'

Colette nodded encouragingly. 'All the stuff we could do anyway,' she said. 'We would be a couple, but nobody would have to know, that we didn't want knowing. As for the rest of it... well, we'll take it as it comes.'

The road dipped, and rose again to cross the railway, and the town was suddenly dark. They had not been talking loudly, but Colette hushed her voice further still. 'Look,' she said. 'The power's still out. Stars over Stancester! You don't see that often.'

'It's put out everything west of the river,' Lydia said. She wanted to stop walking, but Colette drew her onwards, up to the very middle of the bridge.

'Look,' she said again. They looked back the way they had come. The cathedral blazed on the hill in its amber floodlights. Below them, to the south, the station made a scar of fluorescent white. Ahead of them, the dark maze of streets stretched up the hill; and above, the sky was deep blue, and the stars went on for ever.

A train whistle sounded, a long, joyous, bellow, and the train rushed through below their feet, humming and rattling. Lydia turned to face Colette, and somehow forgot to let go of her arm first, and then it seemed only appropriate to slip her other arm around her. They lit the stars for us, she thought, confusedly (could it really have been been one glass of wine?), and drew her closer.

'Truly?' Colette asked.

Lydia knew, somehow, what she meant. 'Truly,' she said, and raised her hand to lay it gently on Colette's cheek. And Colette kissed the fingertips as they crossed her lips and bent her head to meet Lydia's first, urgent, accepting kiss.

Chapter 3

Term started too soon? Books you don't want to read? Essays you don't want to write?

Put it all out of your mind with the FOLKSOC CEILIDH!

What do you mean, you don't dance? Everybody dances!

8pm-10.30pm, Tuesday 8th May, The Venue, SUSU Building

Live band! Undead caller! Beginners welcome!

£3 Folksoc members/£5 non-members

Money back if anyone eats your brains!

Lydia woke the next morning and found the world had changed. For the first time in years, she picked up her Bible without fear. Today, it assured her, *you will know the truth, and the truth will set you free.* That, she thought drily, was a promise and a half; and yet she was willing to believe it. Everything seemed possible, today.

She went down to breakfast and was struck by the improbable beauty of quite ordinary things: the coloured light thrown from the stained-glass window onto the floor of the hall; the curve of a spoon; Gabe humming *did you not hear my lady go down the garden singing* as he waited for his toast.

Armed with her new knowledge, Lydia unwrapped her past, looked at the parts she had tried to suppress. Imogen. Jemma. Naomi. Priya. And, shining brighter than them all, Colette. Colette, who had forgiven her. Colette, who had shown her a way to be. Colette, who had kissed her. Colette, who had sat squashed into an armchair with her, and let her fall asleep on her shoulder. Colette, whom she would be seeing again in two short hours.

Meeting once more in the Coffee House as if nothing were different, Lydia watched Colette cut a slice of Bakewell tart into inch-square pieces with the side of her fork, and felt love and regret swirling together within herself. She only wished that she had known earlier how it would be.

Colette seemed to be eating properly again; her hair would lighten back to gentle brown in time, but the pair of little vertical creases that had appeared between her eyebrows never went away. From the first, Lydia had been struck deeply by Colette's confidence in her own self, her integrity, her security in her sense that she was loved by God. The long weeks of silence had worn all that away. Colette had always been shy, but now there was a lingering hesitancy to her that Lydia knew to be her own work and regretted bitterly. She did not know how to put it right, or even if it could be put right; she could only love her. Lydia, so accustomed to living with pretence that she had forgotten there was a world without it, had not imagined that the strain of three months' denial could do such damage. She could not stop herself asking, 'Was it my fault?'

An ironic smile, over the rim of the mug. 'Not entirely. I mean, not particularly because of what you said or did. It could have been anybody.'

'Really?'

Colette wrinkled her nose thoughtfully. 'Well, I suppose it had to be you, really, but that's only because you were the specific person who was going to be living in my house. All this year it's been absolutely sodden with unrequited love and sexual tension. Olly and Georgia. Peter and me. Not to mention Peter's cassock-clingers, and Georgia insists on mothering them and asking them to lunch. I wish she wouldn't; it only encourages them. And just as I'm consoling myself with the fact that the other three are going to graduate in six months and get out of my house, I go and fall for you and start the whole thing over again. I just couldn't face it. It was obvious – I thought, at least –

that you weren't interested in me. And so, if you were going to move in, I had to not be in love with you. And I couldn't stop that without cutting everything else off as well, and even then I didn't make a particularly good job of it. But it would have worked, just about. I think.'

'So what you're saying,' Lydia said, attempting to lighten the tone, 'is that if we broke up then we would not only make our own lives hell, we would also ruin those of our innocent housemates? Score!'

'Something like that.' Colette laid her fork neatly across the plate.

Lydia said, 'We'd better not break up, then. I can assure you, I have no plans to.'

A sudden, flashing grin. 'I should think not, after only eighteen hours.'

Eighteen hours became three days, a week, a fortnight, and the world was still new and troubling. When she had let herself think about it at all, Lydia had assumed that coming out to Colette would be the hardest part. She had not imagined that, having told one person, two people, she would constantly be wondering if anyone else knew, and if it would be safe to tell them. If *anybody else knowing* was no longer such a terrifying idea, in the other side of the balance sat the leaden weight of *everybody knowing*; and, in particular, the dozen or so *somebodies* who must *never know*.

She had not foreseen that Colette's friends would always be watching her suspiciously, but they were warily protective now. Lydia could not blame them. She could feel them thinking that it was *her fault*. Georgia had turned from mother hen to mother tiger; she took Lydia aside and spelled out in robust terms the likely consequences of Colette's being hurt again. Peter addressed Lydia with impeccable, wounding courtesy, and was ostentatiously considerate of Colette. Only Becky, it seemed, treated Lydia as if nothing had changed, noisy and breezy and cheerful.

Adam came down from Birmingham, and Becky insisted they all four went to the Folksoc ceilidh. 'It's the one place where nobody will notice or care that you're a couple,' she had said to Lydia. 'And Colette loves it. You'll see.'

Now Lydia stood ready watching at her window, dressed in a summery cotton dress patterned with violets, hair back in an optimistically tidy plait, waiting. Colette crossed the lawn at ten past eight; a tall, endearingly ungainly, figure.

My girlfriend, Lydia thought, delighted with the idea. She grabbed her bag and bounded down the stairs. Her sandals clattered on the parquet in the hall; she came to a stop two feet from Colette, who was hovering self-consciously just inside the door.

'Hello,' Lydia said.

Colette's smile was shy and enchanting. 'Hello.'

Lydia felt her heart tighten. 'Shall we go?'

'Let's.'

They met Gabe on the way out; he winked at Lydia and drew a finger across his neck. She hoped it meant *cross my throat and hope to die*, not *fly all is known*.

Becky was already at the Union, holding hands with a long-haired, bearded man, whom Lydia deduced to be the boyfriend Adam. They paid their fivers and went in. The dancing was already in full swing: the floor was alive with pairs and fours, swaying, skipping, chivvied into place by the caller, the music all skirls and runs, the rhythm insistent.

Lydia was too shy to dance at first. Colette sat out with her for the first few numbers, while Becky and Adam danced together, but it was evident from the way she jigged in her chair that she was longing to be out on the floor.

'Colette?' It was a pleasant-faced boy in a checked shirt and jeans. 'Want to do this one?'

She looked at Lydia, clearly torn. 'Would you mind?'

138

'Go on,' Lydia said. 'I'll watch. Really.'

So Colette stepped forward, and Lydia watched her with jealousy and delight. When Colette danced, she shed her habitual awkwardness, moving straight-backed with graceful rhythm. Stepping, swinging, bending to get under an arch or half-running to catch a wayward partner, she seemed to belong to the music, sparkling with laughter. She stayed out for five straight dances, swapping between partners, throwing a glance at Lydia sometimes to see that she was happy. When Adam retreated, exhausted, Colette danced with Becky.

Adam sank into the chair next Lydia and shook his head. 'I can never get my head around stripping the willow,' he said. 'So. You're Colette's girlfriend. Nice to meet you.'

It sounded odd coming from a stranger. Lydia said, 'That's right. Nice to meet you, too. Becky's boyfriend.'

'I understand you're an Evangelical Christian.' He said it as if it were some zoological term. *Unusual specimen.* 'Does that make things difficult?'

'More difficult than you could possibly imagine,' she said shortly. She was watching the dance. Becky and Colette were working their way down the double line of dancers, turning each other in the centre, spinning out to meet the next couple, an arm each to each of them and turning round and back to meet each other, smooth as a zip.

'It shouldn't, should it?'

'Sorry?' Her distraction was not entirely feigned.

'It shouldn't make things difficult. I mean, given that Christianity is meant to be a religion of unconditional love, you would have thought that everybody could just accept and move on.' He raised his eyebrows, questioning, challenging.

Lydia said, patiently, 'That may yet prove to be the case. I haven't told any of my Evangelical friends. Certainly other Christian friends have been lovely.'

'You haven't told any of your Evangelical friends,' he repeated. 'So you are not actually expecting a positive reaction.'

'No,' Lydia admitted. She shuffled her chair backwards until its feet scraped against the skirting board, trying not to wince as her bare legs peeled free of the plastic seat. She nodded at the dancers, Colette and Becky now playing passive rather than active roles, but shoving a less experienced couple in the right direction. 'They dance well,' she said.

He did not take the hint. 'And yet you call those people friends.' He grinned, infuriatingly, as if he had won the argument. As if she had been wanting to argue.

'They are,' she said, wearily. 'They are my friends. The thing is, I know that people will say the most horrible things to me out of a sincere love for me, and out of an absolute conviction that if they don't then I will be heading straight for hell, and that if they fail to do all they can to warn me, they will be held at least partly guilty of my fall.'

The dance finished on a long, defiant chord. There was applause, and some laughter. Lydia said quickly, before it had died down. 'I'm not brave enough to argue, yet. That's all.'

'Well, of course you're entitled to your opinions, but this sounds like it could be very damaging to you...' he was beginning, when Becky strode over, flushed with exertion and irritation.

'Oh, for fuck's sake, Adam,' she said. 'This is exactly what I told you not to do.' She turned to Lydia. 'I do apologise. If it's any consolation, this is not how Quakers are meant to work. We believe in letting the Spirit work in people at its own pace – and theirs – not bashing them over the head with logic.'

Lydia squirmed, but Adam took it in good part. 'I find this very interesting,' he said.

Colette was standing a little way behind Becky, her fine lip curled in amusement. She shook her head slightly. *Ignore them*, she mouthed.

'Now!' the caller shouted, 'we want couples – as many as we can get! This one is the Rozsa.'

'Go on, you two,' Colette said with obvious relief. 'This is your dance.'

Becky and Adam turned to each other, glaring. Becky stuck her tongue out; suddenly both smiled with soppy self-consciousness, and they went up hand in hand.

Colette sat down in the chair next to Lydia as the accordionist played the introduction. 'This is a lovely one,' she said. 'I've never danced it, mind. It's the only one I'd feel weird doing with a partner I wasn't romantically involved with. Which wasn't a hint. I do need to sit out.'

Pleasing as it had been to watch Colette dance, it was more pleasing still to have her sit a bare inch away, close enough to feel the warmth of her body, to share this dance, though they did not dance it. The Rosza was unlike anything she had seen that evening: no promiscuous changing of partners, but a slow waltz, simple and slinky. The couples were swaying from side to side, only fingertips touching, with surprisingly sensuous effect.

'It seems almost indecent to watch, doesn't it?' Colette said. 'They'll do this one at their wedding, I bet.'

(Adam lifted his arms; Becky slipped under them into a close, cross-armed embrace.)

'They're engaged? I didn't know.'

(Stepping sideways, to the left and to the right, and the turn reversed so that they were once again facing each other.)

Colette laughed softly. 'Not yet. Give it time.'

(Right hand to right hand to make arches, the women twisting underneath, and back again.)

'Some day,' Lydia said, reckless, 'I'll get you to teach me this one.'

Colette turned to her. 'I look forward to that. Very much.'

Though the routine was repeated twice or three times more, they did not look back at the dancers until the last chord swelled and slowed to silence.

'For the next one,' the caller was already saying, 'I need sets of four couples.'

Becky and Adam were beckoning them from the middle of the floor.

'What do you think?' Colette asked, anxious. 'I think this is going to be the Cumberland Square Eight.'

This meant nothing to Lydia. She glanced around the room for Fellowship spies and found none, but saw on the other hand at least three other all-female couples. 'It would be a bit pathetic if I went to a ceilidh and didn't dance, wouldn't it?'

'Right,' Colette said, 'I have always wanted to do this, and there aren't enough men to go round, anyway.' She extended a hand to Lydia, who took it with nervous dignity, and regretted it the moment the caller started to describe the steps. Becky took pity on her. 'Watch me,' she said. 'You and I mirror each other. If Colette tries to lead you, let her. You can trust her to know what she's doing.'

Lydia, head whirling, gritted her teeth and hoped for the best. When Colette took her in ballroom hold she felt better. Colette at least knew where they were going, and, until she learned the steps for herself, she would be safe following. Out, and back. Standing still, while the other couples crossed in front of them. Into the middle to meet Becky and the other women in a right hand star; left hand star, back again. Standing back, again, while the men went in, and Colette the best of them. Into the basket: a tight huddle, spinning faster and faster until she could barely keep her feet on the ground. And down, and back to their places, clapping as the side couples went into the basket in their turn. Circle right, circle left; that at least was easy, and then Colette, laughing, was arranging their tangle of hands into promenade hold and leading her in the right direction.

'You're doing well,' she murmured into her ear. 'Are you all right?'

Lydia nodded. 'Confused. But enjoying it, yes.'

On the second run she was more confident, and therefore more prone to moving out of turn, and having to step back, blushing. Colette was expert, though, and, what was more, patient. 'You're trying too hard,' she told her, and tidied her into place. The third cycle was perfect, and, when they went into the basket this time, Becky called 'Fly, Lydia!' and so she kicked back and let the others bear her up, and when they set her down she caught Colette's look and almost wept at the tenderness in it.

'Right, then, guys,' Becky said, 'shall we head home?'

'Actually,' Lydia said, hearing her voice ring suddenly false and hollow, 'if you come back with me, Colette, I can lend you that thing I was talking about.'

'Oh, yes,' Colette said uncomfortably, 'that thing.'

Becky and Adam looked at each other. 'We'll see you at home, then, Colette,' Becky said. 'Lovely evening, Lydia; thank you for coming.' She touched Lydia on the upper arm, to show, perhaps, that she meant it, before leading Adam away.

Lydia looked at Colette, who smiled. They walked together down the steps of the Union building. It had rained, and the night air was soft and sweet, the paths deserted. They continued in silence for some distance, close, but not touching. At last, where the path was darkest, under the cedar tree at the edge of the Richmond lawn, Lydia stopped, and ventured, 'This isn't going to be easy.'

She felt rather than saw Colette's gesture of assent. 'Am I right in thinking that there are people who, should they find out about this, would make your life hell?'

'Near enough.' Lydia began to name them in her mind, and stopped when she thought how long the list would be.

'And that we therefore need to be extremely careful. But that you're otherwise at peace with –' She stopped.

'Who I am? And how things stand between us?' Lydia took Colette's hand and pressed it, briefly.

'Yes.'

'I am.' Very soft, 'I'm scared of them, not ashamed of you.'

'I assume,' Colette said abruptly, 'you don't believe in sex before marriage. I know –' as Lydia was silent – 'it's too early for us to be thinking about either, but I'd like to know where *you* stand, before bringing me into the equation.'

'You are correct,' Lydia admitted, and tried not to follow the logical trail to its unrewarding end.

Colette seemed determined to make it easy for her. 'Our relationship cannot, as things stand, end in marriage as I think either of our Churches would understand it.'

'No,' Lydia agreed.

'Knowing that, are you prepared to keep on with it regardless?' There was a catch in her voice, and no talk of games now.

Lydia stood still, and took both of Colette's hands in her own. 'There is only one thing that I know,' she said. 'This is real. Whatever this relationship with you is, or is going to be, it is as real as my relationship with God; and I am beginning to believe that it comes from the same place.'

'Meaning?' Colette was gripping her fingers hard.

She could hardly summon the words. 'Meaning that God has brought me this far with you, and that I am willing to trust that He will lead us on to wherever He wants us, and reveal His will for us in His good time.'

They met no one on the way up through Richmond Hall, either on the sweeping curve of the grand staircase, or on the steep flight that led to the attics. The lights on the landings flickered into action as they passed, lighting the way behind them. Lydia longed to take Colette's hand again, but this was Fiona's room they were passing now, and that was Simon's. Anyone could emerge, at any time, from any door. She thought: *this is the first time I have brought her here.* It joined a long procession of other first times. *The first time I knew. The first time I prayed against it. The first time I met her...* Colette was chattering lightly, about the evening, about the dances, about the music. Lydia made no answer; she led the way along the narrow top landing and unlocked the door to her room. She stepped in, felt for the light switch, but, remembering she had left the curtains open, did not press it. Instead, she pushed the door shut and she pulled Colette to her.

Colette abandoned whatever it was that she had been saying about the grand chain. Breathing fast, she slid one arm around Lydia's waist and gently brought the other hand behind her head to tilt her face upwards.

The touch of the fingertips was cool in the nape of her neck. Lydia trembled. 'Always in the dark,' she whispered ruefully.

'You should come to mine,' Colette murmured. 'Easier than yours. Nobody cares who I have in my room.'

'Will would.' She pressed closer.

Colette was stroking her hair. 'He's hardly ever in. Always out socialising with you Fellowship guys, or with his hockey lot...'

Will was irrelevant. Here there was only Colette, and Lydia desired more than any earthly thing to kiss her. Her eyes were becoming accustomed to the darkness, and Colette's face was all moonlight and shadows and dark crescents of eyelashes; and Colette's lips were warm and eager on hers.

She would have stayed folded in those arms for ever, or until – no, but she was glad that Colette had so courteously demarcated the boundaries earlier, for she would have been tempted to kick them aside now. Colette was breaking away, disengaging fingers, arms, lips. Lydia protested incoherently.

There was clear air between them; but Colette smiled, and laid a hand either side of Lydia's face. Lydia held her breath.

'Yes,' Colette said, 'that thing. That thing you were going to lend me.'

'Yes,' Lydia said, through a tightening throat.

Colette kissed her once more, this time with finality. 'That. Thank you. I will return it,' she said, 'very soon. Let me know when you want it back.'

And she was gone. Lydia watched from the window until she emerged at the front door and crossed the lawn, twice looking back at the hall, up towards her; then she drew the curtains. She undressed without turning the light on, and lay down under a chilly duvet, to wonder if she would sleep that night.

Some day, she knew, some day quite soon, this would not be enough.

Chapter 4

The full City Circle trail is 25.7 miles, but it can be joined and left at any point around the circumference, and the terrain is not demanding. The route takes in the historic buildings around the cathedral and old town, the beautiful university campus on Markham Hill, the water meadows alongside the River Ivel, and Sharpe Hill, from which the Bristol Channel can be seen on a clear day.

Walks in and around Stancester, Visit Stancester

June chased May out in a flurry of showers and presented Stancester with the first hint of summer just in time for exams. The pressure rose in exam halls and barometer alike. Lydia, distracted by the heady sensation of first love, and secure in the knowledge that most of this year's mark was based on coursework that she had already submitted, was largely immune to the stress. For the finalists it was harder. Colette, whose own finals were a year away, was panicking outright.

'I can't get any of it into my head,' she told Lydia, who had dragged her out on a walk in a last-ditch attempt to take her mind off it. 'I don't think I've learned anything at all this year.'

'Your January results were all right,' Lydia reminded her.

Colette frowned. 'Not great. This is going to be much worse, and now I've lost the whole day when I could have been revising, and even if I *had* spent it in the library it wouldn't have done any good, because I'm just too frazzled.' She flopped on her front in the long grass next the river. 'Whew, it's hot!'

Lydia sat down beside her. 'You're not burning, are you?'

'Don't think so.' Colette was not so easily distracted. 'I just don't *understand* any of it,' she burst out. 'Usually it falls into place if I look at it for long enough, but this just *won't*! It's all letters and dots and lines.'

'Your work always looks like that to me,' Lydia said.

'Ah, well, you do the exam, then!' Colette muttered. Then, repentant, 'I think I may be burning, actually.' She sat up.

Lydia looked. 'Your shoulders are a bit pink. Shall I stick some more suncream on?'

'If you don't mind.'

'Of course not.' They were silent for some little while. Lydia, too well aware that such a moment was rare and precious, took care to appreciate every facet of it. The June sun, the breeze rising from the river, the chirruping of insects. The faint chemical fragrance of the suncream, mingled with the stronger scent of the sun-warmed grass. The warmth of Colette's skin; its smoothness under her fingers. And, rarest of all, the utter solitude.

She shuffled backwards on her knees, and pulled Colette gently towards her so that she lay with her head in her lap. Colette looked up at her, smiling lazily, the little worried lines between her eyebrows gone for once.

Lydia's heart twisted. 'I love you,' she said. 'Whatever happens in your exams, that doesn't change. I know you want to do well, and I want you to, because it will make you happier than not. But even if you don't, I love you.'

Colette caught her hand and held it against her heart. 'Thank you,' she said, very quietly. 'I love you.'

They strolled back to Alma Road together, worked out that Lydia would either have to run back to campus or miss hall dinnertime and decided that it was too hot to run. It turned out that there was no dinner at Alma Road, because it was Georgia's night, and she had an exam, and Olly had told her not to cook, really, he meant it this time. Colette rootled in her section of the cupboard and found a tin of sweetcorn, which she chucked, with tuna begged from Becky, into a pan of white sauce; and she and Lydia ate it with the last of the spaghetti, sitting on the end of her bed, watching the evening clouds gather over the cathedral.

A knock at the door. They sprang apart, and were sitting with a chaste twelve inches between them, Lydia on the chair, Colette on the bed, by the time Becky actually came in and said, 'Sorry to disturb – Colette, did I lend you my post-it notes?'

'You didn't,' Colette said, 'but you can borrow mine if you like. Lydia – by your right hand there...'

'Thanks!' Becky caught the flying pad. 'How's it going?'

'Awful,' Colette said. 'I couldn't remember anything before we went out, and I don't remember anything now. I don't think I ever learnt it in the first place. You?'

Becky shrugged her shoulders. 'I don't think I'm going to *fail*... I'm not really happy about the reproduction module, but maybe it won't come up.'

'When is the exam?' Lydia asked.

'Tomorrow afternoon. There's not much I can do about it now, of course...' She turned at the sound of footsteps on the stairs.

Will did not bother to knock. Lydia was relieved that she and Colette were an innocent distance apart. She felt a stab of guilt at the thought and realised, with a jump, that Will was talking to her. 'Sorry! Miles away.'

'I was saying,' he repeated, patiently, 'that the Union are having a referendum.'

'What on?' Colette asked. 'Joining the Euro? Disaffiliating from the NUS?'

'Independent Socialist Republic of Stancester,' Becky muttered.

'No,' Will said, scowling. 'Since they seem to be unable to accept the democratic decision of the last Students' Union General Meeting, they're throwing it open to the entire student body – who could, of course, have shown up to the meeting if they cared that much.'

Lydia sighed. 'Here we go again.'

'Tossers!' Becky said. 'They don't half pick their moments.'

'So,' Will continued, 'we're making sure to ask everyone to vote in the referendum, to, like, ensure that the democratic decision is, you know, reflected.'

'Will,' Becky said, 'Fellowship rigged the last meeting and you know it.'

Lydia wondered exactly how much Becky knew. She saw Colette wince. 'Not *rigged*,' she suggested.

'Went to considerable lengths to obtain the result they wanted,' Becky amended. 'I'm not saying that any of it was illegal, but I have my doubts about the ethics.'

'Could you perhaps argue about it somewhere else?' Colette asked. 'Somewhere that isn't my room, specifically?'

'Certainly,' Becky said, taking a step towards the door. Will did not budge. She continued, 'Anyway, my actual point was, why on earth is the Union doing this now, when the whole university is stressed out of its mind with exams and frying in the heat? Tossers, I say!'

'It's a plot,' Colette said. 'Someone's trying to drive us all mad. I think they're succeeding, in my case. I mean, look at this: people discussing religion *and* politics at my dinner table.'

'Dinner bed,' Lydia corrected her, smiling, although the strain was back on Colette's face, and she would have liked to march both Will and Becky back down the stairs.

'My point exactly. I must have lost it.'

Becky heard the warning note. 'So,' she said, still moving towards the door, 'what's the plan, Will? Round people up, make them vote? By force, if necessary?'

'Ah,' Will smirked, 'I know that's a trick question. Quakers don't do that sort of thing.'

'Bing! Ten points! Well, I shall vote, and I shall mention to people I know that there's a vote happening, but don't expect a massive turnout, Will boy. The sad truth is, most people don't give a flying fuck. So I suggest that we clear out and leave poor Colette to get on with her revision.' She made a deliberate effort, this time, to bustle Will out of the door, and looked over her shoulder to wink at Lydia as she did so.

Lydia perched next to Colette, kissed her, and whispered, 'Love you. Good luck for tomorrow. See you afterwards.'

For a brief moment, Colette clung to her as if she were drowning; then she released her. 'Love you. Thank you for today.'

Lydia slipped down the narrow stairs, Colette's kiss burning on her lips, and jumped when Will materialised in the hall, blocking her path to the front door.

'Lydia,' he said. 'Lydia.'

'Hello,' she said, warily.

'Hi. Do you mind if I, like, have a word?'

'Of course.'

Will bowed slightly and indicated that she should go into the living room. 'Have a seat,' he said, but remained standing himself.

She sat down, poker-backed, on the one dining chair in the room, and looked at him enquiringly.

'I felt that I ought to tell you about Colette,' Will began.

Lydia felt her face flame, and was thankful that she had at least chosen to sit with her back to the window. 'Oh?'

His brow furrowed in deep concern. 'I don't know if you realise, but Colette is actually homosexual.'

Lydia could not suppress a hysterical giggle. 'Oh, no,' she said. 'You're mistaken.'

'I assure you, I'm not.'

'Really. She's *bi*sexual.' She was still fighting that fatal desire to laugh and give everything away.

'Ah,' Will said, discomfited. 'I wasn't aware that you knew.'

'Oh, she told me ages ago. Back when I first met her, in fact.'

The possibility that she might already be aware of Colette's interest in women had evidently not entered his head. While he rewrote his lecture, she said, pleasantly, 'You might not know, but it's actually considered rather poor form to "out" someone like that. There's no harm done in this case, of course, as I already knew, but if I were Colette I would be –' she searched ostentatiously for the right word – 'I would feel betrayed, if I thought that people were talking about such private things about me.'

Will brushed it aside. 'I do think that there's an obligation, if somebody's got something like that, for them to tell people. You, for example, as a Christian, would need to know that...'

Hating herself, she smiled at him. 'But she did tell me.'

'Oh. Yes.' Will floundered a little, and found his previous thread. 'My point is, though, that you do need to be careful, as a Christian woman, that you do associate with the right – that is, with people who will build you up in the faith.'

She raised her eyebrows. 'Colette *is* a Christian.'

'Yes, yes, of course, that's true, but – well, you do need to be careful, that's all I'm saying. I wouldn't have mentioned it, but you do seem to have been spending a lot of time with Colette, recently.'

She tried to look concerned and dutiful rather than guilty and furious. 'I'll bear it in mind,' she said.

It seemed to satisfy him. 'You will remember to vote in the referendum, won't you?' he said, as she left.

Summer

John JesusSaves Fitzgerald *posted 17 June at 15:06* Yes, but you can't get past the fact that it says in the Bible that women are not to speak in church (1 Cor 14.34-35), that men have authority over women (1 Cor 12.3), and that women are not permitted to teach (1 Timothy 2.12). Not sure why this is so hard to understand.

Peter Nathan *posted 17 June at 15:13* I think it would be a tragedy if we turned away women and the valuable gifts they can offer us – and, yes, those are leadership gifts in some cases.

John JesusSaves Fitzgerald *posted 17 June at 20:09* Nobody's saying that we should be turning women away, and you are right that they do have valuable gifts. However, the Bible says that these gifts should be used in particular settings, for example they can teach but they can only teach other women, or if their husbands are also present and teaching. God has created men and women different and He has given them different gifts and He calls them to do different things. Separate things, yes, but that doesn't mean they're not equal before God.

Peter Nathan *posted 18 June at 00:49* I am going to give you the benefit of the doubt on this occasion, but I very seriously recommend that you Google "separate but equal" "US civil rights movement" before you use that expression again. It is going to do you no favours.

Back on topic: I'd be more convinced by the 'complementarity' argument if there were roles in the Church that were reserved exclusively for women. You can't use the 'separate but equal' spiel when you blatantly aren't offering equal opportunities. (And before **Charlie Bingley** mentions it even as a joke, yes, I have known male flower-arrangers, male crèche volunteers, male coffee rota participants and so on.)

www.stancester-su.org.uk/forums/faith

The referendum on the title of the largest Christian society on campus was duly held. It saw a considerably better turnout than either of the Union meetings at which the question had been debated. The increased interest was generally ascribed to the efforts of the *STANdard*, and Emma Greer in particular, who had devoted several column inches to explaining what the hell was going on, and why on earth anybody should care about it anyway.

The Elections Officer had the honour of verifying the vote. The results were as follows:

A small minority indicated its wish that the society in question should be called the Christian Fellowship, as decided by democratic processes at the April meeting.

A slightly larger minority indicated its wish that the society in question should be called the Evangelical Christian Fellowship, as decided by democratic process at the January meeting.

The vast majority indicated its complete lack of interest in the question by not voting at all.

The Evangelical Christian Fellowship it remained. The Fellowship's Publicity Officer, a prudent soul, had refrained from destroying anything at all after the April meeting, so no more paper was wasted – at least, Becky commented, unless you took a particularly uncharitable view of the *STANdard*.

The day before her parents came to collect her Lydia got her ears pierced; then, finding the effect less startling than she had imagined it would be, had her hair cut for good measure. Relieved of its own weight, it sprang, as she had always thought it would, around her face; but it troubled her less than she had expected it might.

Her father frowned a little when he saw it; her mother said, 'Well, I'm sure it will grow out again.' Lydia would have been irritated, but it gave them something safe to worry about. Moving all her possessions from Richmond to Alma Road, she was barely able to suppress her excitement. Colette had (tactfully, and heartbreakingly) withdrawn to spend a day at the beach and sulk about her disastrous exam results, well away from Stancester, but even so the house seemed to sing of her: her handwriting danced on the shopping list on the fridge; her cardigan sprawled across the back of the sofa; her discarded textbooks propped up the television and shrieked her name.

They stacked Lydia's boxes in the living room, for Olly would not be leaving until after graduation, a few weeks away. She supposed this was just as well: the route to what would be her own room would have taken them past Colette's, again and again, and she was not sure that she could have borne it. She contented herself with a last-minute dash to the top floor to slip a note under Colette's pillow. Resolute, she did not look back as they left Stancester behind. Another summer in Hastings: she could endure it, so long as she picked her battles carefully.

Home was the same as it always had been: the house too small for the four of them; her father's irritability; her mother's twitchiness. Church was the same as it had always been: her free time already snapped up and carved into blocks of band rehearsals and holiday club. Both, now, were overlaid with a smothering fog of deceit. It had been bad enough before, when she had only herself to suppress; now there was a name that could not be mentioned, a volume of stories that could not be told.

She did not altogether resent the time spent in church. It kept her out of the house, and was marginally preferable even when the family was there too. That first Sunday of the vacation, her place in the band gave her an excellent vantage point: she could see the ministers' backs, almost all the congregation, and everyone who came in at the main door. Alex, making a last-minute change to a PowerPoint slide. Her parents and sister, a prim trio in the second row. And, taking a newsletter from one of the Welcomers, Peter.

Lydia's heart leapt; she had hardly believed he would come. He had only travelled from Tonbridge, a scant hour away, but he seemed like a messenger from another world. His incongruous presence was a connection to Colette, a link between the constricted past of Hastings to which she was forced to regress whenever she went home, and her new-found freedom of Stancester.

'I love the new hair,' he said when he came to find her after the service had finished.

She hugged him, and said, 'Thank you – it's gone a bit crazy at the back, but I think I like it.'

'And I never knew you sang.'

She grimaced, pleasantly embarrassed. 'I'm not sure that you would really call what I do *singing*. I don't read music or anything.'

'It sounded pretty good to me,' Peter said.

Frank, the guitarist, said, 'She's very good indeed. Don't you listen to her.'

Lydia shook her head. 'It's very sweet of you to say so. Frank, this is Peter; he's a friend from uni. Peter, this is Frank. He pretty much runs this place.'

Frank winked. 'Lies! All lies! Victoria runs this place!'

'Victoria... your minister?' Peter guessed provocatively.

'No, the church administrator,' Lydia explained. 'She and Frank between them... well, poor Alex, who *is* the minister, hardly gets a look-in.' Over his shoulder, she saw her family approaching; she said, as casually as she could, 'Peter, this is my mum and dad and Rachel, my sister.'

Peter turned, nodded, smiled. Her mother had a faint air of surprise. Hell, Lydia thought: I never told her he was black, and it bothers her. She's not going to let on, though. And indeed, her face was reupholstered almost instantly with an ingratiating smile. Her father lurked behind them, his eyes marble hard. Rachel, too, eyed Peter suspiciously.

'Peter,' Lydia explained, 'used to live in the house that I'm going to live in, next year. I met him through... some of the Christian stuff at Stancester.'

Her parents looked marginally less hostile. Rachel's expression did not change.

'It's very nice to meet you all,' Peter said. 'I came down to see if I could take Lydia out for lunch?' Not, they had agreed, that it was any of her parents' business whether she went out or not, but it was safest to at least make a show of consulting them.

'Oh yes,' her mother said, 'she did mention that. Of course you can.'

'Fantastic.' He nodded awkwardly, surely feeling the deception swimming around them.

'I'll be back for dinner,' Lydia said. 'Come on, Peter.'

Outside, the rain fell in peevish drops, coming in sideways on the wind from the coast. It was a relief to escape from the church. Neither of them had spoken a word that was not true, but the sense of subterfuge lay heavy on them. Peter led the way to the car. Lydia flopped into the passenger seat and sighed gustily. 'How's Stancester?' she asked.

'It was all right on Thursday. Then I came home. Tonbridge is also fine.'

'Graduation went OK?'

'Yes.' He laughed. 'Olly snogged Georgia.'

'Finally.'

'Yes. And way too late.' Peter started the engine.

'Oh, well.' She was silent for a few moments, then looked over her shoulder as if expecting to find her parents in the back seat. 'How's Colette?' she asked.

'I have a letter for you. Hang on a sec.' He brought the car to a halt at the exit of the car park, and felt in his jacket pocket. 'Here.'

A postcard depicting Clee Hill, addressed to *Lydia Hawkins c/o Peter Nathan*.

Dear Lydia
Thank you for your note – lovely surprise. Sorry to miss you though obviously understand you couldn't stick around.
I hope to see you this summer – Peter has a plan – will be back in Stancester from August bank holiday if you're around.

The signature was a squiggle that might as well have read *Colin* or *Carrot*.

Then, in a plain, sealed, envelope, a single sheet of paper:

Dearest Lydia,
I understand that you may need to get rid of this – hence writing separately – but couldn't write to you and not tell you properly, in so many words, that I love you. I am missing you terribly – keep wishing you were up here – would love to show you places + introduce you to people.
It's possible I will be able to get down + stay with Peter – he will tell you more – understand completely if you'd rather I didn't see you so close to home – but hope we can manage it somehow. Didn't want to say on the phone in case it didn't come to anything. If not – I'm going back to Stancester early to do my retakes – maybe you could come back too? Or better not?
I love you so much, and you are so far away.
Colette xxxx

Peter seemed to be concentrating very hard on finding his way through the back streets of Hastings. When Lydia had finished reading he said, 'Any preference where we have lunch?'

'What?' For a blissful five minutes her mind had been in Shropshire. 'Not particularly. Somewhere cheap.'

He laughed. 'In which case I'll find a place to park, and we can wander around until we find something we like the look of. I think Mum left a brolly in the boot.'

'So,' she said, when they were inside a café on the seafront, warm, and dry, and confronting a plateful each of ham, eggs and chips. 'Talk to me about Colette.'

'She went home the day after you did,' Peter prevaricated. 'Ketchup?'

She took the bottle. 'I don't care. There's no one here to whom I can even mention her name.'

'You've not been in touch?'

'We've been phoning. I have her number saved in my phone as plain "C" - I am that paranoid.' She chuckled weakly.

'You know about her results?'

'Yes.' A 70, a 51, and two fails. Lydia bit her lip. 'I know it's not necessarily my fault, but – it probably is.'

Peter shrugged his shoulders. 'I'm not going to guess. Whatever the cause, there's not much to be done about it now.'

'She'll be back in Stancester early, for retakes.' Lydia knew she sounded wistful.

'You could go back early, too.' Peter was the picture of innocence.

'I could,' Lydia agreed. It was a tempting prospect. 'I wouldn't want to distract her, though.'

He raised a suggestive eyebrow. 'I would think it would be more like stopping her dying of boredom spending a month on her own in a house built for a family of eight. Anyway, what I actually wanted to say was: I'm going to ask her to stay with me for a week or two before I go up to Cambridge – so which two weeks would be particularly good for you?'

She thought about it, heart fluttering. 'I assume this week is too soon. After that we're into the school holidays. I'm helping out with the

159

church beach parties – holiday club things – the first two weeks. The second week of August, then?'

'Done,' Peter said.

He dropped her back home at four, graciously declining her mother's offer of a cup of tea. 'I'd better get back,' he said. 'My mum's expecting me for dinner.'

Lydia fielded the subsequent questions as best she could, thankful that she genuinely did not remember the name of the church where Peter was to be a pastoral assistant, but able to agree that yes, he was likely to end up a minister. No, she had no idea which theological college he might be thinking of attending afterwards.

She escaped at last to her room and lay down on her bed to ponder the convergence of her two worlds. Keeping Colette secret was simple so long as she remained safely in Shropshire; 'Colette' meant nothing to Lydia's family, a name on the list of her fellow tenants, that was all. Could she maintain the deception with Colette in the next county? She could not bear not to try.

Downstairs, her father was talking to Rachel. Lydia could hear the disappointed rumble of his voice, but could not make out any of the words. Poor Rae, she thought; what's she got herself into this time? Her mother's nervous interjections seemed, if anything, to be making matters worse. She lay there as long as she dared, holding the postcard against her cheek. Then she put Colette away with her own term-time self and went downstairs for dinner.

Rachel insisted on going to the library with her the next day. Lydia was not sure why. Admittedly, Rachel seemed to have fallen out with all her friends, and Hastings was dull enough when you were sixteen and had no money, but there was surely more to life than the library. Lydia was irritated; she had hoped for an hour of privacy. No, more, the allotted hour on the internet (where Colette would be, she prayed, logged into Messenger, waiting for her in cyberspace), and then to browse the Religion shelves. There might be something about sexuality and Christianity, if she was lucky. It would be difficult to look with Rae there.

Her little sister was clumping along the street with her hands rooted in her pockets and her shoulders hunched. Lydia ventured, 'Is everything OK, Rae?'

'Mm? Oh. Yeah.' The tone did not invite further inquiry. Lydia concluded that she was simply Being A Teenager.

They continued in silence to the library, where they found two computers an incurious distance away from each other; and Lydia did not ask what Rachel looked at for the duration of her booked hour, and did not tell how she had spent her own. Only when the time had run out, and Lydia was looking at the *Religion and Spirituality* section, wondering whether she dared take down *What the Bible Really Says about Homosexuality*, did Rachel display any sign of coming out from under her rock. She slouched up, disdain scrawled across her face. 'You're sticking with it, then.'

Panicking, Lydia grabbed *The Meaning in the Miracles* at random from the shelf. 'With what?'

Rachel pointed at the book. 'All this God stuff.'

'Of course I am. Why wouldn't I?' Lydia bit her lip, waiting for Rachel to say *Well, you're gay, aren't you?* and wondering how to reply, when she did.

But she only shrugged forlorn shoulders and said, 'Oh, no reason.' They walked home in silence.

The beach party passed off in a whirl of sand and Scripture: fifty interchangeable children high on sticky drinks and each other's company. Lydia enjoyed it, in a distracted sort of way, and avoided meeting up with her church friends outside it. She wanted to avoid anything that might progress beyond superficialities; she was too

161

aware of how close-knit were the networks at church. Anything she told Chrissie or Ruth would make it back to her mother by Sunday.

When Colette came to stay with Peter, he and Lydia went up to London together to meet her. Peter devoted his attention to his newspaper; he became very interested in Routemaster buses; he walked a few discreet paces ahead of them when they wandered hand in hand round Bloomsbury; he scrawled his name at the bottom of the postcard they sent Becky from Friends House; he manfully fell asleep on the train home.

Colette stayed a week. On three separate days of it they went down to Hastings and met Lydia there, always heading for the seafront, pretending to be holidaymakers. Lydia was nervous. No hands were held, even under tables. Tonbridge felt safer, and on the two days that Lydia travelled up to join them there, bowling up the main line towards civilisation, Peter managed to discover some urgent errands that only he could do, and left Colette and Lydia with an A-Z street map and each other.

Even so, they had a scare when Alex appeared with his wife Marie outside the supermarket just as they were all three meeting for lunch.

'Why they can't just go to Tesco in Hastings I've no idea,' Lydia said, rattled.

Peter led them to a discreet pub, not the sort that would be attractive to respectable ministers from Hastings, where they got their breath back over crisps and lemonade.

'I suppose,' Lydia said after a while, 'it'll be OK. Even if they did see us, it's more likely to be, "ooh, Judy, who was that nice lad that I saw your Lydia with in Tonbridge the other day, didn't he come to church a few weeks ago?" And Mum will be all, "oh, yes, that's Peter, lovely young man he is too, going to be a minister." They probably didn't even notice us; it's just my guilty conscience.'

Colette laughed. 'Hasn't your mum figured out that Peter's not Saved?' she asked.

'Not yet.'

'I went to your church,' Peter said. 'What more do you want? And who actually has got the double cure, anyway?'

'Oh, goodness,' Lydia said, more flippantly than she would once have dared. 'Let me get this straight. Ellie explained it all to me in great detail a while back. Now. Catholics are right out, obviously, because of the Pope and Mary thing. You're practically a Catholic, Peter, so you're not saved, though if you repented you could be.'

'I knew that. Go on.'

'Some Anglicans are, though they're the sort who tend not to call themselves Anglicans if they can help it. Like me: I used to be saved, though obviously recent developments will alter opinions there; everyone else who goes to St Mark's is probably OK. The Free Churches – fine, most of them. Apart from the Quakers, obviously. Colette, you're beyond the pale. Not only have you passed up the chance to choose a man, but you, a good non-conformist who *could* be saved if she really wanted to, hang around with all these unsaved Catholics and Anglicans, so you're the worst of the lot.'

'And there was me thinking it was something to do with the grace of God,' Colette said.

'I know. I suppose,' Lydia said, 'that should go for Will, too. I mean, back when I first met you lot I thought he was a sort of spiritual canary.'

'I said before that he has a nice singing voice,' Peter acknowledged.

'No – you know how coal miners used to take canaries down the mines? And if there was deadly gas down there then the canary would be the first to die, but if it was happy you knew you were OK?'

Peter snorted with laughter. 'Light dawns. Because Will, who is at least as happy clappy as you, was hopping around chirruping and ringing his bell, you thought it was safe to start hanging out with us heretics?'

'Pretty much,' Lydia admitted.

'What a fool you were,' he said kindly.

'There's a joke to be made somewhere about coal gas and Peter's incense habit,' Colette put in. 'I think Will has coped very well with our household, considering.'

'It gets really complicated, though,' Peter said, 'when two of the opposing forces team up. I remember back in my first year, when All Saints' and St Mark's suddenly decided that they were best friends – coincidentally enough when people were talking about Stancester getting a female archdeacon. And then someone else started talking about homosexuality, and they fell out again.' He shook his head. 'I love All Saints', but there are some people there with some very funny ideas.'

'I think they call them "Biblical",' Lydia said, surprising herself again with her own irreverence.

'"Traditional", more like,' Peter sniffed.

'I thought you were all for tradition,' Colette said, searching for Lydia's hand under the sticky table.

'Yes,' Peter said feebly, 'except where it's wrong.'

'And then you're for...?'

'Oh, I don't know. The Spirit? The right sodding thing, damn it.'

The next time she went to Tonbridge, Lydia had to bring Rachel with her, and they all sat awkwardly in a coffee shop full of yummy mummies and black-eyelinered teenagers. 'I'm not sure,' she said, taking advantage of her sister's brief expedition to the toilet, 'whether she's meant to be chaperoning us – that's you and me, Peter; the family does *not* know, still – or if she's in disgrace and I am meant to stop her having any fun. I seem to have missed a row yesterday. It could go either way.'

'Oh, well,' Peter said, cheerfully. 'That's someone for me to talk to, anyway.'

Actually, Rachel mostly talked to Colette; they took to each other immediately and shared the horror of Chemistry resits. Lydia, reticent in the company of family, conversed primly with Peter about karaoke-style recordings of hymn accompaniments for churches not fortunate enough to have either band or organist. At last, with Rachel and Colette deep in conversation over covalent bonds, Lydia said to Peter, 'I wish I could tell her. This is the nearest thing I've had to a normal life all summer.'

'Sounds grim. What about your beach party? How was that?'

It seemed like a different reality. 'All right. But I spent too long thinking about how this was probably the last one I'll ever do. I'll be out – out of it by next July.'

He raised his eyebrows. 'You think?'

It was a bold statement, but, she realised, probably true. 'I couldn't take another summer like this. Even if I'm wrong about everything – well, being wrong about it here is doing my head in.'

Rachel heard that, and looked up. 'Everything about everything here is doing my head in. Can I come and live with you?'

'I really don't think Dad would approve of that,' Lydia said, and giggled until Rachel asked what was so funny.

They finished the week with another day in London, to put Colette on the train home. Peter abandoned them a few tactful minutes before it left. Lydia kissed Colette at the gate and watched her walk down the platform, and stood there on the other side of the barriers until the doors were sealed and the train pulled out. Then she went to look for Peter, and found him flicking through an ancient *Hello!* in the nearest café.

She sat down opposite him and said, without preamble, 'Last night I managed to convince her. Mum. That we're not together. You and I.'

Peter slid the magazine to the far end of the table. 'Good grief,' he said. 'Are you sure that was a good idea? I got you a coffee. Milk?' He passed her the little stainless steel jug.

'Thank you.' She splashed milk in. 'I didn't go into any more detail than that, don't worry. I just couldn't keep on lying to her. She was so excited about my having a boyfriend at long last, and so disappointed when she finally believed me... I didn't tell her that I will never have a boyfriend. That's a confession for another day. I don't know what I'm going to do. It's not going to be pretty.'

Peter stirred his tea viciously. 'You mess Colette around, and there will be big trouble.'

That stung, the more because she had thought they were past that. 'I wouldn't hurt her for the world.'

'Sorry. That was uncalled for. No, I don't believe you would.'

Lydia pushed a hand through her hair. She said, half-smiling, 'That's why I'm telling you about all this crap, and not her, you see. It would upset her if she thought she was causing me grief.'

He looked more sympathetic. 'Ah, I see. You won't be able to hide that from her for ever, though.'

'No, I know, but it's so soon...'

Peter patted her hand. 'It was never going to be easy. But listen: I will put any money you care to name on the following three things. Firstly, your parents love you, because that's what parents do. Secondly, Colette loves you. She probably hasn't told you so yet, but I know her, and it's screaming to the skies. That might make things better; it might make them a hell of a lot worse. Thirdly – are you listening?'

She rested her chin in her hands and looked up at him, disbelieving, indulgent. 'Yes.'

'Thirdly – what am I trying to say?' He tapped his chin, considering. 'Thirdly, you know this as well as I do: you're bound to come up against some people in the Church – that's the Church with a capital C, the Church in general, not yours in particular – who do think you're a sinner in a big way because of all this, and who will continue to think so.'

'That's encouraging.' She knew she sounded bitter.

'I hadn't finished.' He swigged his tea.

'So?'

'So don't ever forget that the Church here on earth is a collection of human beings, and that as such it fucks up most things on a regular basis. Humans get stuff wrong.' He turned his hands palm upward. 'Lydia, please, please don't ever think that just because one, two, ten, fifty thousand members of the Church say you're not welcome, God is saying that too. He isn't. God is always there, waiting to welcome you, whoever you are and whatever you do. God loves you no matter what, and he's never, never going to turn you away – sod it, I'm getting preachy.'

She shook her head politely. 'No,' she said. Then, because actually he was, 'Yes. It's a helpful sort of preachiness, though. I needed to hear it.'

'I'll write it down on a piece of paper for you if you like,' Peter promised. 'Then you can read it whenever you feel like it.'

Lydia laughed shakily. 'Thanks. Really. Thank you for everything.'

'You're very welcome. If you ever need to talk – well, you have my number. I'm fairly useless, but I'm here.'

'Only *fairly* useless?' She stuck her tongue out at him.

'That sounds more like you,' Peter said approvingly. 'OK. Be nice to your parents. Be nice to your sister. Be nice to Colette, and especially be nice to yourself.'

She nodded. 'OK, I'll do my best.'

He grinned. 'Excellent. Let's go home, then.'

Michaelmas Term

Chapter 1

Love, sex and relationships: the uneasy interaction between these three is one of the biggest challenges facing young people today as they take the first steps out of the shelter of the family home and into the demands and pressures of university or college life. What does the Bible say? How can we talk about it to non-Christians? How can we hold fast to the truth of God's will in the face of the world's expectations? This course aims to explore the Bible's teaching on God's will for young men and women and to equip them with spiritual armour as they interact with each other and the world.

Treasure Store: God's will for human relationships (Course Leader's Handbook), Sheep Door Publishing 2005

It was a truism that frequently circulated within the Evangelical Christian Fellowship, that living in the same house as one's partner would inevitably result in the pair of you *ceasing to live a godly life*. The details were not usually elaborated, but one had a reasonable idea of what this expression referred to in this particular context. The temptation, it was implied, would be too great.

And if the temptation that arose from merely having one's separate beds in the same house was irresistible, that which was induced from having the whole house to yourselves... well, Lydia thought, amused, it didn't bear thinking about.

However, Colette spent the days in intense revision, and by nine o'clock in the evening she was worn out. Lydia, meanwhile, got ahead with her reading and, when she grew restless, went to the White Hart to talk to Mel across the bar. Or she went out walking, exploring Stancester more thoroughly than she had ever bothered when she lived in halls, and coming home with no thought more fleshly than soaking her tired body in a hot bath, or perhaps going out for a drink at Curzon's after dinner.

Opportunity was therefore more limited than a cynical observer might suspect; and though motive might be strong (she did not quite dare to ask Colette's thoughts on the issue, but for her own part she was conscious of a hunger she was still not ready to name) it was not insuperable. After her summer of dissembling, this September it was paradise merely to be here with Colette; to blow kisses at her across the dinner table or to look over her shoulder at the adverts for PhD places in the back of *New Scientist*; to snuggle up to her on the threadbare sofa as they watched terrible television in the evenings; to play at house together and make believe that these few weeks alone together could somehow stretch to a lifetime.

Their intimacy was marred only slightly by Stuart's arrival. He treated the pair of them with a respect that surprised Lydia at first, and accepted their obvious relationship as a matter of established fact. Becky roared in from the north, all red curls and black leather, delighted to find that Colette and Lydia had made it through the summer. Georgia wrote Lydia into the cooking rota and behaved generally as if nothing was odd. Lydia began to get used to the idea not so much of *coming* out, as of *being* out. No: the trouble with being a couple who lived in the same house was, Lydia discovered, that they forgot that there were people who should not know that they were any more than housemates – and then, if one of those people came back into the house...

She had become careless. That was all there was to it. She alone? Could she not say that Colette had been careless too? But Colette had nothing of her own to hide, and while she was diligent in doing nothing that might disturb Lydia, she had not that long-nurtured, bone-deep fear of other people seeing her true self, and so she did not jump at shadows; she was not the one to scoot to the far end of the sofa when someone else came in; she talked proudly, if evasively, of 'my girlfriend'. Lydia admired her calmness, her confidence in her identity; she was just beginning to emulate it herself, and then –

It was the Monday of Freshers' Week. Colette's retakes were over. Term proper had not yet started. The AngthMURC social had been comprehensively organised by Georgia, and there was nothing to worry about for the Fellowship welcome event until tomorrow. Lydia dozed on the sofa after lunch, defeated for the moment by *The Faerie Queene*. She was lying with her head pillowed in Colette's lap; it barely occurred to her that this was a pose that could not have been construed as platonic even had their hands not been firmly interlocked.

The sound of footsteps on the path outside, the jingle of keys, were, after all, perfectly normal noises, now that there were other people in the house.

Had Lydia been less sleepy she might have remembered that all the other people were already in the house, and sat up in time. She might have recognised the affable snigger, the light drawl that said, 'No, Dad, it's *this* one...' She might have connected the expensive growl of the car engine with the expected arrival –

As it was, she opened her eyes when Colette jumped with shock, and by then it was too late, because Will had opened the door, and was just *looking*.

She could not move. She would not move. Caught out, she would at least have the honesty not to deny Colette. She opened her eyes wide, tipped her head slightly backwards and, so inverted, met Will's gaze without flinching, daring him to challenge her. She felt Colette become very still, withdrawing silently from the fight. This was between Lydia and Will. Not one of them moved for – what? seconds? minutes? – she could not have said. The moment stretched unbearably, and still she gazed up, stared him down. She would deny nothing, but neither would she surrender any advantage, volunteer any admission unless it was demanded.

She felt a petty satisfaction when he turned and left the room without speaking, but it was swamped immediately by terror. She gripped Colette's hand. 'Oh, God,' she whispered.

Colette said, as casually if she were talking about what to have for dinner, 'What would you like to do, then?'

'I don't know,' Lydia said. She sat up delicately. 'I don't know,' she said again. 'What's he going to do?'

'That's his business,' Colette said. She was still motionless, and Lydia was reminded of the way she had been at the beginning. Whatever happened now, it would be Lydia's decision; Colette, she knew, would not risk pushing her one inch, would not ask her to do anything, for fear of trespassing on forbidden ground. Infuriated by the pair of them, she threw herself into Colette's arms and kissed her hard. Let Will see that, if he wanted to see something.

He cornered her the next morning when she was washing up after breakfast. 'Lyds? I wanted to talk to you.'

'Mm?' She scoured savagely at a coffee-stained mug.

'I spent a lot of yesterday praying, about, you know, about your thing with Colette, and your role within Fellowship. Do you really think that God wants you to continue as a hall officer?' Will asked. 'Do you think it's appropriate when you're clearly not leading a Christian lifestyle?'

'He didn't appear to have a problem with it before,' Lydia said shortly. She supposed Will wanted to convert her to heterosexuality. She was in no mood for it; she had a headache and was dangerously close to being late for her stint at the Fellowship GodTent.

'Well, yes, but before you weren't living with your, er, *girlfriend*.'

She snorted. 'I wasn't living with you, either.'

'What does that have to do with it?'

She swirled the dishcloth through the dirty water. 'About as much as my living in the same house as Colette does. After all, you didn't have a problem with Nick living with Jo, even though they were a couple.'

'Nick was the Fellowship president at the time,' Will pointed out. 'I think we could all trust him to behave in accordance with Biblical teaching.'

'Really.'

'Anyway, that's not the point,' Will ploughed on, before he could be disillusioned. 'We're talking about *you*.'

Lydia squeezed the cloth dry, hung it over the tap, and dried her hands on her skirt before she turned to him and answered. 'Ah, yes. Me. Well, confusing as it may seem, I'm pretty much the same person I was when I was living in halls. I was a lesbian last year, and it made precisely no difference to my gifts or integrity as a hall officer. And, not that it's any of your business, I'm not having sex with Colette. I have done my own praying about who I am and what I do with that, but I'm late for Mel and the GodTent. Perhaps we can pick this up later?'

They never did, though; not face to face, at least. Which, Lydia thought, was a pity: she would have much preferred to deal directly with Will. Or Jake. Even Ellie. Instead, she now had Colette hovering on the landing, apparently unsure whether to come into Lydia's room or retreat into her own, mumbling something about *the best thing* and *it isn't fair on you, so...*

She understood all in one disbelieving, furious moment. 'You're trying to break up with me?'

Colette nodded, her face taut with misery.

'Will's been talking to you, hasn't he.' It was hardly worth making it into a question.

'Yes, but...'

Lydia frowned. 'Come in. Shut the door. Tell me.'

Will had made a fatal tactical error in talking to Lydia before Colette. She could understand why he had made it: being aware that they shared a background (at least in the respect that was currently at stake) he had assumed that, his interpretation of said background being of course the correct one, he need only talk at her until she agreed with him. He had not counted on her having spent several months thinking and praying about this, and it had done nothing worse than irritate her.

It meant, however, that now, when Colette came to her in an agony of remorse and suggested breaking up, she knew exactly what had happened. Will had been more imaginative when it came to Colette; knowing that the Biblical touchstones and conventional social mores that he would have tried on Lydia would be ineffective, he went for observable facts:

That Lydia's friends were beginning to look askance at her, and, while they might not know *why* she had withdrawn from them, they were aware that something had changed. That Lydia missed those friends. That there was a part of Lydia that, deep down, desired a normal, Christian, relationship. That Lydia would never deliberately hurt somebody. That Lydia would never let on how much she was being hurt. That Lydia was deceiving her parents, and hating herself for it. That it fell to Colette to do the decent thing and end the misery.

He had, all in all, made a very thorough job of it, and it took Lydia a while to extract the whole truth. When she had, she was almost amused under her boiling righteous wrath. She sat down on the bed, hoping that Colette would sit next to her. 'You are so gullible,' she said, knowing that nothing would dissolve all this cloying martyrdom so well as a refusal to take it seriously.

Colette, who was busy being noble, remained standing and looked hurt. 'I'm doing what I think best.'

'You're not,' Lydia said, and thanked God for the insight. 'You're doing what Will thinks best. He's an idiot. You're a worse one. Whatever he's told you about us, forget it. He hasn't a clue.'

'Not about us,' Colette protested. She would not meet Lydia's eye; she prodded at the fringe of the rug with her toe.

'What he's told you about *you*, then? No. You still know who you are. What he's told you about me. Ignore him. He doesn't know a thing about me.'

'He said you're not happy.'

Lydia barked a laugh. 'He has a point. I'm not. I would be quite a bit happier, though, if he had the courtesy to stop interfering in my life. Smug bastard,' she said, and enjoyed saying it.

Colette looked stricken, and folded suddenly onto the bed. 'I worry that your being with me is just making your life miserable.'

'I believe,' Lydia said, inconsequentially, 'that in the Big Handbook of How To Be A Lesbian, there is a page on Bisexuals. It tells you that you should never date a Bisexual, because she will inevitably leave you to run off with a Man. Now, either I'm going to have to ask for my money back, because it turns out that a Bisexual will actually leave you for some misguided, pig-headed idea of what is the right thing to do, regardless of whether you actually want her to – or Will has been even more subtle and manipulative than I thought possible, and you're actually trying to run off and leave me for him –'

To which the only possible response was a cushion, hurled with some force.

Lydia swatted it aside, laughing. 'Come here,' she said, and they collapsed, cushion and all, in a heap on the bed.

'You're right,' Colette said into her jumper. 'I am an idiot.'

Lydia stroked her hair. 'He's sneakier than I thought,' she said. 'That was really quite clever, getting you right in the guilt complex. And of course you would try to do it without actually talking about it, because you always do.'

'Ouch,' Colette murmured.

Lydia said rapidly, 'I knew it would be like this, and I did it anyway.' She needed Colette to understand. 'Say, for the sake of argument, that you did break up with me, for an actual good reason. I wouldn't start looking for a boyfriend, because I know now that's not who I am.'

'Oh, Lydia.' Colette looked up at her, grey eyes bright. 'I'm sorry. I'm a selfish coward, and I thought I was doing it for you, I honestly did… I couldn't bear the thought of things being said about you and knowing it was because you were with me.'

'But it isn't. It's not because of you. It's because of me. I've burned my boats,' Lydia said, quieter than ever. 'I can't go back now – or, if I could, I would know it was a lie. I could say that you seduced me. I could repent and be accepted back, but the repentance would be a worse sin: it would be covering up what I know I am. Colette, darling Colette, while I appreciate that in your own bizarre way you've been trying to set me free, it just isn't going to work like that. I'm not going to repent for something that's not a sin, and if that makes me an outcast, so be it. Either I'm with you, or I'm an outcast alone.'

Chapter 2

The Bible is clear on the most Godly pattern for human relationships. Over and over again, Paul tells us that husbands should love their wives as Jesus loved us; wives, in turn, should submit to their husbands – a duty that becomes a joy where God's will is truly done.

But we have to go back to Genesis for the archetype of human relationships. God says that it is not good for man to be alone, and immediately creates a helper, a companion, a wife, for Adam, the crown of His creation. And, so long as Adam and Eve are obedient to God's will, they live, quite literally, in Paradise.

What, we must ask ourselves, does this have to say to Christian students, in their late teens or early twenties? Most of them won't yet have met the person that God has chosen for them to spend their life with. Marriage may be a long way off for them. How, until they can commit themselves in the holy partnership of marriage, can they live lives of Godly integrity?

Treasure Store: God's will for human relationships (Course Leader's Handbook), Sheep Door Publishing 2005

Membership of the new hall group hovered around seven or eight: practising Christians from her own sort of background, refreshingly – sometimes alarmingly – fresh-faced and innocent. Untainted by last year's political distractions, they were unaccustomed to discerning subtle nuances or understanding that things were sometimes more complicated than first appeared.

With a year's experience under her belt, Lydia found that the stage fright had gone, but she was much less sure of having the answers than she had been when she began. It was strange, not living in the same hall as them. She found that she had to make a conscious effort to keep up with the gossip that had flowed naturally around her last year –

and she had to know what was going on, if she was going to do anything to help her group with the problems they were facing.

Given the new logistical difficulties, she considered it vital to ensure that they had a regular routine. Tuesday worked best for the group? Very well, hall group would always be on a Tuesday, and she would always be free on a Tuesday. If the group wanted to reschedule, that was up to them, but it would be their choice, not hers. It was, therefore, just too bad that the first meeting of the Teaching and Study Committee fell on a Tuesday. And it was just as well that Will was an enthusiastic member of that same committee, and able both to attend the meeting and to report back on it for her.

'Say hi to Kris and Fiona for me. And let me know if anything interesting happens,' she had said, before dashing out of the door leaving her dinner half-eaten.

'I will do!' Will assured her, breezily. She could not help suspecting a hint of disapproval at the back of his mind; so long as it stayed there, she thought crossly, she did not much care. No doubt he would take her failure to attend the committee meeting as further proof of her complete moral disintegration. It was rather irritating, given her plan to spend the evening engaged in the consumption of hot chocolate and sound biblical teaching.

She made sure to arrive home before him, and spread her teaching notes out on her desk, just to prove that she had been engaged in equally Christian pursuits. It was petty, she knew; this was the last thing in the world that she should be competitive about, but there it was. Will had a positive talent for bringing this kind of behaviour out in people.

He looked in on her when he got back. She had left her door open in the hope that he would.

'How did hall group go?' he asked.

She smiled. 'Very well, thank you. I'm really pleased with this bunch; I think God's doing some fantastic work in Richmond this year. How was Teaching and Study? Anything I should know?'

'Oh, yah, it was good,' he said. 'We had a look at some resources for next term, to get a feel for them before anybody ordered anything, you know?'

'Yes? Any good stuff there?'

Will shifted from one foot to the other. 'I thought so. You – well, yeah, you'll see. It's actually a series that Ellie advised us to have a look at – so comes with recommendation from our superiors, you see!' For Ellie had graduated and moved on to higher things – specifically, the Federation of Christian Student Societies. However, she was based in the West of England division, and Stancester continued to see a lot of her.

'I'll look forward to it,' Lydia said, secretly annoyed that Will had not asked for details of their (really quite interesting) study on Colossians.

'Yes. Good. Oh well. Good night, then.' He looked suddenly, inexplicably, guilty, but Lydia was still too cross with him to want to seem curious.

'Night!' she said, and shut the door after him.

It arrived just less than a fortnight later, a lazy Saturday morning. Lydia was flicking idly through the *Stancester Comet* while Colette caught up on her washing up duty, until the peace was broken by the rattle of the letterbox and the ring of the doorbell.

'I'll go,' Colette said, wiping her hands on a tea towel, and went down to take delivery of the post. She brought it upstairs to sort on the kitchen table. 'Phone bill – Georgia can work that out. You've got a postcard from your friend Mel; how did she swing a field trip to Mexico? That parcel will be my Burrows. And another for you.'

It was a bulging A4 manilla envelope, packed with brightly coloured glossy booklets, and reeking of new ink. 'That's my hall group materials for next term,' Lydia said. 'Let's have a look.'

Colette returned to the washing up. 'Why do I never do this after dinner, instead of letting it all stick to the plates?'

'Because you're always half asleep after dinner,' Lydia said. Then, as she looked more closely at the contents of the envelope, 'Oh, God.'

Colette looked up. 'What?'

Frantic, she flipped through the shiny pages, praying that it was not what it looked like. But, 'I can't use these.'

Colette came over and perched on the end of the kitchen table. 'Why not?'

'Look. Just... look.' She shoved the booklet at her.

'*Treasure Store: God's will for human relationships,*' Colette read. 'Oh, Lord. No sex before marriage? Women, obey your husbands?'

Lydia held it at arm's length. 'I've not read it yet. I don't want to.'

'Don't you get any say in what you teach your group?'

'Yes, we discuss it at Teaching and Study, but I missed the last meeting, and they ordered it then...' It slipped from her fingers.

Colette picked it up, sat down at the table, and took Lydia's trembling hand in her damp one. 'Do you have to use all this, or can you do your own thing?'

'Well, up to a point, but I can't directly contradict what I've been given. I don't think I can do a whole term of this...' She could hear the panic in her own voice. 'What am I going to do?'

Colette's tone was artificially reasonable. 'I hate to say this, but what about reading it? See how bad it really is?'

'And if it is? If it's something I can't teach from with a clear conscience?'

Colette opened and closed her mouth several times. 'Well, there are several things you could do,' she said at last. 'You could bring this lot along as an example, but also have some alternative viewpoints handy, from, um, the Quakers, for example. You could just resign. You could talk about how far you agree with this, and leave the rest as silence. You could talk about *why* you find it difficult.'

Out herself to her hall group? 'No! Oh, God, I know I should, but I can't.'

Colette ploughed on. 'You could say you're doing it without notes this term, and just let the group loose with a Bible. They can read, can't they? Talk about the different Biblical models of relationship.'

'Yeah, let's start with Solomon and all his wives and concubines,' Lydia muttered. 'Or we could argue all term over just what David and Jonathan were up to...'

'Ruth was totally bisexual,' Colette said. 'Look, read it first. I'll hold your hand if you like. Then we can see what to do with it.'

It was exactly as bad as Lydia had expected. She jabbed a finger at a line in one of the supplements. 'Look at this. *Eighteen to twenty-five year olds who claim to be homosexual are eight times more likely to attempt suicide than normal young people.'*

'I think that's about right, actually,' Colette said, 'apart from the *normal* thing. Obviously it would depend on the study they used...'

'No, listen. *This frightening statistic on its own tells us that homosexuality is not in God's plan for His people, and that any attempt to pursue it can only end in unhappiness and separation from Him.'*

Colette said, 'Oh, well, we're doomed, then. On the bright side, we're not going to get pregnant out of wedlock. Not accidentally, anyway.'

'There is that,' Lydia said. She tried to laugh.

Colette picked up another insert and read it swiftly. 'Good grief,' she said. 'I honestly didn't realise that people still got so hung up on Leviticus. I thought that all got straightened out round about the year AD40, with the sheet full of animals.'

It felt like a small earthquake. '*Oh*. Go on.'

Colette raised her eyebrows. 'It's obvious. Isn't it? Peter thinks he's been sent to the Jews and only to the Jews. And then he goes to stay with this Roman and he has a vision.'

Trembling, Lydia knelt beside Colette, stretched her arms around her waist, and laid her face in her lap. 'A sheet comes down from heaven, full of all sorts of animals, some of which are unclean. And he hears a voice saying, Peter, kill and eat. And he says, no, they're unclean. And the voice says...' She broke off.

Colette laid a hand on Lydia's head, and finished it for her. 'Do not call anything unclean that God has called clean. And then Peter realises that it's not about the food; it's about the people. The people that Peter previously thought were unclean, are clean, because God made them, too.' Then, more urgently, 'And they realise, later, that the Gentile believers don't have to be circumcised. They are welcome exactly as they are.'

Lydia cried for a little while. 'I didn't realise it was about me,' she said at last. 'Thank you.'

Colette stroked her hair. 'A pleasure. A privilege. I'm sorry we haven't talked about it before.' She paused, and then said, 'Lydia.'

She looked up. 'Mm?'

'Do you think this was deliberate?' Colette's forehead was furrowed.

She chewed her lower lip. 'No,' she said at last, '– but I don't think it was accidental.'

'That's an interesting distinction,' Colette said, her voice heavy with cynicism.

Lydia got to her feet. 'I am trying really hard to not think that anybody deliberately thought, right, how do we show Lydia the error of her ways, well, maybe some teaching on heterosexuality might do the trick. I don't think it's as pointed as that, and I don't think Will's told anyone. I'd have had something more direct if he had. *A quiet word.* Hadn't I better resign, for the good of Fellowship. No, this isn't a sniper rifle.'

'What is it, then?'

She searched for an appropriate metaphor. 'A cluster bomb. Let it off and see what damage is done. Damage to legitimate targets, or otherwise. After all, it's not just me – it's Rose, who's got an atheist boyfriend, and Mazz and Kris, who everybody knows are sleeping together. It wouldn't surprise me if someone suggested this particular set of materials with a view to making me – and some other people – *think*. As if I hadn't been thinking every day since I was thirteen.'

'So how is that not deliberate?' Colette demanded, angrily logical.

'Not malicious, then. They – whoever they are – think they're doing the right thing.'

'What's that saying about the road to hell?'

'Paved with yellow bricks, if you read this lot,' Lydia said with a desperate giggle. 'You don't know how I envy you – not having to try to believe the best of everyone.'

'None of this "hate the sin, love the sinner" lark,' Colette agreed. 'It's a tolerable idea, if you've accepted the inbuilt bigotry as inevitable, but it doesn't work in practice. It ends up as "hate the sin, despise the fool who's too weak-willed to resist temptation". You get used to it in time. Oh, darling, don't cry... look, I know what we'll do: we'll take it to Becky. If anyone can talk sense into Will, she can.'

Becky was not impressed, and said so at length.

'Nevertheless,' Colette said when she had finished, 'the committee has still chosen it.'

'That was pretty fucking stupid of it, then,' Becky said. 'It's not as if Fellowship is flavour of the month with the Union Equalities Rep...'

Lydia shuddered.

'What?' Colette said.

Becky sighed. 'It's not flavour of *any* month with the Equalities Rep. Do keep up. If it's not homophobia it's sexism, and if it's not sexism it's faith healing, and if it's not faith healing it's requesting exemptions from the equality clauses in the Union constitution. All the same,' glancing down the offending page, 'I don't get it. How can they possibly think that this is in any way helpful? How is being a bunch of misogynist, homophobic gits going to help them spread the good news?'

'Ah, well, you see, they win both ways.' Colette made no attempt to disguise the bitterness in her voice. 'If things are going well, that's God blessing them, but if the rest of the world is queueing up to smack some sense into them, well, didn't Jesus say, Blessed are you when men revile and persecute you?'

'But they're the ones reviling and persecuting!' Becky said.

They merely looked at her.

'… sorry, yes, you're already well aware of that.' Becky looked at the pamphlet again, frowning. 'No, I can't imagine it's much fun.'

'No,' Colette said. 'But Fellowship are good at that kind of circular logic. Like, gay sex is wrong because there's no such thing as same-sex marriage, so it would be sex outside marriage, but you can't have same-sex marriage because gay sex is wrong.'

Lydia wanted to scream.

Becky sighed. 'Right. And this lot think the Catholics aren't Christian why?'

Colette scowled. 'At least the Catholics are consistent – they reckon gay sex is wrong because there's no way of getting pregnant, which is the same reason that they don't like contraception. I disagree with them entirely, but considered in a vacuum it makes sense.'

Becky's face hardened. 'So they're the least worst. I see.'

'Anyway,' Colette said, 'I'm not talking about the Catholics.'

'Indeed.' Becky turned the pamphlet over and over. 'Leave it with me.'

Chapter 3

From: r.m.seymour@stan.ac.uk

To: e.greer@stan.ac.uk

18 October, 10:31

Dear Emma,

Please see attached a scan of a double-page spread from a publication entitled 'Treasure Store'. The Evangelical Christian Fellowship is intending to use this as a basis for its hall group course next term. As you will see, this raises all sorts of concerns as this course advocates a 'traditionalist' view of the role of women and of same-sex relationships.

I have emailed Paul Coster, Students Union Equalities Officer, regarding this, but have received no reply as yet.

I would be happy to meet you to discuss this further.

Yours sincerely,

Becky Seymour.

From: e.greer@stan.ac.uk

To: r.m.seymour@stan.ac.uk

18 October, 16:14

Hi Becky,

Thank you for your email. I'd be keen to meet – as you say, it's very relevant to the STANdard that this sort of hateful filth is being peddled to our Freshers.

Let me know when you're free to meet up and I'll try and get Paul involved myself. The paid officers are very good at what they do, but completely useless at replying to emails!

Best wishes,

Emma Greer

The Evangelical Christian Fellowship's Teaching and Study Committee crammed itself into the living room at Balton Street, together with the Area Representative for the Federation of Student Christian Societies, and the President. There was no written agenda, but it was understood that they had come together to discuss Emma Greer's latest article in the *STANdard*, to apportion blame, and to formulate a damage limitation strategy. Jake stationed Mel at the front door to ensure that only committee members were admitted; it gave the affair the flavour of a secret society. Lydia was amused and apprehensive in equal measure. She had been jumping at shadows ever since the article appeared, terrified that someone would link it with her or Colette, or Becky, or Will. This was at least a chance to get it over with.

The meeting opened with prayer and continued with shrill indignation.

'Did you *see* the *STANdard*?' But of course they all had, or were pretending to have done.

Kris had a copy with him, and began reading out loud: *'It's a good job that the organisation formerly known as the "Christian Fellowship" added that "Evangelical" to its title. Reading its proposed curriculum for next term, you might be forgiven for wondering whether the intended audience was the late Fred Phelps. I can't think of many Christians who would put their signature to the hateful bigotry the ECF has approved, but it seems there's a minority who think that their right to freedom of so-called religion outweighs my right not to be called 'perverted and unnatural'...'*

'It's a travesty,' Will said. He had come straight from hockey practice and looked damp and irritable.

Fiona, now officer for Freeman Hall, squeaked, 'It's a disaster!'

'Never mind what it is,' Ellie said, icily. 'How did they get hold of it?'

Suspicious eyes moved slowly, appraisingly, around the room. *One of you at table with me...* Will was shifting in his seat, but everybody looked uncomfortable.

'It could have been anyone,' Kris said, and shut up suddenly as they all turned to look at him.

'Actually,' Will said, 'I have a pretty good idea who it was, and so does Lydia, but she's too nice to say without proof.'

They all turned to look at him, now, Lydia among them.

'Who?' Jake asked, urgently.

Will was choosing his words with care. 'One of my housemates – our housemates, I mean. I don't know where they got it from, but I don't think either Lydia or I was as careful about keeping it secret as we clearly should have been.'

'You can't trust people, can you?' Ellie said, mournfully, her eyes still bent on Lydia.

'What can we do?' Jake asked, not really expecting an answer.

'Leave it,' Will said reluctantly. 'Seriously. I've looked at the Union constitution. We can't do anything to someone who's not a Fellowship member, and we've got no proof.'

'Do we run the course?' Fiona asked.

Jake looked to Ellie.

'Probably. See what happens,' she advised. 'Have an alternative ready in case the Union is really unreasonable, but I think God is calling us to stick to our guns on this.'

Jake nodded emphatically. 'That was my feeling.'

There were a few other bits of business, but nobody had much stomach for them, and the meeting subsided into aimless grumbling.

'Well,' said Kris, the nominal chairman, 'I guess that's it. Shall we pray?... Lord Jesus, we just want to thank You for this opportunity to come together to do Your work. You know the challenges we are facing here, You know the battles we are fighting, You know the stumbling blocks that are being set up in front of us. But we believe, Lord, that You are working through all this, we trust You that You will bring your people through this, and we know that You will use this to glorify Your name in this place. Amen!'

'Amen!' they echoed, and the meeting dispersed.

Will slung his sports bag over his shoulder. Lydia followed him. They walked several morose streets before she said, 'I suppose she thought it was for the best.'

'I guess so,' Will said. Righteous indignation gleamed in his eye. He would, Lydia had no doubt, be having words with Becky, and both would enjoy the scrap. She intended to speak to Becky herself, but she was not looking forward to it. She had not the stomach to fight with Will any more, and anyway, he had not said nearly as much as he might have done.

'Well, anyway. Thank you.'

'You're welcome,' he said, blandly, as if he had no idea for what she was thanking him.

Becky seemed to have been expecting one or the other of them; her bedroom door was open and she was quick to jump up and pause the film she was watching when Lydia came in. On the screen, a laser beam was halted halfway to a gleaming spacecraft.

'It's blown,' Lydia said. 'I don't think any of us were expecting you to go that far.'

'Will called my bluff,' Becky said. 'I honestly thought he'd back down, if I threatened him with the Union.'

Lydia shook her head. 'Even if he had, I doubt the rest of them would have listened.'

188

Becky pressed on. 'Anyway, he didn't, so I had to get the Union involved, and then they were no fucking use so I had to go through the *STANdard.*'

'Had to,' Lydia repeated grimly.

'I know,' Becky said. 'I know. I should have let it die. I haven't changed anything and I've probably made it worse for you. I'm sorry.'

Lydia sighed. She was still angry, still scared, but it hardly seemed fair to be angry with Becky. What had she done, except bring to light the things hidden in darkness? If Fellowship objected to its course appearing in the *STANdard*, perhaps it ought to have chosen a different course. What was that old bromide? *If you have nothing to hide, you have nothing to fear...*

Oh, but she had plenty to hide, and plenty to fear – though it seemed that nobody in Fellowship knew that she and Colette were a couple – nobody except Will, and he, for some reason of his own, wasn't telling.

Chapter 4

Freedom of speech is a concept that is misunderstood depressingly frequently. Yes, I am free to write whatever I like, and you are free to say whatever you like. However, my editor is equally at liberty to refuse to print what I write, if he deems it inappropriate, offensive, or just plain crap, and any person speaking in a way to stir up hatred against any particular group is acting outside the law of this land, and can expect the consequences to be severe.

'Stirring up hatred' is perhaps putting it a little strongly. However, when my Students' Union resources appear to be funding the purchase of materials that state explicitly that women are inferior to men, that lesbian, gay, and bisexual people are a deviation from nature, and that homosexuality is a mental illness, I am deeply concerned.

I welcome, therefore, the decision by the Students' Union Executive to conduct an audit into all SUSU society activities, with a view to ensuring that all of them comply with the Equal Opportunities policy, which, we remember, all of them have committed to honour. Should any society be found to be ignoring their side of the agreement, it seems only fair that the SUSU should be at liberty to withdraw any privileges it sees fit from the society in question.

Setting our house in order, Emma Greer (*STANdard*, 9 November)

Lydia arrived at Markham Grange to find that her housemates accounted for half the attendees at the AngthMURC meeting: Colette, Georgia, Becky and Stuart. The others were the speaker (fussing with some handouts on persecuted Christians in China), Zoe, Anna Blackie, and a Fresher called David. They seemed excited.

'Lydia! Have you seen this?' Stuart was brandishing a copy of the *STANdard*, folded back to the Opinion page. 'Yeah. Another Emma Greer special. Apparently the Union is doing an Equal Opps audit of all the societies, and they're so keen on this idea that it's already under way. I don't know what the Equalities Officer's motivation is, but the subtext of the article is that Fellowship had better clean up its act if it knows what's good for it.'

Suppressing a shudder, Lydia hung her coat on the back of a chair and sat down. 'It had better clean up its act or what?'

Stuart shrugged his shoulders. 'Who knows? It says here the Union can forcibly disaffiliate Fellowship from it – what would that mean?'

She thought about it. 'Money. Facilities. Advertising. Goodwill. I don't really know how the funding works, but it's something to do with the size of the membership, and we're the biggest society on campus. We'd lose a lot of money if they did chuck us out. Not that I think that's very likely.'

'You do get funding from elsewhere, though?' Stuart looked interested.

'Oh, yes. Some of the city churches, and the FSCS as well. It wouldn't kill Fellowship; it would just make life a bit difficult until we worked out a way around it.'

'Heaven help us all,' Colette said. 'Georgia – you're looking worried.'

Georgia jumped. 'Me? Oh, I was thinking about the Anglican chapel, and the disabled access. Just wondering if it's really such a good idea to do so much AngthMURC stuff there, given what a nightmare it is for wheelchairs...'

'Tanya's been trying to sort that out for ages, hasn't she?' Stuart said. 'I remember Peter moaning about it last year.'

'Yes – it's a listed building.'

'I wouldn't worry,' Colette said. 'The Union won't start picking on us, because that would *prove* they were anti-Christian, you see. They like having us and Cathsoc around, as examples of How Christian Societies Should Be Run.'

'What, be... inoffensive and miniscule?' Lydia grinned.

Colette flapped a hand at her. 'You know very well what I mean. Anyway, G, don't worry: most of our stuff is in the Grange, and therefore accessible.'

'Had we better talk about the audit at the committee meeting?' Stuart asked.

'I suppose we ought to,' Colette groaned, 'though I wanted to get home before midnight and I feel it only fair to warn you that my brotherly love towards my fellow Christians is being stretched almost to breaking point. I doubt that anything coming out of this will do much to improve things. I don't mind being Vice President, but I don't feel very Ecumenical at the moment.'

'Well,' said Becky, who had been uncharacteristically quiet through the preceding conversation, 'I hope they pick up on that poster of the rugby team's, that's all I can say. It's a fucking outrage.'

Colette's room was dim in the evening shadows. The blank screen glared white. 'How,' Colette asked, 'did "I am not writing this thing" get minuted as "Colette to draft AngthMURC statement to *STANdard*"? I knew I should never have given up being Secretary.'

'Have you been fretting about this all day?' Lydia looked over her shoulder. 'You were probably asleep at the time. Be as cunning as snakes and as innocent as doves. To be fair, it does say, "To be signed by whole committee".'

'Hmm. Well, it had better be. I don't *mind* being the University's Token Queer Christian,' she said. 'I mean, it's irritating, and I don't see why Tim bloody Benton can't be it, given that he started all this mess in the first place, but I can live with it.' She sighed. 'I'm just worried about you. If this thing blows any further your parents will hear. And that's assuming that Will *doesn't* see fit to email the whole of Fellowship to tell them you're gay, which to be quite frank I'm surprised he hasn't done already. Even if your family only find out that you live in the same house as a depraved bisexual like me, there'll be hell to pay. If anybody catches on that you're my girlfriend...'

'I'm going to tell them,' Lydia said, hoping that Colette was being pessimistic. 'Better me than anyone else.'

'You think that's wise?'

'It's the only thing I can do. You're quite right: sooner or later someone's going to out me, and if it's not me, it'll be the Christian gossip network.'

'It'll be a very well-intentioned outing, if so.' Colette's tone was acid.

'Probably via the medium of the prayer telephone tree. *Dear friends in Christ, please pray for Lydia, that she would be cleansed from sin and see God's plan for her, and for Judy and Alan in this difficult time...*'

Colette laughed, without humour. 'Do you want to help me write AngthMURC's statement?'

It was a relief to think about someone else's problems. 'Yeah, if you like. Did you want me to translate it into Evangelical, or just check your spelling?'

Colette leaned backwards and caught her in an inverted embrace. 'Rather the opposite. I think we just want something boring and absolutely *glowing* with Christian charity. You know: God loves everybody, particularly the people nobody else loves, and AngthMURC attempts to reflect that. Also some of us might actually not be straight, but we're not telling you who, because we don't think it's any of your business.'

'I don't think that's boring at all.' Lydia bent and kissed her. 'I wish someone had told me that years ago.'

Chapter 5

The row that engulfed the Stancester University Students' Union earlier this year has broken out again, with the Union announcing an equal opportunities audit which has been interpreted by many as directly targeting the university's Christian Fellowship. Paul Coster, the SUSU Equalities Officer, said, 'Sadly, in the course of our investigation we have discovered that the Evangelical Christian Fellowship has asked its officers to use deeply offensive and homophobic materials. We have requested that the ECF doesn't use these materials, but if they do not comply we will have no alternative but to remove their Union privileges.' These privileges could, Mr Coster confirmed, include funding and use of the Students' Union building.

The Bishop of Stancester, Right Reverend Robert Antcliff, said, 'It is deeply concerning to see faith coming under such savage attack. Despite the increasing secularisation of Britain, this is still a Christian nation, and if we do not protest against the erosion of our rights to teach the moral lessons of our faith, we will soon find ourselves very much the poorer.'

Ellie Ford, a student at the University of Stancester and a representative of the Christian Fellowship, said, 'Not content with forcibly changing our society's name, the Students' Union is now attacking our beliefs. We are not preaching hate. Everyone who will be learning the course that has apparently caused so much offence has willingly chosen to attend it, just as every member of the Christian Fellowship is a Christian. Like the society's name, the content of the course is surely therefore a matter for Fellowship and Fellowship alone.'

New Faith War Breaks Out at Uni, Jackie Lloyd, *Stancester Comet,* 16 November

Colette's birthday fell in the middle of November. Peter returned to Stancester for the occasion, dressed in a new, severely cut, black coat, and looking lankier than ever.

'How's Cambridge?' Lydia asked him as the household gathered in the kitchen.

'How's Cambridge? Bloody freezing and full of rahs and tourists and bicycles. In fact, it's just like here, but five degrees colder and without any hills. Not that I'm complaining about about there not being any hills, you understand.' He stopped to draw breath. 'Oh, and speaking of rahs, I ran into Phil the other day!'

'Phil-the-last-sacristan-but-one?' Georgia asked. She turned to Lydia. 'He was the AngthMURC publicity officer, and then the treasurer, and he basically ran the chapel. Imagine a white version of Peter, give him Will's accent, and then turn the incense up to eleven.'

'Yes – he's at Staggers, but –' Peter had always been fond of dramatic pauses – 'he was in Cambridge visiting his boyfriend at Westcott.'

After a stunned second, Georgia laughed. 'Well – that's three months of my life I'm never getting back.'

'I did tell you at the time,' Peter said.

'Such is the tragedy of the spinster of this parish,' Georgia agreed. 'The men you fancy always turn out to be gay. The women – so I hear – never do. You can stop grinning and all, Colette.'

'I wasn't grinning,' Colette said.

'Really,' Georgia said. She turned to Peter. 'Which are you going to, then?'

'Who knows? Staggers suits my style but not my politics, and I'm told Oxford's horribly damp.' He rubbed his nose, and said, in a different tone, 'It's a long way off, anyway. I might have changed my mind by then.'

'About which to go to?'

Peter frowned. 'About going anywhere.' Before Georgia could pursue that, he said, 'So, what's new with the Fellowship mess?'

Georgia scrabbled in the pile of junk mail on the kitchen table and passed him a newspaper. 'This will amuse you: it's the *Comet*'s take on the story. They're thrilled, of course – some actual news, even if they don't understand any of it. Look, front page. Complete with the Bishop of Stancester missing the point completely, *and* comment from your old nemesis, Ellie Ford.'

Peter took the paper. 'Oh, is she still in Stancester?'

'Not really,' Georgia said. 'She's become the area rep for the Federation of whatever it is, Christian Societies, and rushes all over the West Country telling Christian students what they should be doing to further the work of the Kingdom.'

Lydia, who still went to some effort to think of Ellie as a friend, cleared her throat. 'I believe she's actually doing a lot of good work.'

'*I* bet,' Peter snorted.

'She's very efficient when she puts her mind to getting something done,' Lydia protested. 'Seriously, I bet she'll be shaking up some committees...'

'Hang on a sec,' he exclaimed. 'Ellie Ford getting people to do what she wants I can see, but Ellie Ford *telling* people, specifically *male* people, specifically Evangelical Christian male people in positions of authority? She was always very into male headship – stop sniggering, Colette – and here you are telling me she's effectively acting as archdeacon when she doesn't believe in women priests?'

Lydia was not sure what an archdeacon was. 'I think,' she said carefully, 'she sees herself more as an administrator. And you mean ministers. She wouldn't talk about priests.'

'Hmm.' Peter began reading the article. 'Good grief, I see what you mean about the Bishop.'

'Oh, God, yes,' Colette said. 'Isn't it brilliant? I saw Tim earlier; he's fuming.'

'I'm not surprised,' Georgia said; 'it's quite impressive. Nasty atheist Students' Union throws poor persecuted Christians to the lions and steals all their money.'

Peter chuckled. 'I'd take the lions over Ellie any day. Wait – why's she pretending to be a student?'

'She used to be a student, to be fair,' Georgia said, amused by his irritation.

Peter frowned. 'It's a bit disingenuous. I wouldn't mind so much if she were just a concerned outsider, but she's getting paid for this. She ought to say so. Do you think *I* should make a comment posing as a Christian student at the University of Stancester?'

'Oh, grow up,' Georgia said. 'We've already done one from AngthMURC, not that anyone cares what we think. Anyway, do you think God really worries about all this political shit?'

'Yes,' Lydia said at once. 'Yes, I do actually. Not about who wins or what the society ends up being called, but I think God does care about all this – rubbish – because just think what it means for His work on campus. You're right, Georgia – nobody understands what's going on here, apart from those who are basically obsessed by it, and nobody cares, and all they see is Christians fighting other Christians, and how is that going to bring anyone to Jesus? Why aren't we getting this worked up about the stuff that really matters?'

'But, God knows, this *does* matter,' Peter growled. 'You, of all people, should –'

'Should what?' Colette too was looking at him severely, daring him to complete the sentence. With the two of them facing him, he subsided with a meaningless, 'Well, you know...'

'There is an argument,' Georgia said delicately, 'that we owe it to Christians and – how do I put this? - potential Christians – to present the best possible face of Christianity that we can. The problem is that nobody agrees what the "best possible" face is – whether it's the most united, or the most welcoming, or the most consistent, or whatever.'

'Your point being?' Colette asked.

'Well, that so far as I'm concerned, all *I* can do about that is make sure that as many people as possible know that AngthMURC exists, and continue to work within it to promote that sort of loving tolerance that *I* think Christianity is all about. Because trying to explain student

198

politics to the newspapers is a waste of breath.' She continued, with a distinct change in tone, 'I just wish people would stop going on about how you wouldn't expect anybody who wasn't studying Maths to join Mathsoc. I mean, have these people ever been to a Freshers' Squash? Nobody except Fellowship cares what you believe or what you study, so long as you're happy to pay them a fiver and stick your email address on a list.'

'I'm still a member of Cathsoc,' Colette said.

'So is the rest of AngthMURC,' Georgia said. 'And the whole of Cathsoc joined AngthMURC – including Jay-the-atheist.'

'Which is proof in itself that it is entirely appropriate for someone who is not technically a Christian to join a Christian society,' Colette concluded triumphantly.

'Ellie Ford would say that Roman Catholics aren't technically Christian,' Peter put in, amused.

Colette said, 'And then there's whatshisface? That Fresher – Billy, that's the one I mean – who is not Anglican, Methodist or United Reformed, but just doesn't agree with organised religion.'

'Nobody could call AngthMURC organised,' Lydia said with a grin. 'I admit he probably wouldn't fit in at Fellowship, though.'

'They're not overly impressed by AngthMURC, either,' Colette said.

'I'm not surprised,' Peter said. 'Coming over here, stealing their women... ow! Georgia!'

'He's got a point,' Colette said, giggling. 'This is all my fault. Nothing like this ever happened before I led Lydia astray.'

Peter raised his eyes to heaven. 'See? So far as the Christian Fellowship is concerned, AngthMURC could be sacrificing virgins on the High Altar of the cathedral, and they wouldn't bat an eyelid; but start seducing their hall officers into loving, committed, monogamous relationships, and all hell breaks loose.'

'I'm not sure that the seducing happened on the AngthMURC side,' Lydia said. 'Not that it's really... *anyway*.'

'I don't care about facts,' Peter protested. 'I'm simply telling it the way that Fellowship will.'

'It's not about us, though, is it?' Colette said.

Lydia nodded. 'I really hope not. This is Tim Benton's fight. Why do *you* care, anyway, Peter? You're well out of all this.'

'I know,' he said, ruefully.

'Don't you believe it,' Georgia said. 'He's following it more obsessively than any genuine student.'

Peter looked guilty. 'The perils of Facebook...'

'Perhaps I should come up to Cambridge and disable your wi-fi,' Colette suggested.

Georgia looked ostentatiously at her watch and said, 'Come on. Colette, you said the table was booked for seven. Coats!'

The four of them traipsed out onto the landing. 'Becky!' Georgia bellowed. 'Will! Stuart!'

Stuart stuck his head out of his room and peered up at them through the banisters. 'Becky's talking to Adam,' he hissed. 'It's not going well, judging by all the shouting.'

'Oh. Well, are you ready to go out, at least?'

He nodded. 'As I'll ever be. I've pretty much resigned myself to this essay being a disaster.'

'Will you shut the fuck up and listen to me for *just one second*?' Becky was clearly audible through the closed door.

'Shit,' Georgia said. 'I see what you mean.'

'They've been going on like that for the past quarter of an hour,' Stuart told her. 'I'm surprised you lot didn't hear.'

Becky yelled, 'No, it's just a tiny bit more complicated than that – *Will you listen to me?* – not that it's any of your business anyway – yes, thank you for that. Yes, of course it is – Look, Colette is my best friend *and I do not dispute for one moment* that Will has acted like a complete dick – What? No, it's not perfectly simple... well, you try living in this house... Well, yes, because Will is my friend. No, I know you don't like

200

him – to be quite frank, that's your problem, not mine... What?... No, you fucking well do not get to tell me who I do and don't call my friends...

'Well, if that's the way you feel, perhaps we'd better not...

'No, I won't stay with you this weekend, then... No, you needn't ask Sam. I will... Yes, I'd much rather spend my time with someone who actually respects my decisions...

'Bye.'

A metallic crash, as if Becky had relieved her feelings by throwing something violently into her waste paper bin. Then a scrabbling noise, as if she were retrieving it.

'Shit,' Georgia said again.

Up on the top flight of stairs, Will cleared his throat.

'Is everything, like, OK?' he asked.

Chapter 6

And so news comes of another skirmish in the war that rages on campuses across the country, where our children's souls are attacked on every side. This is an old battleground: we are in Stancester once more, where the enemy, in the form of aggressive secularism, has already claimed one victory and is greedy for more. We hear that homosexual Christians – now there's a contradiction in terms – are offended by the content of a course that seeks to lead Christians into relationships that mirror the pattern that God has provided. So they should be.

Christians, campus and censorship, Richard Trefusis, Faith Now, 19 November

Rose emailed her the link during their American Lit lecture. Lydia read it under the cover of the desk, and ran all the way back from campus. Hurt, angry, scared, she pelted up the stairs and burst into Colette's room without knocking. 'This is it.'

Colette jumped.

Lydia collapsed against the doorframe, half-panting, half-sobbing. 'I have to do it, now,' she said.

Colette said, 'Hang on a minute,' and put a ruler in the textbook to keep the page. 'What's up?'

'This.' Lydia thrust her phone at her, shut the door, and sank down on the floor with her back against it. 'This one will get to my parents, even if nothing else has. Alex will be sending Dad the link right now.'

'Let me have a look. What does it say?' Colette was infuriatingly reasonable. Lydia wondered why she was bothering to approach this with an open mind. Everything that she had shown her had been exactly as horrible as she'd said, if not worse.

'Blah blah... *earlier this year instructed the Christian Fellowship to change its name to the Evangelical Christian Fellowship*... blah blah... *blackmail*... oh, God, I see what you mean. *Our aim is simply to teach students about godly relationships, said Ellie Ford, Christian Fellowship representative. Sadly, there are so-called Christian groups on campus which promote sex outside marriage and homosexual relationships...* Is that libel?'

Lydia mustered a half-hearted grin. 'Dunno: ask Will.'

Colette kept reading. '*Even worse, Christian students, at the very beginning of their journey of faith, are hearing this and believing it...* blah blah... *It's not a minor disagreement between denominations. This is fundamentally about Christian truth and the suppression of facts that the secular world would rather not hear...* I'd pay quite a lot to shut her up, I have to admit... blah blah...'

'My parents will be putting two and two together now. There's no way they won't see this.' She imagined her father squinting granite-eyed at the computer screen. 'I've got to tell them.'

'Ellie Ford doesn't know about you. Us. That's a shot in the dark.'

'How do you know?' Lydia looked up at her, wanting desperately to believe her.

Colette hardly looked convinced herself. 'Ah. Right. Wouldn't she have confronted you? I mean, Will did.'

'Not her style,' Lydia said. 'She's sneaky.'

'Fine, but to go straight to these clowns? You'd have heard about it elsewhere. It would have trickled down through the layers and you'd have been chucked out of your hall officer position by now.'

Lydia had to admit that this made sense.

'And,' Colette continued, more confidently, 'it says *beginning of their journey of faith*. She's obviously got someone in mind, but it's not you.'

It seemed all too likely. Relief flooded through her, then remorse for the relief. 'Oh. You're right. I wonder who it is? The poor scrap; they don't deserve this.'

'Deserve what?' Becky said through the door. 'Can I come in?'

Colette looked inquiringly at Lydia, who shuffled across the carpet to make room for the door to open. 'Of course you can,' she said.

The handle turned very cautiously. Becky sidled in. 'Sorry, girls; I didn't mean to disturb you if you were being private.' She must have got straight off the bike and into the shower; she was wrapped in her dressing gown. Drops of water coalesced at the tips of her curls.

'Oh, don't worry,' Lydia said bitterly. 'We were talking about the necessity of going public. How were the Young Friends?'

Becky grinned. 'Indecisive, as usual. Did you know that even Quakers can have too many committees? And I had another row with Adam.'

Colette looked at her sharply. 'What about? Are you two still...?'

'Ostensibly it was about the venue for the next meeting, but it was really about... something else. And yes, we are. Still. Apart.'

'That sucks,' Colette said.

Becky flicked it off. 'It's OK. Anyway, what do you mean, going public?'

'I'm coming out to my parents, before they read Ellie's latest and start having ideas of their own.'

'Wow,' Becky said. 'That's brave. Are you sure you want to?'

She was already wavering. 'I don't want to, but it's got to be done.'

Becky looked at Colette, who shook her head. 'If Lydia needs to do it, Lydia needs to do it.'

Lydia got up, grabbing at the footboard of the bed for support. 'Come on, then. Will you two be my backup?'

'You're going to do it now?' Colette asked, impressed. 'Now as in right this minute?'

Lydia smiled, without humour. 'Why not? There's never going to be a good time, is there?' She marched downstairs. The other two followed three yards behind like mismatched bridesmaids.

Georgia put her head out from her bedroom door as they passed. 'Off on a jolly?' she asked.

'I wouldn't exactly call this a jolly,' Colette told her. Lydia snatched the telephone receiver from its rest. Stuart, coming out of the kitchen with a bucket-like mug of tea, found the landing blocked by the four of them, Lydia next the window, and the others clustered a yard back from her. While she was dialling, jabbing each key with determined accuracy, Colette explained to Georgia and Stuart what was going on.

'Oh,' Stuart said, when he had grasped the vital points. 'Does she really want all of us here?'

Lydia nodded vigorously. 'Yes, please,' she said through her teeth. 'Keep me honest...'

Then, as someone picked up at the other end, 'Hello?'

'Lydia! Darling!'

That was good. She had hoped it would be her mother. Or, rather, she had feared it might be her father.

'Oh, hi Mum. Hi. It's me...'

'How are you?'

Her heart was hammering. 'I'm very well, thank you. How's everyone there?'

'Oh, you know, sweetie, same as ever! You've just missed your father; he's gone off on retreat with the Men's Group. And Rachel's fine. And so am I. And you probably haven't heard, but Abby's pregnant!'

Lydia swallowed. Fond as she was of her cousin, she was not quite in the mood to react as she might have wished. 'Oh, wow, that's fantastic news! I must give her a call, then...'

'Oh, yes, you must... Well, this is lovely. You don't call much these days. Was there something special?'

The other four arranged themselves into a rough semi-circle behind her. She did not look at any of them, gazing, instead, straight out through the window. 'Yes, well, no, I actually did have a reason for calling...'

Tinny laughter. 'Oh, yes, I thought you might. Of course we're all doing the same as usual...'

'What?... oh, *Christmas* – no, that wasn't it, but that's fine. Christmas at home and then do the rounds afterwards? But Mum, what I really wanted to say was about all the stuff that's going on here in Stancester, and...'

Her mother's voice became grim. 'Ah, yes. We've heard about that.'

Lydia looked at Colette, raising her eyebrows and half-sighing. 'Yes, I thought you would. That's why I'm phoning...'

'We've all been praying, of course. The Enemy is at work.'

She gritted her teeth. 'The thing is that everybody who's really upset about this is a Christian; that's why it's so awful...'

'I'd heard it was the atheists. Political correctness gone mad.'

She thought of Olly, happily out of the mess, and laughed. 'Oh, there are atheists involved, but that's not where it started... The thing is, Mum, it's the teaching notes for next term. It's by Sheep Door... I don't know if you've ever heard of them.'

Considerably less disapproving: 'They're very sound. We've just ordered a whole set of *In the Spirit!* for the youth group.'

Lydia's shoulders hunched. 'Oh. Oh, I see. Did Alex think they were, you know, suitable, for the teenagers? They're quite detailed...'

'Yes, he's very keen on them. He says they're very thorough.'

'Oh.' But she supposed she had expected as much.

'What's the matter? Don't you like them?'

The words formed in her mind: *No, I don't. I'm a lesbian.* She could not spit them out. 'I just think it's going to be difficult teaching out of them, that's all. The thing is...'

'You'll be fine, darling. Remember, you're not doing this in your own strength.' Only her mother could turn reassurance into disapproval.

Desperately, she squeaked, 'Mum, there's one more thing I need to tell you...'

A sharp intake of breath. Lydia just had time to think, *Oh, thank God. She's guessed.* 'Lydia! *You're* not pregnant, are you?'

It threw her completely. 'What?... No, no, of course not! I don't even have a boyfriend... I've never had a boyfriend, you know that! In fact...'

But her mother was babbling, 'Well, that's all right, then! Oh, sorry, sweetheart: there's someone at the door. Love you!'

She sighed. 'OK, Mum. Love you, too. Give my love to Dad and Rae...'

'Will do! Bye!'

'Speak to you soon...' Lydia dropped the receiver and turned to face the others. 'You don't need to tell me: I'm pathetic. I had at least three chances there and I didn't take any of them.'

Becky was the first to step towards her. 'It's all right,' she said as she held out her arms. 'It's all right. Today wasn't the right time, that's all.'

But Lydia, ready to weep for shame, looked at the four loving, concerned faces, and knew that any of them would have done it without thinking, and one of them had.

Chapter 7

The Chaplaincy team provides pastoral support to students of all religions and none. Please contact the Chaplaincy Assistant (chaplaincy@stan.ac.uk) to arrange an appointment.

In an emergency, the duty Chaplain (usually Rev. Tanya Darcy, but other members of the Chaplaincy team cover this when she is absent) can be contacted on the mobile phone number below.

www.stan.ac.uk/chaplaincy

'Well, this house, obviously,' Colette said. 'What about Olly?'

Lydia shook her head. 'I don't think so. I never really got to know him.'

Colette smiled. 'Probably best. He'll be at daggers drawn with Will all evening, and Georgia will be so tense if he's there.'

Having spent her twentieth birthday tied up in Students' Union bureaucracy, Lydia was determined not to let her twenty-first go the same way. She was dreading Christmas, and she vowed that there would be something to look forward to even if she had to organise every last detail herself – which, when it came to it, she had not. Georgia had got herself joyfully involved, booking a bar, negotiating a generous discount on the drinks, and advising on the theme.

'I need a theme?' Lydia had asked, feeling, as she often did around Georgia, a long way out of her depth.

'Purple and gold,' Georgia had told her airily. 'It's only what you'd go for yourself. I'm making it official, that's all. And don't worry: I won't let it look tacky.'

It was with some difficulty that Lydia had retained control of the guest list. Now it felt rather sparse. 'Rose,' she said. 'Mel. My group from last year.'

Colette grimaced. 'Really? I mean, Zoe's OK, but the rest of them...'

'They're my friends,' Lydia protested. 'I know you don't like them, but I think they should be there.'

'It's not that I don't *like* them,' Colette said dubiously. 'It's just that I don't think your party's going to be much fun if they're there.'

A sudden, sharp hankering for the simpler times of first year. 'But they are fun! Mel's great, you just haven't got to know her properly.'

Colette threw the pen down. 'You're being wilfully ignorant now.'

That was the sin against the Holy Spirit in Colette's eyes, and Lydia suddenly realised that this was serious. 'Please. Tell me what you mean.'

'You know what I mean.'

'Do I?' She had an idea, now, but Colette's impatience was irritating her, and she was determined that she would say it explicitly.

'Lydia.' An exaggeratedly forbearing sigh. 'Have you actually thought how this is going to work?'

Two could play at that game. 'How what's going to work?'

Colette cracked. She bent her head; her hair fell forward into her face as she muttered, 'I mean, am I going to be there as your girlfriend, or am I going to be there as your housemate?'

'Oh...' This was exactly what Lydia had expected; yet suddenly she could not answer. She pictured herself dancing with Colette, kissing her, low lights, soft music, long swishing skirts. It was an enticing scene. She thought of the guests around them, and tried to fit faces on the anonymous bodies: Rose – Will – Jake – Mel – Simon – Fiona. She could not make them stick. The masks twisted in disgust and slid to the floor.

'In my head,' she said at last, 'I've come out by then. And so anybody who's there knows, and doesn't care. But how I'm going to get from here to there I have no idea.'

'Really? Perhaps you're planning a literal coming-out party? Débutantes? Long gloves and tiaras? The Queen, or just *a* queen? I can suggest a few from among the ranks of the LG-so-called-BT society. I'd be quite grateful, to be honest.' Colette became bitterly sarcastic. 'My God, look, here's an actual bisexual, with a real live girlfriend who's not ashamed to admit to her existence. I thought they were a myth.'

Lydia tried to assign the pronoun appropriately; it kept her from thinking about the implication of the whole speech. 'I don't know, Colette. I tried, remember.'

'Not –' Colette bit her lip.

She knew how that sentence had to end. 'Go on. Say it.'

Colette sighed. 'Not hard enough.'

Lydia tried not to flinch. 'I didn't realise it bothered you so much.'

'Oh, it *bothers me*,' she mimicked. 'It bothers me a hell of a lot.'

'Why didn't you say so?' Lydia asked, knowing she would regret it.

Colette looked wounded. 'I didn't want to upset you.'

Lydia was angry now. 'You never do. So you never say a bloody thing, and then you act all offended when I do something that upsets *you* and I haven't any idea how I've done it. Or you just take matters into your own hands. Oh no, Lydia can't possibly have an opinion that deviates from conventional teaching, let's just take it for granted and make our own unilateral decisions, shall we?'

Colette's eyes narrowed. 'Yes, well, you're quite good at never saying a thing yourself, aren't you? You could have told the whole world by this time. You lied and lied and lied about who you are – even to me, and you knew I had to be sympathetic – and you're still lying to everyone you can get away with.'

There was a twisted sort of truth in it; and yet surely Colette must know why she kept silence. 'I don't think you quite appreciate,' Lydia said, hearing her own voice querulous and pedantic, 'how very difficult it is. And how even more difficult it's going to be. My mum would probably have told me not to bother coming home for Christmas.'

Colette said, with a smug, conscious recklessness that made Lydia want to slap her, 'You're exaggerating. It's not the fifties any more. Most people's parents come round within days.'

Lydia answered as if it had been meant seriously, as if she thought Colette really believed that. 'Most people's parents aren't evangelical Christians.'

'No. And yet you are.' A cool, detached observation. Lydia might have been a colourless liquid in a test tube.

She drew a long breath. 'Oh. So that's what this is about, is it?'

Colette was very precise, very controlled. 'It had to come up sooner or later, didn't it? I'd been hoping that you'd be able to integrate the two, somehow, but it clearly isn't possible. I suppose it was stupid of me to think it ever might be. You're never going to give it up, even though it's going to rip you to pieces. And I can't bear...'

She did not finish that sentence, and Lydia was treacherously glad of it. She could not start feeling sorry for Colette. 'And if it is going to rip me to pieces,' she said instead, 'whose fault is that? God knows it wasn't much fun last term, but I wasn't living like an illegal immigrant, always wondering who was going to catch on to me next. Why did you insist on getting Becky involved?'

'I asked. You agreed.' Colette shot that down with the minimum of effort. 'And that's exactly what I'm saying. You're making yourself live in constant fear, whereas if you'd just say it out loud once you'd never have to worry again.'

'You don't believe that,' Lydia flashed back. 'You know as well as I do that I'd have Fellowship on my back for ever. You didn't like what Will did? That's a pinprick compared to what's coming my way when I hand myself over. You, too. You'll get it. You'll get the well-meaning exposition of scripture. You'll get the guilt trips and the prayer groups camped on your doorstep. You'll get the inbox full of tracts. You'll get prayed against – denounced –'

'Don't start pretending this is for – oh, fuck it.' Gone was all pretence of not understanding, of not believing. 'How do you know this happens? Or do I not want to know? Why the hell do you still have anything to do with this bunch of psychos?'

Lydia said patiently, 'I can't give it up. It's the truth, and you know it is as well as I do. Just because the two of us come at it from opposite directions...'

Colette snatched at that. 'Yes, that's the trouble, isn't it? There's still a bit of you that thinks you're going to hell simply for being who you are. And she thinks I'm going there with you, and she resents me for booking the tickets.'

'That's come out of your own head,' Lydia protested. But it had indeed hit closer to the heart than she was prepared to admit.

'Prove it, then,' Colette challenged. 'Prove you've accepted who you are.'

'Please, Colette. You've got to give me time.' Pathetic, to beg; and she hated Colette for making her do it.

'How about until the end of January?' Colette's face was grim; there were dark shadows under her eyes. 'Look. It comes down to this. If I don't go to your party as your girlfriend, I don't go at all. With one exception.'

'Yes?' Lydia heard the idiotic hope in her own voice.

'I'll go as your housemate if that's all I am to you. If you don't want to be my girlfriend, that's fine. I'll let you think about it.'

The door clicked shut behind her.

Dawn broke and dulled to drizzle. Lydia stayed in bed until past eleven, until she could be sure that Colette would have left the house; she lay there watching the narrow line of light creep across the ceiling, listening to the rain spitting listlessly against the window. She heard Colette's footsteps creep down the stairs; voices in the kitchen; the crash of the front door. Nothing for a little while, then Will's heavier tread; the gush of the shower, and a full-throated baritone mingled with the running water.

Will tramped back upstairs, and the house fell silent again.

If only it were possible to stay in bed all day. Lydia sighed, threw off the duvet, and found her dressing gown. A tepid shower and a damp towel, and the tiles chilly underfoot. Not feeling much refreshed, she trudged to the kitchen.

'Hello,' said Colette.

She was uncharacteristically neat, her hair combed flat against her head and tied back severely, her shirt buttoned to the neck. She looked Lydia in the eye, impassive as an effigy. On the table in front of her lay the remains of a pizza delivery menu, torn into tiny squares.

Lydia forced herself to return Colette's gaze. 'I thought you'd gone shopping with Becky,' she said.

'She said I had to apologise to you,' Colette said.

What, Lydia wanted to say, for letting her interfere in my life? Colette must have seen the irony, for she amended her statement. 'At least, she said not to worry, she'll meet up with Georgia for lunch instead, and I should do whatever I needed to do. It's me who thinks I should apologise.'

'Oh,' Lydia said.

'So. I'm sorry.'

Lydia sat down and said nothing.

'I shouldn't be pressuring you; it doesn't help either of us. Of course you should do exactly what you need to in your own time.' She tore one of the scraps of paper in half, and half again. 'I thought it would be enough just to know you loved me. I thought I would be able to make it be enough. I'm angry with lots of people, mostly myself. Not you at all. At least, not very much. I'm sorry you got the lot.'

'I see,' Lydia said to buy herself time. She ought to accept the apology. She ought also to welcome the opportunity to extricate herself from the whole intolerable situation. She could do neither. She could not ignore her own doubts; nor could she write off the whole of the last year and go back to who she was before. Unwilling to say anything that might commit her to either path, she sat there and dragged fragments of the shredded pizza menu across the table with the tip of her finger. Colette watched her, having, apparently, nothing more to say.

The phone sliced the silence. Lydia laughed from sheer relief.

'Georgia,' Colette said, 'wanting to know if we have enough bog roll.' She winked sardonically and was suddenly herself again.

Lydia felt a twinge of hope. Even if this is the end, she thought, we can carry on. She said, 'We're nearly out of milk.'

And she knew it was not the end. They ran for it. Colette got there first, twisting as she snatched up the receiver, and coming to rest with her back against the windowsill. Lydia, laughing, was close behind her, close enough to hear the voice through the receiver.

'Hello?' Colette said, smiling shakily at Lydia.

A strained gulp gasped down the line, and then, 'Hello? Colette.'

'Georgia?' Of course it was Georgia; but she sounded distant, muzzy.

'Colette, it's Georgia. I –'

She was crying. Lydia had never known Georgia cry.

Colette said, sharply, 'Georgia, are you OK? What's happened? Where are you?'

'I'm OK – I'm at the hospital – There's been an accident – a car – Becky –'

'No.' Suddenly, in that expelled breath, Lydia knew. They both knew. She watched Colette's face turn to a mask of horror, and felt her own mind separate itself into two layers: her rational brain trying to hear Georgia, and thinking what must be done, and, below that, a tidal wave of shock. Later. She would deal with that later.

'I don't think she knew who I was,' Georgia was saying. She was unfocussed, darting at random pieces of information and pecking them up. Not like Georgia, Lydia thought. Georgia was not coping. Colette was not coping. Somebody had to cope.

'It's Becky,' Colette said. She could only repeat Georgia's words. 'An accident. Becky. Will ought to know. Get Will.'

Lydia squeezed her hand and pit-patted back upstairs to tap gently at the door of his room.

Yes. Will ought to know. He was red-faced, simmering with quiet anger. 'Lyds. Have you seen this? Can you believe it?'

She could not help peering at his screen. The union logo blazed bright red. She did not know how to say it. 'Will, it doesn't matter now. Becky – Georgia's on the phone, Becky's been hit by a car.'

Will's voice changed. 'Oh. My God. But she's all right. Isn't she?'

Downstairs, Colette was asking intelligent questions.'Do her parents know? Oh God, what about Adam?'

Lydia tried to picture Georgia white-faced and red-eyed. She did not want to think about what Becky might look like. She tiptoed back downstairs; took Colette's hand and held it to her heart. Will had followed her meekly.

Colette said into the phone. 'I suppose there's – no point in us coming up there?'

They all heard the breathed, reluctant, 'No.'

'What are you going to do?'

She would have a plan, Lydia thought. Georgia always had a plan.

Colette said, 'There's nothing else we can do for her?' And then, hating the answer, 'Come home.'

Will had, silently, started to cry. His massive shoulders shook slightly; apart from that, he was motionless. Lydia put her free hand into Will's, drew him closer in. She felt a sudden wave of exasperated affection for him. At any other time that would have surprised her.

'Come home,' Colette said again, and laid the phone down.

'We should tell Stuart,' Lydia said quietly. 'And Olly. And Peter.'

Colette nodded. 'And the Quakers. I – oh, sod it. I'm going to phone…' She swallowed, hard, and took her mobile phone out of her pocket. She phoned Stuart. She got hold of Peter at his church office. She left a message on Olly's answerphone. *Ring back.* She called Tanya. All the while Lydia held her hand, and Will's, and they stood there together on the landing until at last there was no one left to phone and Colette broke down in tears. Stuart came home. Tanya turned up and made cups of strong, sweet tea. Georgia arrived, silent and ravaged-looking. They sat together in the kitchen and said nothing, all afternoon.

Later, it occurred to Lydia to wonder what had so annoyed Will, in those last few seconds before he knew. In their two years together as Christians at Stancester she had seen him irritated, she had seen him dissatisfied; she had been the unwilling subject of his attempts to force the world into the shape he thought it should be; but she could not remember seeing him so angry, and she was curious.

Or perhaps she was not really curious. Perhaps she just needed something – anything – to think about that was not Becky. And because the night was dark, and there was an empty place at the table, and because she had just put Colette to bed with a hot whisky and lemon, and she did not want to start thinking about things on her own, and she supposed *he* could do with his mind taking off it, she knocked gently on Will's door.

He opened it at once. 'Lydia.'

'Can I come in?'

He gestured vaguely behind him. 'Of course.' But he did not move, and she had to take his arm and turn him around, lead him into his own room, sit him down on the side of the bed. He submitted unquestioningly.

'You look like I feel,' she said.

'I don't think I feel anything at all,' he said, puzzled. His eyes were pink with weeping, but the strangest thing was his complete passivity, so unlike him that it was almost frightening.

She said, 'What was it you were reading earlier? That you were so cross about?'

It could very easily have been the wrong thing to say. For a moment she thought it was. But he said, 'It doesn't seem very important now.'

'You were really furious.' At that moment it seemed vital to remind him.

'I was,' he agreed. 'I was. It's the bloody Union again.' He said it without feeling, as if he were reading from a script.

'What's happened?' she prompted. She needed other news to exist. The world had shrunk to the size of their house, and Becky's absence was vast and unbearable.

'Oh, they've suspended our funding. They've done it. They've fucking done it.'

'*What*? Fellowship's funding, you mean?' Which was a stupid question. Of course it was going to be Fellowship.

'Our funding and our Union privileges. Use of rooms. With immediate effect, until after the audit is finished.'

Will sounded as if he really did not care. Lydia wished she could feel relieved about that. 'They can't do that, though, surely? Not without warning?'

'They did warn us,' Will said, dully. 'Anyway, does it really matter?'

'Maybe it doesn't,' Lydia said. 'Not tonight, anyway.'

'No.'

She squeezed his hand.

He looked blank, broken. 'Pray, Lydia. Please. I can't.'

Oh, God, she remembered how that felt. 'Of course I will,' she said. 'Of course.'

Chapter 8

Following a family funeral in her home town of Lancaster, a memorial meeting for **Becky Seymour** will be held at Stancester Friends Meeting House on Thursday. All who knew Becky in any capacity are warmly invited to attend. Donations to Amnesty International.

STANdard, 6 December

Lydia had never been to the Quaker Meeting House before. It was a pleasant, airy building, a converted warehouse just on the cathedral side of the river, with tall windows that stretched even the stunted light of December into a semblance of radiance and warmth. It spilled like water across the wooden floor, extended long fingers over the circles of chairs, washed the table at the centre and fell on the scarlet leaves of the poinsettia, illuminating, too, the maroon covers of the Bible and *Quaker Faith and Practice* that lay there, until all three danced bright blood-red.

They had arrived early, but the room was already strewn with mourners. More crept in. Becky's family sat in a tight clump towards the middle of the room. Lydia started looking for students, and lost count after thirty-seven. Older people were, she supposed, lecturers, or family friends, or Quakers. There was barely an empty seat left when two o'clock slid past and the murmur of preparation changed, almost without warning, to the silence of remembrance.

Lydia was becoming more comfortable with silence, but this one was overwhelming. So many people sharing it, such inexpressible emotion at the core of it. Saying nothing because there was nothing that could say it. There was grief in there, there was fury, there was a desperate, exhausted, awful sort of peace. It was easier when people began testifying (no, she corrected herself: *ministering*), each word spoken chipping away at the vast slab of meaninglessness. There was nothing that could make sense of this, nothing to bridge the gap

219

between cold facts (*Renault Clio, Bridge Street, Saturday*) and colder platitude (*everything happens for a reason, it's all in God's plan*); but they spoke, her friends, her family, of Becky living, and pulled her story back from the nonsense of her death.

A woman in her seventies, wearing a long black coat. (Will murmured, 'That's Shirley, from the soup kitchen.')

Shirley was saying, 'Becky had a fantastic memory for names. You never had to introduce anyone to her twice. And she always remembered what was going on in your life.'

A girl of their own age, with a strong Northern accent. A school friend, Lydia supposed. 'Principle. If she disagreed with you, you knew about it. Probably in no uncertain terms, either. But she never let that get in the way of being your friend.'

Rob, from Campus Quakers. 'She never wasted anything. I don't just mean things like recycling. If she was angry, if she was scared, if she was bored, whatever, she would *do something* with that. Write a letter, write a poem, find something that needed doing...'

Lydia had not expected to have anything to say, but words came bubbling up inside her. She rose. 'The first time I met Becky,' she said, 'she asked me to join the Western Road traffic crossing protest. Since that time, I've never known her not to be involved in some campaign or other, up to her elbows in whichever battle needs fighting at the moment. She was incredibly generous with her time and energy, and she would throw herself into anything, if she thought that her doing that would help...' She hesitated. 'Even for those of us who... She would take up a fight on behalf of people who were too tired, or too scared, to do it themselves. And sometimes you resented that and felt it showed you up, and sometimes you were just grateful that somebody else *cared*.' She finished in a rush, and sat down. Colette, weeping quietly, took her hand.

A middle-aged man stood up in her place. 'Becky was an attender of this Meeting for more than two years,' he said. 'I too recognise that quality of hers that has just been spoken about, that intense devotion to justice, to love, to equality – that empathy and solidarity, and the passion that she brought to everything in which she was involved...'

Lydia let her gaze wander around the room. On and on the service rolled – testimonies, stories, edged by cold bergs of silence at whose heart lay the grief and anger that could not be expressed. She marvelled at the facets of Becky's personality that were emerging.

Georgia was almost the last person to speak. 'I was there at the end,' she said. 'I saw it. I saw the accident. I wasn't going to say anything about that. It seemed so important to me that we get away from the tragedy, but, listening to you all, I want you to know this:

'*She laughed.*

'She wasn't conscious for very long after the accident. She only opened her eyes once that I saw, and she was looking straight at me. Through me. I don't think she knew I was there, but *she laughed*. It was a surprised sort of laugh, as if she'd suddenly seen a joke she'd heard years ago. As if she'd seen the funny side of everything,' She choked a sob. 'It sounds ridiculous. But that was so very Becky.'

Lydia could not sleep that night. She sat up with *The Allegory of Love* and, just as she became aware that her eyes had passed over the same page three times and absorbed nothing, she heard a muffled sob break out from Colette's room and sneak onto the landing.

She put down her book and got out of bed; stood, barefoot, outside the door for a moment before murmuring, 'Colette? Sweetheart, can I come in?'

There was a sort of indistinct grunt. Lydia took it for consent. With infinite care, she tiptoed into the bedroom and closed the door behind her. 'Don't cry alone,' she whispered, and knelt down beside the bed, and kissed Colette's forehead and cheeks, and managed an awkward half-hug.

'I feel,' Colette mumbled, 'as if it should have been me. Completely illogical position, of course. Why blame God for what can perfectly easily be attributed to human stupidity and recklessness?'

Lydia clambered into bed beside Colette. 'I think maybe we all feel like that,' she said. 'I do, sometimes. Or that it would have been easier for everyone if it had been me.'

Colette shuddered. 'Don't. I couldn't –'

Had she been going to say, *choose between you?* 'Nobody's asking you to.'

'No. Random chance. There's no reason it should be any of us rather than Becky. No reason it should have been Becky. No reason it was anyone at all. And I always thought it would be the bike...' She pressed her face into Lydia's shoulder and cried, silently, for a while before she slept.

After that, every dark night that was left in the term, Lydia lay in her own bed with the lights off, and listened. After the third time she stopped asking for permission to enter, but simply slipped through the door and into Colette's bed, to take her in her arms and hold her until the tears ceased to flow.

Lydia loved it. It was not merely gratitude for the power to comfort the one she loved; it was not merely companionship in grief; she loved it too on the animal, sensual level, feeling Colette's body lying along the length of her own, sharing their warmth, closer than they ever could be in daylight.

'Lydia,' Colette murmured, one night.

'I'm here.'

'Oh, I know that.' There was the ghost of a chuckle in her voice. Lydia clutched at that like a child chasing a piece of thistledown fluff.

'Good.' She stroked Colette's hair.

'I love you.'

Lydia paused. There was a *but* coming; she could hear it breathing in the wings, waiting for its cue. 'I love *you*,' she said.

She felt Colette nod. 'I know. This – this is going to sound awful.'

'Go on.'

'I am finding this very difficult.'

'Which particular *this*?'

Colette became very still. 'This particular this,' she said, almost in a whisper. 'You. Me. In bed. Now.'

'You know,' Lydia said, trying to be helpful and understanding, 'you can ask me to leave whenever you want, if you'd rather I weren't here.'

'My love, if it were up to me, you'd never leave.' Her eyes gleamed in the darkness; she caught Lydia's lower lip in an angry kiss.

'So...?'

'So even though I know you are in my bed because you are trying to cheer me up because my best friend is dead, I mostly want – oh God – well, what everyone will assume you're in my bed for.'

Lydia felt the blood dancing in her fingertips, and wondered what she could possibly reply that would not be either untrue or misleading. But Colette was speaking, quietly and swiftly, her eyes tight shut. 'Every night you're here I want you to do more than hold me. I want to lie like this without pyjamas between us. I want your hands everywhere you don't put them at the moment. I want you to kiss me and not stop. I want everything.

'And I want *you* to do it. I want you to lead the way, because I always know that I am ready to go further than you are, because I always fear that doing anything more with you than I've already done will be going Too Far. I know you feel we're sailing close to the wind as it is, and I know that I'll always want more, and it is so hard to lie here and not do it.'

Lydia tried to control her quickened breathing. 'Oh, Colette, do you think I'm made of stone?' she groaned.

'This would all be much easier if *I* was,' Colette said. 'Honestly, I know what you feel about sex before marriage, and I respect that, and God knows I would never, *never* want you to do anything you didn't want to, but I feel like I need a sword down the middle of the bed or something.'

Lydia thought about it. 'The trouble is,' she said, 'that part of me is very much up for the programme you just described, but the rest of me is fretting – as you say – about sex before marriage, and it doesn't help that I've not yet come up with a working definition either for sex or for marriage, insomuch as either applies to us.'

'Which is why we're both erring wildly on the side of caution,' Colette said, though she sounded more optimistic. 'But what is marriage, anyway? We live together; we love each other; we intend it to last. What's missing?'

'God's blessing,' Lydia said at once, 'and nobody knows about us. Oh, I know there are secret marriages, but – I don't know. I need people to know, and on my terms, not by gossip. And you know what happened last time we talked about this...'

'Peter says the ministers of a marriage are the couple themselves. The priest's only there to give the blessing and be a legal witness.'

Lydia was incredulous. '*Peter?* Mr oh-no-I-can't-say-these-four-lines-I'm-not-ordained?'

Colette laughed. 'The very same.'

'Hm,' Lydia said, unconvinced. 'I don't want to be like those American teenagers who go almost all the way and then claim they're still virgins. I mean, by that definition you and I could be having a fully sexual relationship and it wouldn't mean a thing. I do want it to mean something. I don't want to devalue what we will have by getting away with it now.'

'I like that "will have",' Colette said. She sighed. 'And yet the way things stand at the moment, we're never going to get to the point where that's a possibility, because no Church will let us get married

224

even if we do manage to decide what the sex would be that we were going to have after it.'

'Would you want to?' Lydia asked, without entirely meaning to.

'What, get married? Yes, I think so. I mean, if I'd fallen off the other side of the fence I would probably end up getting married eventually, and if it was something that was important to you... yes, I would. But it's never going to happen, is it? There's civil weddings, now, but – It annoys me so much that if I were marrying a man I'd get a choice, and if I were marrying you, I wouldn't. And you'd want to do it in church...?'

'Yes,' Lydia said.

'So we have three choices: either we say 'sod it' and have sex now, or we find some sort of unofficial blessing ceremony or something, and manage it in the next five years, maybe, or we wait for the Church – yours or mine – to get its act together and decide that we exist. Which will be never.'

'Never's longer than I want to wait,' Lydia acknowledged. 'And I can't help remembering that there are people at my church who would think I am already bound for hell just for being in bed with you and having kissed you.'

Colette shifted onto her back. 'Do you think about it yourself? When I'm not asking you, I mean?'

Lydia felt the blood leap to her face. 'Which part of "I'm not made of stone" didn't you understand?' she asked, as lightly as she could manage.

The low, sleepy, chuckle did not help matters. 'No – though it's a relief to know you're not a saint... I meant, do you take much time out of your day to think about the logistics of all this relationship stuff, and wonder how it's all going to pan out?'

Lydia turned up the corner of the pillow and got an inch of purchase for her elbow on the edge of the bed. She propped her chin on her hand. 'Only recently,' she said. 'I never used to think about it at all. It was filed away in the "God will sort it out" box, along with, you know, Finding a Man.'

'God probably will sort it out,' Colette said. 'Or possibly already has, and we just haven't noticed. I find that happens a lot.'

'Could be,' Lydia said. 'Could be.' She dropped a kiss on Colette's forehead. 'Of course, if I had found a Man I wouldn't have had to worry about this whole marriage issue in the first place. Why does God never sort things out the simple way?'

'I can hear you smiling,' Colette said severely. 'Anyway, it might not have been simple. The man might have been married already, or Muslim, or something. And I'll tell you this for free: you'd still be angsting about what exactly constitutes sex. It's what good Christians do.'

Lydia felt vaguely hurt. 'Are you not a good Christian?'

Colette was wiggling a hand between her waist and the mattress. 'Debateable. I'm just not angsting, because, whatever sex is, I've already had it. Unless there absolutely positively has to be a man involved, of course....'

Lydia's elbow gave way and she flopped onto Colette. 'I'd love you to demonstrate,' she said into her shoulder. 'Just... not yet.'

'I know,' Colette said. 'I know.' She lapsed into silence, and wrapped her arms around Lydia, and they lay there, motionless, in the darkness.

'OK,' Lydia said at last. 'Here's one thing I can promise you. I won't wait until my church will marry us. I don't know about anything else, but I have a horrible feeling you're right about that.'

And she kissed the soft skin of Colette's neck and wondered how she could bear to wait at all.

Christmas

From: peternathan@yourmail.co.uk

To: w.h.f.seton@stan.ac.uk

21 December, 19:58

Hi Will,

Good to hear from you. I'm sorry we didn't talk much at the funeral. Yes, it was a bit out of my comfort zone, too, but I am glad I went – it has helped me make a bit more sense out of who Becky was and what made her tick. I don't think any of us will get over this completely. It will change us all.

Sorry to hear the other guys are being so shitty about it. As you say, they didn't know Becky, and it's a horrible way to behave about anyone's death, no matter what you might think of what they did in their life. Tell them to remind themselves what Jesus said about the Tower of Siloam.

What is the feeling at Fellowship around the funding suspension? I think it's going a little far, myself. I don't think the SU should have imposed it without warning and without giving Fellowship a chance to make any changes. It assumes bad faith. No doubt everyone is fuming. It's certainly all got a bit handbaggy on Facebook and the forums!

'Happy Christmas' feels a bit off, under the circumstances, but I hope yours is as good as it can be.

Peter

Nobody wanted to be the last one left in the house. Will's mother arrived early on the last day of term and swept him away; Stuart's parents were next. Georgia walked down to the station alone, travelling very light.

Lydia had dissuaded her parents from coming to collect her, and had bought a return ticket home. Now she and Colette sat in the living-room, carrier bags full of Christmas presents stacked around them, and waited for Dr Russell to arrive, trying not to notice how quiet the house was.

'You could come home with me?' Colette suggested, not for the first time.

Lydia bit her lip. 'I would love to. You know I would. And you know I can't, not until I've – done this.'

Colette reached to take her hand. 'I could point out that coming home with me would effectively achieve that.'

'But you won't, because you know I've got to do it properly. Get behind me, Satan. Besides, you told me to do it in the first place.'

'Well, you can at least come to lunch with me and Mum, and have a lift to the station. I just wish you could – skip the next part.'

'It's probably going to be horrible,' Lydia agreed, 'but – well. You know. You were right. I've got to do it, if I'm ever going to look myself in the face again... And I'd rather they find out the truth from me, than some twisted horror from somebody else. And I just think, what would Becky have done, if it were her?'

She did not want to ruin Christmas. And then on Boxing Day they were visiting Nan and Granddad, and then Uncle Ron on the 27th, and then Abby and Paul came to visit on the 28th; and then on the 29th there were no more excuses.

She thought about telling Rachel first, separately, but decided against it. Rae was not reliable at the moment. Lydia was under no illusion that her parents would receive the news with unalloyed delight, but – no, it was better to do the lot together, and get it over with.

Her mother was out at church half the day, setting up for the children's Christmas party. Lydia went shopping with her father, which occupied the afternoon. Striding up and down the fluorescent-lit supermarket aisles, she tried to quell the rising tide of apprehension. Eight months of lying to her parents was quite enough. Eight months. Seven years.

She said nothing through dinner; she cleared the plates and made the coffee, and waited until nobody had a cup in their hand before saying, 'I have something to tell you three.'

'What's that, darling?' her mother asked.

Lydia took a breath. Was there any other way to do this than the cliff-top plunge into the raging, icy, ocean? If there was, she couldn't think of it. She watched their expressions change from curiosity to concern; was tempted to say, *it doesn't matter.*

It did matter.

'I'm a lesbian,' she said.

Her mother screamed.

Her sister laughed.

Her father did nothing at all.

She breathed out. Breathed in. Said, 'I have a girlfriend.'

'And about time,' said Rachel.

Lydia sat down, very deliberately, and sipped her own coffee. Her mother had stopped screaming. That was a good thing, she supposed. She looked at her sister, who was watching their parents narrowly.

'It'll be OK,' their mother said, hoarse. 'It'll be OK. I'll talk to Alex. He'll know of someone who can help. There are places in America, special camps, they're very good, I'm told. I'm sure we could manage it.'

Lydia was suddenly furious. She had not thought of this, and she should have done. 'I'm not going to America, Mum. We can't afford it.'

Flailing hands. 'We could, for something as serious as this –'

'I'm not going to America,' she repeated. 'I think maybe you don't understand. I'm still a Christian. My girlfriend is a Christian. I know –'

Her father rose from his chair like an atomic bomb. 'Liar,' he said, and struck her in the face.

She gasped. Almost overwhelmed by the roaring pain in her cheek, and stung as much by the insult as by the blow, it took all her willpower to say, calmly, 'I'm not lying. I don't lie, any more. This is who I am. This is who God wants me to be.'

'Meanwhile,' Rachel said, conversationally, 'Lydia may still be a Christian, but I'm not.' She lolled insolently back in her chair.

Their father growled, 'You're what?'

Lydia's ears were singing, but she had heard, and she knew that the worst had not passed. She moved to stand between Rachel and her father. 'Take it back, please,' she said to him, pleasantly.

He was looking at his hand as if it belonged to somebody else.

'Oh, girls, girls – what did we do wrong?' their mother wailed.

'Hitting Lydia was a bad move, for a start,' Rachel told her. 'And you lot are surprised I'm an atheist?'

'I'm sorry,' their father said. 'But you can't – you just can't be a Christian and be homosexual. It's not possible.'

'It is who I am,' Lydia said, as gently as she could manage, though her face was throbbing. 'I've come to understand that God doesn't want me to pretend to be something I'm not – Mum?'

'It's not too late! It doesn't have to be like this, darling,' she burst out. 'I know this isn't really you! It's this woman, whoever she is, she's brainwashed you, she's made you believe you're a lesbian! Of course you're not! I know you best, you're my child, I know you could never really –'

'That is not true,' Lydia said.

'But it must be!' her mother exclaimed, desperately. 'Oh, if I could only get hold of her, I'd show her!'

'One more word...' Lydia hissed, knowing that she had no ground to stand on, and a universe to move.

Her mother was hysterical. 'Oh, darling, you can't even see it! This isn't my Lydia speaking, it's this wicked, perverted woman who's tricked you, dragged you off the way. Who is she?'

'You don't deserve to know her name,' Lydia said, furious.

Their father sat down again. There was a flinty calm in his voice when he spoke. 'Perhaps you had better not go back to Stancester. The Enemy is clearly at work there. Bible-believing Christians are persecuted for proclaiming the word of God. You are taught to disrespect Scripture. You've fallen into bad company. Your insolent attitude is leading your sister astray. No, I don't think it is God's will that you return to Stancester.'

For the first time that evening, Lydia was truly frightened. She did not doubt that they would keep her here if they could. Rachel's eyes were wide and horrified.

I cannot stay here, Lydia thought. But she hesitated. 'Oh, Jesus,' she breathed. Then, *'Becky...'* She hugged the names close to her heart; of all her friends, those two were the only ones who, being nowhere and everywhere, could be here, now, in the middle of this wreck of her life. What would Jesus do? What would Becky say?

Jesus would, she supposed, turn the other cheek. Jesus would take whatever came to Him. But He would not deny who He was. Becky would say... she could almost hear it in her voice: *Get the fuck out of there, now. There's a time to fight and there's a time to run. This is definitely the time to run.*

Lydia looked at each of them in turn. Her father, majestic, unyielding, one massive hand laid on either thigh. Her mother, huddled in her chair, whimpering in denial. Her sister, sitting up straight now, naked fear in her face, the urge to be flippant long fled. Lydia looked, and knew that the time had come to leave.

'Rae,' she said. 'We're going. Come on.'

Rachel darted a terrified look at their parents, and got up and followed Lydia. They hurried back into the kitchen and out into the hall. Lydia snatched her handbag from the newel post as she passed. Rachel pulled a pair of coats from the hooks and slammed the front door behind them.

Outside, a sea-mist choked the street. Lydia moved with a swift, angry stride, faster than was wise in the fog, with only a nebulous plan in her mind. *Away. Train. Ticket? Yes.*

Rachel pattered alongside her. 'Are you *leaving* leaving?' she asked.

'You heard them, Rae. I'm leaving while I still can.'

'Then at least put your coat on.' Rachel thrust it at her; her face was streaked with tears. 'They didn't mean it!'

'You know they did. And you're coming with me.'

'I'm not. It's going to be all right, really. Really. I'll come with you as far as... wherever, but I'm going back.'

Lydia bit her lip. 'Are you going to be safe there?'

'I have been, so far. And where are *you* going to go? I'm not leaving you until you've got somewhere safe to spend the night.' Rachel's little pixie-face was stubborn.

'Stancester. No. There won't be a train out of London. I'll phone Colette,' Lydia said. 'She'll know what to do.'

They rounded the corner of the street. 'Oh, is it Colette?' Rachel was smiling, suddenly. 'I'm glad. I liked her a lot.'

Lydia scrabbled in her bag for her phone. She was beginning to think that perhaps it would be all right.

Peter phoned Lydia perhaps ten minutes after Colette rang off, with a clear list of instructions and the assurance that of course his parents would be delighted to welcome a complete stranger, and possibly the complete stranger's little sister, at ten o'clock at night.

They sat in the station foyer and watched the lights coming and going through the fog.

'You're sure you won't come?' Lydia said. 'I'm going to worry so much if you stay here.'

Rachel kicked her gently. 'Lydia. Shut up. You realise that Dad thinks it's for your own good that he's keeping you at home? You don't have to start on me.'

'Touché.' Lydia chuckled, though it was not particularly funny. 'And I'm putting Peter's family out enough as it is.'

'You can go on to Stancester in the morning,' Rachel said bleakly.

'Come and stay,' Lydia said. 'Any time you want. As long as you want.'

'Thanks.' Rachel's smile was too bright to be true. 'I'll be OK.'

'If you're not, let me know.' Horrible visions, plausible and implausible, raged through her mind. 'I don't think they'll kick you out. They might take your phone. They can't keep you off school, though... You've got email there, haven't you?' She put a hand to her cheek. 'You've got friends you can stay with, right, if Dad ever tries anything like that on you...?'

'Yes. But it's fine. It's Mum and Dad, and they won't kick me out, because they're not actually as crazy as you think they are. Oh – they are crazy, but they won't be dangerously crazy towards me. No terrifying American camps.'

Lydia summoned a memory of a smile. 'How do you work that one out?'

'Well, they've let us go, for a start,' Rachel pointed out. 'And I've been arguing with Dad about every three days and he hasn't hit me yet. But my point is, they're used to dealing with atheists. They have no idea what to do with you, so they're more likely to ship you off to someone who does. They'll just keep on preaching at me. You've got more to lose than I have.'

'Rae – how can you say that? Your exams – you could lose your whole future!'

'I could, but I won't. Trust me! Now –' suddenly businesslike – 'is there anything you've left at home that you're wishing you hadn't?'

'Pyjamas. Toothbrush. I'm going to turn up like a bloody refugee...'

'You are, sort of,' Rachel said, unhelpfully. 'But, you know, if Peter's family are as nice as Peter, you'll be fine... Is he single?'

'Rae! He's far too old for you!'

'Joking!' Rachel grinned at her, unrepentant.

Lydia fanned herself. 'Don't do that to me.'

'Made you laugh, though. Seriously – anything I need to send on to you?'

'I could do with my essay notes on *Ruth* – they're on my desk, I think. Don't worry about the book itself. I can easily pick up another copy.'

'No problem.' A half-hearted chime heralded a bored announcement that the next train to depart from platform three would be the 2050 to London Charing Cross. 'You'd better go through to the platform, look.'

'Yes...' She pulled her sister to her in a swift, tight hug. 'Thank you for being such a sweetheart. I'll text you when I get there. And for God's sake let me know if you get any trouble.'

'Don't stress, Lyd,' Rachel said. 'Look after yourself, OK?'

Lydia ruffled her sister's hair in an attempt to reclaim seniority, then passed through the ticket gates, trying not to notice how light her only bag felt, leaving home for ever.

It was not so far to Tonbridge. An hour on the train, the same journey that she had made on joyous summer mornings, the landscape spread out in possibilities and the minutes trickling past honey-slow, with Colette waiting for her. Now that she was fleeing the darkness rushed past, and there was nothing to see but her own face, smudged and yellow, reflected in the window. This hour, dwarfed by the mass of years and decades queueing up behind it, rendered meaningless by the lack of a landscape to give it reference, was at once an instant and forever. She alighted from the train with shaky legs. The station was deserted except for Peter's mother.

'Lydia? I thought so,' brushing aside her halting thanks and apologies, 'no, it's a pleasure to have you. Now, I'm parked massively illegally, so...'

Molly Nathan was tactfully, mercifully, talkative, keeping up a stream of innocuous chatter to which Lydia had only to reply, 'Yes,' 'No,' and 'Oh?' all the way to the house.

'You'll have eaten?' she asked as she reversed tidily up the drive. 'Yes, Peter thought you would have done. Would you like a cup of tea? Coffee? Hot chocolate? You don't have to talk to anyone if you don't feel up to conversation. No, of course that's fine! God knows I wouldn't. Let me put you in here...'

Lydia drifted around the living room, too nervous to take a seat. She looked at the bookshelves, the ornaments, the photographs. Two in particular caught her eye: one, black-and-white, a dashing-looking minister with Brylcreemed hair, dressed in priestly robes and standing in a church doorway. Next to it, a colour photo, much more recent: a head-and-shoulders portrait of a black woman with a dog collar and a shy smile.

Molly came in with the coffee and laughed when she saw her looking. 'That's my father-in-law on the left, and my sister on the right.'

'Wow,' Lydia said. 'I can see why Peter doesn't have a chance.'

His mother grinned. 'Yes, it does seem to run in the family. Not necessarily harmoniously. I swear, Richard – Peter's granddad – always used to get a little bit twitchy when he saw Dorrie's photo up there next his own, all vicared up like that. He's got used to the idea now; there's a woman curate in the parish he retired to, but, my goodness, there were a few fraught years there!'

Lydia nodded.

'It's interesting,' Molly mused, apparently accidentally, 'how it's actually quite possible to respect someone as a good and wise Christian

235

who has a lot to teach other Christians, while also acknowledging that on some subjects they're just dead *wrong* – and aren't realising how their wrongness is hurting people...' She coughed. 'Would you like to use the phone?'

Lydia slept, in borrowed pyjamas, in Peter's bed, long and deep, waking only once from a confused dream to wonder, terrified, what was wrong with her face, and where the dinosaurs had come from. Concluding that this too must be a dream, she slept again, and only worked out in the morning that Peter had not changed his wallpaper since about the age of eight. There were, she supposed, worse ways to wake up.

Molly came in with a cup of tea and a tube of arnica gel, and fussed over her in a general sort of manner for some little while before coming to the point. 'I was thinking,' she said, 'about your sister.'

Lydia sat up in bed and sipped the tea. 'Rachel? Why?'

'Peter mentioned her – I think he half thought you might bring her with you.'

She frowned. It made her cheek hurt. 'I would have liked to – you've been so kind, of course, I couldn't ask – I am worried – but she wouldn't do it. She didn't want me to go. She understood why I did, but she wouldn't go herself.'

Molly looked at her, her expression serious. 'You know I'm a teacher, and so's Peter's dad?'

'Yes.' She must have looked mystified.

'Between the two of us we made a list, last night, of all the secondary schools and colleges in Hastings. There isn't a single one where one or the other of us didn't know someone who we thought would be useful. More than one, in most cases. And if you wanted one of us to have a quiet word...'

'She won't want to do anything formal,' Lydia said anxiously.

'It wouldn't have to be. Just so there's someone keeping an eye on her – and who she knows she can go to if, God forbid, anything escalates. Look – here's our list.'

Lydia looked down the columns of clear, round, teacher handwriting, scanning for her old school, and pointed to a name. 'Yes,' she said. 'Mr Norris. He'd do nicely.' She was ready to cry with gratitude. 'Thank you so much. I couldn't think of anyone who wasn't churchy, and I couldn't even begin to explain...'

'Hey, hey. It's no trouble at all.' Molly passed a box of tissues. 'Now. Do you still want to go on to Stancester today? I can run you down to the station whenever you like.'

'Thank you. Yes, please, I would. I just want to get back, now...' It was the only place in the world that might feel like home.

She left Molly on the concourse and crossed the footbridge at Tonbridge station. Loneliness washed over her. All across the South East, she thought, as she paced the platform, she had left her allies behind her, waving her off on the other side of the ticket barriers. Ahead of her, an empty house.

'The rest of my life begins here,' she said, out loud, and wished she hadn't. She pushed the thought away and boarded the train.

It was busy, crowded with gaggles of teenage girls off to the sales; families with overexcited children (the Natural History Museum and then a pantomime?); older couples (a musical, perhaps, the tickets a present from the grown-up children who had long since run out of other ideas)... Nobody else on their own, not that she could see. She managed to get a window seat, and squashed herself up close to the pillar to hide the bruise on her cheek. If she kept her eyes on the view outside the window, it would look like hardly more than a shadow; and anyway, no one was particularly interested in her.

Through the town, over the Medway, under the North Downs, towards London, she thought about the rest of her life.

She had never thought to leave home so suddenly. (She had, she supposed, avoided thinking what would come after the revelation. Revelations came at the end, but now she was living in a new earth, if not a new heaven, and was annoyed with herself for not planning for it.) It was as if she had skipped six months without warning. When she got back to Stancester, her housemates would still be students, but she would be an adult.

(Except Becky. Oh, God. Becky.)

She would never move back home. Not home. Her parents'. Lurking at the back of her mind she found a sense that she ought to feel more ambivalence towards the idea, but it would not materialise, and she had no desire to summon it.

That was all very well, but there were practical matters to consider. Money, for a start. Thank God, her rent was paid for next term, and the next instalment of her student loan would come in shortly. All the same, she needed a job as soon as possible. Bar work, perhaps, or something administrative, part-time, that she could fit around lectures. Then she would need to change her address with – everything. Bank account. Driving license. Credit card. The university, the doctor, her mobile phone.

More immediately, she would need to buy some food. There would be nothing fit to eat at Alma Road. Despite her resolve, she shuddered at the thought of a week in an empty house. It would be cold; it was always cold, and it would be worse with nobody else there. Frowning slightly, she tried to remember which clothes she had brought home – back to Sussex – with her, and what she had left in Stancester.

'Cheer up, love,' said the man next to her. 'It may never happen.'

She turned to face him, and felt a wicked satisfaction as his smirk flowed away like melting butter on sight of her bruised cheek. 'It did,' she said. 'It won't happen again, though.'

She was left in peace until they reached London. Nor did anyone speak to her on the Tube. Here at least her lack of luggage was an advantage. Her sense of isolation intensified as she drifted along the travelator at Waterloo. All that stainless steel, she thought, abstracted. Very science fiction. Strange new world.

At Paddington she found that she had just missed a train. Not that it made any difference, really. She left the station to find a cheaper source of coffee, and then gave ten pounds to a homeless man, in an act that was something between charity and a loan to the universe, the hope that some day, if she came to the same pass, she might get it back. And then, perhaps in the same spirit of investment, perhaps simply because she was lonely now, she bought them both a coffee, and sat down with him on the edge of his doorstep.

'Cheers, love,' he said, and she did not mind *his* 'love' half so much. He nodded at the station. 'Where are you off to, then?'

'Back to uni. Stancester.' She slipped the lid from her paper cup and blew at the coffee to cool it.

'Ah – lovely town, that. Used to have an auntie there.'

'It is,' she agreed. 'Did you see your auntie often?'

He wrapped his fingers luxuriously around the hot cup. 'Once or twice a year, maybe. She died, though – 99, was it? It might have been 2000.' He could not have been more than 15 back then, but even wondering felt intrusive.

'I'm sorry.'

'Thanks. So,' he said, 'where's home really?'

She hesitated. 'I grew up in Hastings,' she said, which was as close to the truth, and an answer, as she could manage.

'That's another nice place. Like the seaside, do you?'

'I'll miss it,' she agreed.

'So – Stancester's the future, then?' He was as tactful as she was trying to be.

'Probably. This is my last year, but I think I want to stay there after I graduate.' It all depended on Colette. It had to, now.

He was drinking his coffee slowly, making it last, she thought. She had almost finished hers. He noticed. 'Don't miss your train,' he said.

She checked her watch. 'I've got a quarter of an hour,' she said.

'You'll need ten minutes of that to get back to the bloody platforms, in my experience.' He paused. 'If you don't mind my asking – who hit you?'

Somewhat to her surprise, she didn't mind. (He must have seen worse, after all.) 'My dad.' She drained the coffee and crushed the cup in her hand.

'Ah.' He looked on the verge of giving her some good advice, but evidently thought better of it. 'In which case, all the very best.'

'Thank you very much,' she said, as she got to her feet. 'And to you too. I hope things look up for you.'

'Thank you. Happy New Year for tomorrow!'

'Happy New Year!' She had almost forgotten.

The Stancester train was less crowded, although the profusion of 'reserved seat' labels made it equally challenging to find a seat. Lydia eventually slid into a corner at a table, where she was joined by a woman who kept looking at her face, pretending she hadn't seen, and then looking back at her. Lydia tired of this swiftly and, having nothing to read (how had she come away without even a book?), pretended to go to sleep.

Feigned sleep became real. She woke with a jolt at Reading, and then dozed intermittently. The train sped westwards then, crossing into Somerset, abruptly slowed and became a stopper. Lydia sat up straight in her seat, and let herself look out of the window. So what if the nosy cow did see her face?

It was becoming a clear, sun-watered afternoon, the blue sky dissolving into pearl-white, the landscape enriched by the pale winter light. The red-brown of the ploughed earth, the washed-out beige of the stubble, the bright green tractor crawling along the far edge of the

240

field like a determined beetle – it all felt very alien, so very far from the chalk and the grey sheep-trimmed grass of her south coast. 'Home,' she said, silently.

She felt better as the train drew into Stancester Main. Lydia stepped boldly off the train. No year had ever ended or begun like this. The flat sound of footsteps on concrete, the scrabbling in her handbag for her ticket, this much was familiar; far less so was the awareness that this was a new life as well as a new year.

She came down from the philosophical to the practical. She needed food. Now was not the moment to do a full-scale supermarket raid, but she stopped at the off-licence on the corner of Station Road to buy milk, bread, a frozen pizza and a packet of watery sliced ham. That meant walking the long way round rather than cutting through the back of the station, but it seemed appropriate that the walk should be a significant one. All the same, she thought wryly, she could have done without the corner of the pizza box splitting the carrier bag, leaving her to trot up the road clasping the whole lot to her chest in an awkward bundle. She tried not to think of it as an omen for her newly-begun independent life.

Had she ever gone to number twenty-seven and found it empty? Certainly not before she lived there. All of last term, had she never been the first one back? She could not think of a single occasion – and knew that she was only trying so hard because she did not want to think of it empty now. (Her big blue Aran jumper, she remembered, the only one that kept her really warm, was in Hastings. Bugger. And it would cost a fortune to heat the house properly with only her in it, and Georgia would look disappointed, and she was going to have to economise more anyway. How much would it cost to post? More than Rae could afford. Well: she could find something in a charity shop tomorrow, and it wasn't as if it really mattered what she looked like, with no one there to see her.)

She turned off Western Road onto Halton Gate Road, noticing how forlorn the streets looked now that she was in the student quarter. A lone jogger passed her as she reached the deceptive little dip half-way down the road. Even the one family of real people at the bottom of Sevastopol Terrace seemed to have gone away for Christmas; there was no sign of life there, not even the dog.

Alma Road, then. She was regretting going the long way now. The hill was gentler, but it went on further, and the ham packet was cutting into her finger and the bread would be squashed out of all recognition. Sighing, she extracted the milk bottle from the remains of the carrier bag and hooked the handle over the little finger of her left hand. Nearly there.

Twenty-seven came into view, its red door bold against the white frame. Something caught her eye – a little movement, behind the living-room curtains. Her heart raced. Visions of burglars – squatters – her family, come to take her back to Hastings – even, ridiculously, mice – rushed through her head. But the front door swung open, and Colette was racing down the path to take her in her arms, and at last Lydia wept.

'You came back,' Lydia said, when she was able. 'You came back for me.'

'Of course I did,' Colette said. She kept a very gentle hold of Lydia's hand as they bent to pick up the groceries. 'Good job you didn't have any eggs in here, eh?'

Lydia laughed, in a wobbly sort of way. 'Yes.' She could see Colette looking at her face. 'It's all right,' she said, in a ham-fisted show of bravado, '*I* don't break that easily.'

Colette caught her in a great clumsy hug, and they lost the pizza again. 'Oh, my darling, my darling,' Lydia could hear her saying. 'I knew I should have come down to get you last night...'

Lydia extricated herself and sat down on the low wall, until such time as her legs might support her. She held a hand out, and Colette joined her. 'This happened before I phoned you,' she said. 'Anyway, even if you started driving the minute you hung up, you couldn't have got to me before three in the morning – by which time I was safely tucked up in bed at Peter's parents' house.'

'I could have –' Colette stopped. 'There wasn't really anything I could do, was there?'

'Except what you did. And to be here, now...' She could not carry on. 'Hush. Hush.'

She felt Colette's arms wrapped around her, and relaxed in the sheer unbelievable gift of her presence. 'When did you get here?' she mumbled.

'Oh, about half past eight.' Colette sounded embarrassed. 'My family agreed to bring all the arrangements forward by three hours and leave at the crack of dawn, as compensation for not letting me drive to Sussex last night. They've all gone on to lunch with Uncle Laurie and Auntie Wendy in Plymouth.'

So they would pick her up again on the way back. Lydia tried to keep the disappointment out of her voice. 'Oh?'

'I shall be sorry not to see Laurie and Wendy, of course,' Colette mused, 'and also miss seeing in the New Year with my college friends – but if you think for one moment that I'm going to leave you here on your own after what must have been the most disastrous Christmas in human history... Also, someone's got to be here for the gasman.'

'Gasman?' Puzzled, Lydia craned her neck to see Colette's face.

'The boiler's gone. I've tried all the obvious solutions, and no joy. I'm afraid we're going to freeze tonight – I plan to steal everyone else's blankets, and wear socks to bed. And I'm either going to take you out to dinner, or buy something expensive and lazy from Marks and Spencer. We can eat it wearing three jumpers each, and talk about the epic that will be your birthday party.'

Lydia wondered idly how she would have managed the inactive boiler, found the prospect terrifying, and then decided that she was being pathetic. She turned her attention to Colette's implied question. 'I don't think I could face going out,' she said. 'Too many people.'

Colette nodded. 'Come on in, then. It is actually marginally warmer inside than out.'

That night, as they snuggled together in the nest that Colette had made out of their two mattresses and all their bedclothes, Lydia asked, softly, 'Would you even know how to get to Hastings?'

She could feel Colette's breath warm against the back of her neck.

'There is such a thing as sat-nav, you know,' Colette said, very gently sarcastic. 'Anyway, you just drive south until you hit the coast, then you turn left. Poole, Southampton, Portsmouth, Brighton, Eastbourne... oh, my love, what is it?'

For Lydia had not been able to suppress a start. At last she said, 'Eastbourne. The last time I was in Eastbourne – no, that's complete rubbish, I've been there hundreds of times – but the last time I was in Eastbourne and having to think about being homosexual and Christian – oh, God. It was the first time I was in love, and the first time I understood what that meant for me.'

'Tell me?' Colette asked.

Lydia swallowed a sob. 'Imogen. This girl from church. Three, maybe four, years older than me. I suppose I must have been in year nine. I thought she was amazing. She *was* amazing. She was going to go to Bible college and then she was going to be a missionary and she was the perfect Christian woman.'

Colette's silence was like the water in a well, still and unexpectant, and it was impossible to resist the temptation to drop another stone down and see if that one would make a splash. 'All that summer we'd been volunteering for the church holiday club, and every spare minute when I wasn't mopping up poster paint I'd been coming up with these far-fetched fantasies that would somehow have her feeling the same way about me that I did about her, and, God knows how, admitting

244

that to me, and somehow we'd find a way to be together. Of course I couldn't tell her that. I used to lie awake at night, terrified that I'd somehow managed to give myself away, and she would have to explain to me gently how lesbianism wasn't in God's plan. Can you imagine the humiliation?'

A sympathetic chuckle. 'And Eastbourne?'

'Eastbourne. I can't even remember why we were there, now, but it was the day after she'd gone off to college, and I just knew that she was never coming back, and that had to be the end of it. Mum and Dad went into town, took Rae with them, and let me wander off on my own. I went up the pier. I walked all the way up to the end, and I looked out over the sea. It was a horrible day – always looking like rain but never managing to actually do it – and the sea was like lead and the horizon was completely black. And I stood there, and I had a completely rational conversation with myself as to whether I actually wanted to jump off the pier and swim out until I couldn't swim any further.'

Colette stiffened, and Lydia cursed herself. The loss of Becky was too raw, the mark on her own cheek too fresh; she should have edited the story.

'I didn't,' she said. 'I was as miserable as I've been in my whole life. I was convinced that I was an abomination to God and to the human race. My heart was broken as only a fourteen year old's can be. But I didn't want to die. I was in love, after all, and love is worth living for. On some level I was enjoying every moment of the agony. I was enjoying being noble and renouncing my feelings. Showing her how much I cared by never telling her. That would have to mean something, wouldn't it? Except she could never know. I was praying every day to stop loving her, but I never managed to mean it.'

'And then?' Still cautious.

As casual as she could manage, 'There isn't much of an "and then". I haven't seen Imogen since – in person, I mean; there used to be regular

245

email updates at church. She did become a missionary, she got married and lives out in Africa permanently now. After about six months of moping I got over her, the way you do when it's a teenage crush. And then I met you.'

'You've skipped about five years there,' Colette murmured.

Lydia wriggled around to face her. 'My love life was not very interesting,' she said. 'There were maybe three other crushes. None of them was as serious as Imogen. Imogen was nothing compared to you.'

'Sweetheart,' Colette said, and kissed her forehead.

They lay close in the darkness for some while, until Colette said, 'You're not going back.'

'No,' Lydia agreed. 'I was thinking about it on the train. I will start all over again, from here.'

She was trying to sound braver than she felt; evidently without success, because Colette suddenly hugged her tight. 'Oh, my love,' she said, 'you're so alone.'

'I don't feel alone,' Lydia said, 'I've got you.'

This was somehow the wrong thing to say: Colette became rigid. Lydia was nearly sure that she was holding her breath. Hurt, she rolled to the right, so that Colette lay almost under her, and laid a hand upon her cheek, and kissed her with considerable deliberateness. *If you wanted to, now,* she was trying to say, *I would.*

But Colette evidently did not want to; her breathing was quick, but she flopped like a rag doll, accepting but not responding. And suddenly Lydia understood: too much, too soon. If she had grown a year in the space of a day, then Colette was suddenly a year behind her. She might have left her father and her mother, but she could not expect to become one flesh with someone who was not nearly ready to become her wife. There must be a way to close the distance, but this was not it.

She rolled onto her back, searched for Colette's hand, found it, raised it to her lips. 'Sorry,' she said. 'Not the time, was it?'

246

'I love you,' Colette said, so quietly that Lydia could hardly hear her, 'and I'm sorry, and I'm scared.'

'I love you,' Lydia said, 'and I am scared. And –' she picked her words like pearls for a string – 'I need you to know that none of this is your fault. And that if it is all too much I will understand. And that your having come down to meet me today is the most wonderful thing that anyone has ever done for me.'

Colette only squeezed her hand in reply, but it was enough to build a hope on.

Lent Term

Chapter 1

It is clear that God does not bless homosexual relationships; the Bible, biology and logic alike tell us that. The physical differences between men and women alone would be enough to show us that relationships between same-sex couples quite literally cannot be fruitful.

The course leader may encounter differing views on homosexuality, which should be resisted gently but firmly. There may be course participants who themselves struggle with homosexual desires. 'Love the sinner, hate the sin' should be your motto here. Encourage the student to seek pastoral help – you should be ready to recommend a sound minister or more mature layperson who will be able to give them advice and support in their struggle against their inclinations.

Treasure Store: God's will for human relationships (Course Leader's Handbook), Sheep Door Publishing 2005

Lydia was very happy to be back at St Mark's. That was what made it so awful.

She had hoped – believed? – that it would make no difference to her friends at St Mark's. Having fled one home and returned to another that was irrevocably changed, she needed this at least to stay the same.

She was torn. On the one hand, she was conscious of the need to release all her pain, her regret, her loss, into the safe containment of the love of her church family; on the other, the fear that, when they knew the reason for her leaving, this one also would cast her out. And she knew that there was still a blotchy purple shadow below her eye, and she could feel people looking at it.

She remembered how Colette had told her... *my ex-girlfriend... bisexual, actually...* How easy it had looked, that take-it-or-leave-it honesty (not, Lydia could admit, entirely innocent of the desire to shock), that stubborn insistence on her identity. *Queer Christians. We exist. Do you have a problem with that?* A challenge unspoken, and, even now, not fully answered. *We exist.* And the clear autumn breeze lifting the hem of the curtain, and Peter singing in the garden, and her soul standing on the threshold of its self-made prison, not yet ready to step out, but knowing for the first time that there was a world outside it.

She shook her head. That was a year ago and more, and she sat here alone, with bodies pressed around her. Not knowing who knew, who might have guessed. Knowing that every minute spent pretending, letting people believe that she was merely what they thought her, took her further from herself and further from God.

The suspicion in the air mingled with the dusty stuffiness rising from the radiators. She felt sick. She had to speak, and she could not. Colette had had it easy: a captive audience of one, bound to pay the respect owed to the host by the guest, and little to lose if the reaction was cold. Here, every body in the throng seemed hostile; every hand might have held a stone.

'Let's pray,' and a thick silence settled.

Must she do it now? She could ask one of the prayer team to spend five minutes with her afterwards. But prayer was not really the point of this. (That seemed heretical; but she was already being prayed for. Peter was probably lighting a candle for her this very minute; Georgia perhaps writing a cryptic note whose meaning God alone would understand, and pinning it to the board at the back of Wardle Street Methodist; Colette praying fiercely and silently with her eyes wide open.) This was about making people know, in a space where they could not immediately turn on her. They could pray for her, and she well knew what that prayer would be; but at least they would know. And so she stood.

'Brothers and sisters,' she said, 'I ask for your prayers for myself and for my family. This Christmas, I – it became clear that I could no longer live at home. Please pray for me. Pray for my parents, and for my little sister Rachel...' Her throat was closing up. 'There are things about me that they can't accept, and I can't change...'

She could not continue. She could not expose herself to public denunciation, but she sensed in the thickening atmosphere that she was understood. 'Pray for me,' she concluded feebly, and swayed a little on her feet before she remembered that she was meant to sit down now.

The rest of the service swirled past her. She followed it mechanically, standing when others stood, sitting when others sat, singing thinly words that had become meaningless, catching an eye here and there, reading in it revolted fascination or disappointed pity. At the end she sank back into her chair, screwed her eyes tight shut, and hoped that they would think that she was praying.

The moment she looked up Chris bustled up to her, his face pink above his dog-collar and lime green shirt. 'Lydia. It sounds as if you and I should have a chat some time soon.'

She stood. *A chat.* Had that euphemism ever been convincing? It could have been worse, she supposed; it could have been *a word.* Absurdly, she smiled at the thought, and managed to turn it into a meek, acquiescent smirk as she held out her hand to take his card.

'Give me a ring, OK? Any time this week will be fine. Monday is my day off, but with something as serious as this of course I'd be happy to see you...' Perhaps, she thought, she was being paranoid; perhaps he was simply concerned about her having left home. Wouldn't anyone be worried? But he continued, 'God can change things, Lydia. Remember that. God can turn lives around. We all struggle with the flesh, and you're very brave to have admitted it.'

She supposed she ought to be grateful.

'Chris, if you've got a moment...' Jill, the church secretary, had come to twitter about the projector or something. Lydia welcomed the escape, but not the curious stare that Jill directed at her. She stood, lost, in the middle of the aisle. Around her, they were talking about her. She could feel every sharp, distasteful glance like an arrow in the back; and she could hear fragments: 'Her dad beat her up...' And the reply, 'No! I can't believe that... Well, it must have been serious, then. I mean, my dad would *never*...' Mumbled dissent, too low to make out; then a proof text, swung like a sledgehammer, 'Honour your father and your mother...'

She was not going to cry. She promised herself that she was not going to cry. At least nobody else was speaking to her. She wanted to leave without having to talk to anyone. But Mel was bearing down on her with two brightly-coloured mugs. 'Here you go, Lyds. Coffee. I got the impression that you would rather not have to talk to everyone in the queue. You don't have to talk to me, either, if you don't want.'

Lydia smiled gratefully. 'You star. Thank you.' She took the cup, and drank deep.

Suddenly Rose was there. 'It's true, then? You're a homosexual?'

Lydia swung around. She tried to read Rose's face: disgust, hurt, simple anger? She could not tell, and so she only nodded, waiting with detached interest to see what would happen next.

'*Practising*?' Rose demanded.

That was an old joke. She resisted the temptation to reply *No, I'm an expert.* It would have been neither true nor helpful. 'I have a partner,' she said. She would not, she resolved, be drawn further.

'Rose,' Mel ventured, 'this really isn't the time and place.'

Rose ignored that. 'I thought you were my friend. You've been lying to me for the last two years.'

Lydia felt miserably weary. 'I'd been lying to myself all my life,' she said. 'I don't want to talk about this now. I've got it straight between myself and God. You don't need to worry.'

'*I don't need to worry?*' Rose hissed. 'I am not *worried.* I am *terrified.* Do you know what is going to happen to you, Lydia? Do you know where you're going to end up? You are going to suffer in hell for all eternity. I assume you abandoned your family because they told you that. They told you the truth and you ignored them. You are going to suffer for that.'

Provoked beyond endurance, Lydia snapped, 'Do you know how much there is in the Bible to support that view? Sod all. Meanwhile, I seem to remember somebody ignoring *Do not be yoked together with unbelievers...*'

Rose laughed derisively. 'You've got some nerve. There's one thing about *your* relationship that no amount of prayer is ever going to change, isn't there? There's no way *your* relationship can be part of God's plan for anybody. You're disgusting.'

Lydia gasped, as at a blow. She had expected her parents' displeasure. She had not wanted to expect it from her friends, and it hurt far worse.

But Mel was saying, in sweetly reasonable tones: 'Rose, just because you got a lot of crap from Jake and Ellie about going out with an atheist, there's no need to be a vindictive cow and take it all out on Lydia. And if you're going to call yourself her friend you ought to act like one. I think –' this to Lydia – 'we had better get out of here, because nobody is being at all sensible.' She led her to the edge of the church.

Lydia folded obediently into a chair. Somewhere, she could hear Mel saying, 'Adrian, could you be an angel and give me and Lydia a lift up to York Road? And not ask questions...?'

God bless Mel, Lydia thought. God bless Adrian. 'Thank you,' she muttered. 'I appreciate this.'

'Don't worry about it,' Mel said. 'But why didn't you tell us before? We could all have prayed for you.'

Lydia wanted to scream. She told herself that was unreasonable; it was only what she had asked of them herself. Instead, she followed Adrian mutely across the car park and prayed to get away from all of them.

Adrian dropped them at the end of Alma Road. Mel walked to the house with her, but would not come in. 'I'll pray,' she said. She looked desperately worried.

Lydia stumbled through the door. Colette was there in the hall. She held her arms out. Lydia fell, blindly, into them.

'It didn't go well, then?'

Lydia shook her head. Colette led her upstairs to the kitchen and gently removed her coat, then shovelled three spoons of sugar into her own tea and set it before her. 'Drink this.'

Lydia obeyed. 'It's horrible.'

'I know. That's the point. What happened?'

She sipped at the tea. 'It was awful. Rose... oh, God, it was awful. And Mel was trying so hard to be nice, but she doesn't get it at all...'

At the door, someone cleared his throat. Lydia looked up. Will.

'What?' Colette demanded.

He ignored her and spoke directly to Lydia. 'I can see this is not a good time,' he said, 'but you need to know as soon as possible. I tried to catch you last night, but you'd already gone to bed.'

Lydia blew her nose on a sheet of kitchen roll. 'What is it?'

'The Sheep Door course. I went round to Jake's on my way back here. He's decided that we're going ahead with the full thing as writ. Including the – you know. That bit.'

She knew. They both knew. 'Oh,' Lydia said. 'Oh, God.'

Will grimaced. 'I tried to get them to drop it. Not because – at least, I just don't know any more. But they're doing it for, like, the wrong reasons, aren't they? It's not about right teaching any more. It's about this petty little human power struggle. I'm sorry. You don't need to believe me, and it doesn't make any difference now, but I did try.'

'But it's going ahead,' Colette said, unable to forgive so easily.

'But it's going ahead,' Will agreed bleakly.

Lydia was sobbing outright, barely hearing either of them.

'I did try,' Will said again.

Colette said, slowly. 'They didn't know. Nobody knew until today. But you've known for months. And you didn't tell anybody. I'm impressed.'

Will rallied. 'Well, of course I didn't. It's very poor form to out anybody. Didn't you know?'

Lydia got up and blundered out of the kitchen and up the stairs to her room. She threw herself face-down on the bed, weeping furiously into the pillow. Colette raced after her. She sat down on the edge of the bed and laid a gentle hand on Lydia's shoulder.

Lydia choked, rolled onto her side, and sat up. 'I never realised,' she said wonderingly, 'how much it was going to *hurt*. It goes right into the heart. They don't want me. They were OK with the person they thought I was, so long as she stayed in her place. They don't want the person I really am. I always knew, in theory, that I was only there on sufferance, that as soon as anyone worked out who I really was I'd be out on my ear, but oh God, it hurts when you understand the reality. Nobody wants you.'

'God wants you,' Colette said. 'I want you.'

But Lydia shrank into her crossed arms, closed in upon herself, and wept.

'They're wrong,' Colette said flatly. 'They're well-meaning, they're devout, they truly believe that they're doing what God wants. But they are one hundred per cent wrong, because they have forgotten that God loves you exactly as you are *this very minute*. I know this,' she added, 'because I love you.'

'I don't know what to do,' Lydia said. 'There isn't a place for me. They don't want me at Fellowship, and they don't want me at St Mark's, but I have to go somewhere. And it would be just the same anywhere else. Even your lot: I know they cope with the idea of you, but it'll be different when you show up with a woman in tow. You don't realise until it all comes true.'

'*This* is true,' Colette said. 'There's more reality than you're seeing at the moment, that's all.'

But it was too big for Lydia, then, and she only cried.

After a while, she said, 'Maybe they're right. Maybe I should be teaching it. I honestly can't see any way out of this. It's going to be like this for the rest of our lives, isn't it? Why do you even stick with it? Why stay with me to get cursed when you could get together with some bloke?'

'Because I happen to have fallen in love with you,' Colette said shortly. She put her arms around her.

Lydia said, 'Well, yes, *now*, but are we going to last? Because between all my so-called friends lining up to tell me how ungodly I am, my family on the verge of dispossessing me, you wanting to be out, and my not seeing how I can bear to do all that again, the only possible outcomes I can see are my losing faith in God, or us losing faith in each other.'

'Oh, God,' Colette said, quietly.

'Can you?' Lydia persisted. 'Can you see any other way out?'

'I think,' Colette said, stroking her hair, 'that an awful lot of people are putting stumbling blocks in front of you. I, and a lot of other people who love you – not all of them in the same way that I do – are trying to take them away again. The trouble is that they're very tempting to believe in...'

'I'm the one with the stumbling block,' Lydia said. 'I stuck it down right in Rae's way.'

Colette blinked, then said, 'No. Are you the one telling her that God only loves certain people? Are you the one telling her that her own sister isn't loved and welcomed by God just the way she is? No. If she's examined the evidence – and your parents' and Church's behaviour is part of the evidence – and found that she can't see God in the way you're being treated, that's not your fault.'

'And now,' Lydia said, letting the last demon out of its cage, 'Fellowship will know.' She shivered.

'I don't understand,' Colette said, 'why you didn't resign from Fellowship months ago.'

Lydia drew a breath. 'Because, leaving aside the little matter of my being abhorrent to certain members, this is what I believe in. I want to bring the Good News to everybody, and sometimes the only way to get things done is to hold your nose and stick with the people who are in a position to do them. No group is perfect. Not in Church. Not in politics. Student or otherwise.'

Colette turned passionate eyes to her. 'But they're trampling you into the ground!'

She considered that. 'Yes. I don't know whether I can stay now. I want to. The reason that it hurts so much is that this is where I belong.'

'Not with me?' Colette looked worried.

'Oh, yes,' Lydia hastened to reassure her, 'but – look. Your God and my God are the same, but your people aren't my people. Yours are lovely – if a bit weird, and deeply suspicious of me – but we don't really understand each other.'

Colette nodded reluctantly. 'What are you going to do, then?'

'Pray, I suppose,' Lydia said, bleakly. She thought a moment and continued, 'It's not as if your lot are always right either. I mean, I know that at any given time half the Church of England thinks that the other half is going to Hell, but I've heard you rant about the Methodists too.'

'We'll probably end up back with you lot within ten years,' Colette grunted.

It was an oddly enticing prospect. 'You think? Anyway, my point is, you can't change something from the outside. You either keep working on the inside, or you give up on it completely. You won't believe how tempted I am to jump ship, but I'm not going to. Not until I've thought about it properly, and maybe not then. All I know,' Lydia said, 'is that I can't teach that course, because I don't believe it. I don't know what I'm going to do about that.'

Chapter 2

Hi Lydia – you busy on Sat? if not wd love to take you + Colette for lunch for your early bday. Let me know! meanwhile R + i have a plan for yr party... Abby xxx

Rachel had been in touch via email to confirm that her phone had indeed been confiscated, but that things were not as bad as Lydia might think, really. It did not have the reassuring effect that had probably been intended. Lydia cheered up considerably upon receiving the first communication from another family member.

Colette was less enthusiastic. 'Lunch. With your cousin. Your married, perfect, *Christian* cousin.' She sounded deeply suspicious.

Lydia laughed. 'You needn't be so scared! She's lovely.'

This did not convince Colette. 'Actually lovely? Because yesterday is fresh in my memory, and I can't help remembering that your parents threw you out on the street at Christmas, and if that's the way all your family carry on...'

Lydia said, with more conviction than she felt, 'It wasn't Christmas, it was the day before New Year's Eve, and anyway, I walked out. Don't worry, her side are definitely the least crazy branch. Besides, Abby is the sort of person you can tell anything.'

'Right. Do you think she knows?'

'I know she knows,' Lydia said, with studied carelessness. 'She knew your name. Which means either that she's on side and Rae knows that, or that Rae has cracked under torture and it's got around everyone. We'll find out soon enough. Anyway, don't worry. It'll be fine. You'll love her.'

Colette was noisily reluctant all week, but she went. Lydia saw that her footsteps were dragging as they approached Angelo's. Trying to see through Colette's eyes, she conceded the point. Abby was the perfect

Christian wife. Blonde (a paler blonde than Lydia), pretty (but not too pretty), very clean-looking, and lit with that internal glow that characterises the most irritating sort of saint (not that Abby would ever call herself that). A pink top, for God's sake. (Colette was wearing pink herself, but that was hardly the point.) A plain silver cross on a plain silver chain. Short, but unbitten, nails; wedding ring, engagement ring (boring diamond). And of course, she'd almost forgotten, Abby was five months pregnant.

And then she was so damn *nice*. She said, 'Hello Colette, it's lovely to meet you,' and enveloped Lydia in an enthusiastic hug.

'Good to meet you, too,' Colette said. 'Lydia's been telling me how lovely you are.' Thank God, she was going to behave.

'All true,' Lydia said, too cheerfully. 'You're my best cousin.'

Abby laughed. 'Just because I buy you lunch.'

'Well, that and the fact that you're the only one who's spoken to me since Christmas,' Lydia said, fumbling, trying to break the subject. 'Though I suppose it's only been three weeks, and I wouldn't hear from most of them in that time if things were normal – but it must have got around, surely?'

'It did,' Abby said. 'Look. I have something I want to say – I promise it's not horrible – but I didn't want to get into it before you'd even got your coats off. Can I suggest we order and then get into the serious stuff?'

Lydia would rather have got it over with, but she said, 'Sure.'

'Fine with me,' Colette said, though Lydia could see the tension in her hunched shoulders.

'Now,' Abby said, when the drinks had arrived and the waiter had departed, 'I wanted to tell you something.'

Here it came. 'Well, I'm assuming that since you asked me and Colette out to lunch together it's *not* that you disapprove of us and think we're a disgrace to the family...' Lydia was babbling.

Abby looked rather shocked. 'God, no. Quite the opposite.'

'Quite the opposite?'

'What I wanted to say,' Abby said, 'was that I know that our family is not at all helpful when it comes to relationships that happen in anything like the real world, and that I know that your parents are if anything less helpful than my parents and that – if you wanted me to – I would come out.'

Lydia choked on her prosecco. '*What?*'

Abby told Colette, in a stage whisper, 'I said it wasn't a helpful family.' Then, in more serious tones. 'I'm bi.'

Lydia could think of nothing to say. Colette, clearly amused, said, 'She looked less shocked when I told her I had a crush on her.'

Abby smiled, though it looked like an effort. 'I wasn't ever going to tell anyone. Not in the family, at least. It never occurred to me that I might not be the only one.'

'Same,' Lydia just managed to squeak. 'Does Paul know?'

'Of course – I wouldn't have married him if I couldn't tell him that.'

'People must do,' Lydia said. 'Oh, God, this must happen all the time.'

Abby nodded. 'I know four or five – happily married, most of us, still in love, still Christian, still trying to find a way to be truthful, always knowing how bloody *lucky* we are: that we could so easily have gone the other way, fallen for someone we couldn't take to church with us...'

'I'm not sure it *would* help,' Lydia said, in a rush. 'I appreciate the offer and everything, but...'

'Too much risk of my being held up as a shining example?' Abby said. 'If *she* can suck it up and get married, why can't you?'

Lydia laughed. 'Something like that. I don't want it to be in my hands, anyway. This is your decision.'

Abby said, 'It always has been.'

The waiter arrived with the food, and broke the tension with the usual palaver of pepper grinders and parmesan cheese. Meanwhile, a plan unwound itself in Lydia's mind. 'Tell me the truth,' she said to Abby. 'If you didn't know about me, would you come out? Ever?'

A spasm of dread flashed across Abby's face. 'Not unless something else changed,' she admitted. 'You're a braver woman than I am.'

Lydia found that she was very calm now. 'Like I say, I don't want your life to be down to me. Anyway, I don't think you can help me more than you already have. But...' She trailed her fork through her spaghetti.

Abby laid her cutlery down. 'What?'

'I am worried sick about Rachel.' It was a relief to admit it. 'I don't know if you heard this, too, but, when I came out as gay, she – well, yes, she came out as atheist. I am really not sure that she is safe at home. I was threatened with not being allowed back to Stancester – well, I'm an adult, and there's not much they can do to enforce it.'

'So I see,' Abby said, drily. 'But Rae?'

'She's got a year to go before she can leave home, and she can't come to me, not unless she's really desperate. Can you be a safe house for her?'

Abby reached across the table and squeezed her hand. 'Like you had to ask. And she's coming to your birthday party. We both are.'

Lydia said, 'All I need is someone on my side. Someone who comes from where I've come from, but who can wish me God speed where I'm going.'

'That,' Abby said, 'I can also do.'

Lydia said, 'Thank you.' Then, feeling it past time to change the subject, 'So – are you ready?'

Abby glanced down at her own belly. 'That depends what you mean by *ready*,' she said. 'If you mean, is the house full of disgusting hand-me-downs from every child in the entire Hawkins clan, then yes, I'm ready. If you mean, am I psychologically prepared to have my life

262

invaded by a tiny, screaming, helpless creature that I'm probably going to love more than anything else in the world, then no, I'm not remotely ready.'

'Oh,' Lydia said.

Abby grinned. 'It's perfectly normal. I've never been ready for anything. Baptism, for instance.'

'Yes, but *you* were baptised as a baby.' Lydia was rather pleased with that answer.

'Are you going to tell me you were ready when you were baptised?' Abby retorted. 'No, I thought not. Moreover, I wasn't ready for confirmation, marriage, or coming out.'

'Wow,' Colette said. 'I thought I was the only one who did things that way round.'

Abby shook her head. 'Nobody's ever ready, not for the really important things. That's where grace comes into it. You do it, and about six months later – if you're lucky – you find you're just about in the place where it would have been a good idea.' She cleared her throat. 'Another thing, Lydia. I know you've left home. I know money's tight. When we've finished I am going to take you shopping and buy you something absolutely fabulous to wear to your birthday party. Call it a trophy for quasi-suicidal bravery, if you like. You don't get to look at the price tags, and you don't get to argue about this.'

Lydia thought about arguing, but not for very long.

She got home to find the email she had been dreading. It was almost a relief.

Dear Lydia,

I have been told that you are (and have been for some time) in a relationship that is not in accordance with God's will as clearly revealed in the Bible. I am shocked and disturbed by this and cannot help feeling that there has been some mistake. *If there has been any misunderstanding please do not hesitate to let me know.*

If however you are engaged in a homosexual relationship it is clearly inappropriate for you to continue as hall group officer. I have asked Ellie Ford for advice on this and she recommends, given the recent negative publicity smears on Fellowship, that you make it clear that this is a resignation rather than an expulsion. I am sure that you would not want your behaviour to cause any further hindrance to God's work here at Stancester. Ellie thinks it best that this is done in public, and as soon as possible. Can you make next week's meeting? I've attached a suggested statement.

All the best – I will be praying for you, of course.

Jake Warner

President, Evangelical Christian Fellowship

She read it twice, the first time to gasp, the second to laugh. Then, 'Colette!' she called. And, when Colette appeared, 'They want a resignation.'

'Well, we knew they would,' Colette said.

'No, in person. At the meeting. *And* it's my birthday party. I wasn't going to go.'

'Ah,' said Colette, 'a shaming.'

Lydia laughed again. 'You think you're joking. He's sent some suggested words.'

Colette looked, and whistled. 'He can fuck right off. You should tell him that from me.'

Lydia thought about it, then smiled slowly and shook her head. 'He shall have his resignation.' She got up and shouted down the stairs. 'Georgia! Are you busy? I need to talk to you about my party...'

Chapter 3

Lydia Hawkins requests the pleasure of the company of

...

at her twenty-first birthday party

from 8.30pm, Friday 25th January

at Tiger Eye (112-115 Northgate Street, Stancester)

Dress code: formal

'Lydia. Can you zip me up?' Colette sidled in, holding her dress in place with one hand.

'Come here,' Lydia said, 'and stop wriggling. Let go.' She twitched the narrow straps into place, settled the shimmering organza over the lining, and fastened the zip. Then she kissed Colette's shoulder and turned her round. 'There. You're lovely.'

'You're not bad yourself,' Colette said.

Lydia looked at their reflections in the mirror: Colette tall and anxious in icy lavender; herself, regal in the severely cut, matte gold, dress that Abby had insisted on buying her, bare shoulders veiled with a sheer shawl. At her throat, Colette's gold wire cross hung from a white velvet ribbon, its purple bead glowing in the lamplight.

She tried a smile. 'So I'm doing this.'

'Apparently.'

They looked at each other for a long moment, then Lydia led Colette down the two flights of stairs to the front room.

Georgia was chattering anxiously and ironing somebody's shirt. It must belong, Lydia deduced, either to Peter, just arrived from Cambridge and yet to take his coat off, or Will, who was wearing a scowl and his dress trousers and not much else. Stuart was already dressed, kneeling backwards in an armchair and peering between the curtains into the street.

'We've got twenty minutes before the taxi comes,' Georgia said. 'Oh, good, you two are ready. So, Peter, to recap, this is what happens: all of us except Stuart go to the Fellowship meeting. Lydia does her thing. I've booked another couple of taxis to take us straight from the Freeman Building down to Tiger Eye. Stuart, when we're all out of the house, you head down to finish setting up. And make sure to lock the back door as well as the front. And remember the cake!'

'Don't stress, G,' Colette said. 'The party's the least of our worries.'

Peter moved to hug Lydia. 'Happy birthday,' he said. 'Congratulations, key of the door, and all that. You look fantastic.'

'Thank you,' she said, and hugged him back. 'Thank you for coming down for this.'

Colette was fidgeting with her bracelet, pushing her hair back, adjusting her shoulder straps. 'Ready to be eaten alive?' she murmured.

Peter hugged her, too. 'Yes,' he said. 'Georgia told me the plan. I have to say I've never been to a Fellowship meeting in a dinner jacket before, but there's a first time for everything.'

'First and last, I hope,' Colette said. 'We who are about to die...'

Peter laughed. 'But if we're the Christians, then who are... the Christians?'

Georgia snorted. 'Here you go, Will.'

'Thanks – you're an angel.' He took the shirt from her and put it straight on.

'Ooh, a real bow tie,' Georgia said. 'Classy.'

'I feel rather inadequate,' Peter said, bringing out of his suitcase his own, ready-tied, specimen.

Will's expression lightened momentarily. 'I'd say you ought to learn to tie one yourself, but I guess it's hardly worth it if you'll be entitled to a dog collar in a couple of years.'

'Presumably you don't have to wear a bow tie once you're ordained?' Colette asked.

'No,' Peter said. 'I get a dog collar and a black shirt. Much less hassle. But I'm not counting my chickens. Show me how you tie that thing?'

Will demonstrated. 'It's very easy, once you've got the hang of it. You just have to keep the ends straight in your mind.'

'There's no time for a masterclass, Will,' Georgia said. 'Peter has about six minutes in which to change.'

Lydia found that she was shivering.

An hour and a half of upbeat worship songs and 'Yes, Jesus!', and everyone was slightly hysterical by the time it got to the notices.

The president claimed the microphone. 'Firstly, I've got some very good news! The Students' Union has decided to reinstate our funding and everything else, so we're back in the Venue as from next week!'

Loud applause. Peter sniffed. 'I can't believe they caved,' he hissed to Georgia, who jabbed him in the ribs.

Jake waited for the din to die down, and then said, 'Now, I'd like to welcome Lydia Hawkins to give one more... personal notice. For those of you who don't know her, Lydia is a member of the Teaching and Study Committee and she's the officer for Richmond Hall.'

The Richmond group cheered. Heart pounding, Lydia glided forwards and did her best to smile as she took the microphone.

'Thank you very much, Jake,' Lydia said. Her voice was steadier than she had feared it might be.

She waited for a murmur to die down, and then said, 'This is difficult for me. I can't quite believe that I'm about to say this. But it's vital that I do.'

A stir of interest. Was that a look of concern on Jake's face? Emma Greer was seated in the middle of the front row; her notebook, which had lain conspicuously closed through worship and preaching, was now open, and she was scribbling furiously. Lydia tried not to notice. 'I have two things to tell you this evening. The first is that I'm resigning as a hall officer, and from the Evangelical Christian Fellowship's Teaching and Study Committee.'

Nobody seemed surprised.

'The second is *why*. Before that, though, I want to thank my group in public. You lot are the best. I've loved working with you. I am sure that you'll do really well with Kris, your new hall officer, and I will keep praying for you – as I hope you will for me.'

A murmur of approval; a pattering of applause from the Richmond row.

Lydia smiled slightly. 'Thank you. Let me, then, explain my reasons for resigning. As you are all aware, this has been a difficult time for Fellowship, and I'm anxious that it doesn't become any more so through any misunderstanding that is in my power to correct.'

She waited while Emma Greer turned over a page.

'I'm gay,' she said, and counted two breaths while the words hung in the air.

'I dare say that isn't news to many people. Anyway, I want to make that absolutely clear: whoever you heard it from, it isn't a malicious rumour, because in this case it happens to be true. I'm also a Christian. I'm still gay and I'm still Christian. I'm Christian and I'm gay. I want *everybody* to know that both these things are true, simultaneously, right now, and the universe isn't collapsing in on itself. It is possible.'

Embarrassed laughter. Also, she fancied, the beginnings of a boo, hurriedly shushed. No matter. She had said the important thing.

'As hall officer,' Lydia continued, 'I am expected to teach my group, and, quite rightly, to use the themes and materials that have been agreed by the Teaching and Study Committee, so that the whole of

Fellowship is thinking about, talking about, and *praying* about the same thing at the same time. For eighteen months I have had the immense privilege of being part of that, and with God's help have, I hope, done a reasonably good job.'

'Hear! hear!' from the Richmond row and elsewhere.

'For nine of those months I have been in a relationship with another woman. Colette –' she turned to face her – 'I want to say now, here, before all these people I am blessed to count as my friends and all these people who may not approve: I love you.'

Colette was blushing beetroot red; she looked as if she wanted to hide, but she held Lydia's eye with a reassuring smile.

'What I have with Colette is a relationship that is deeply serious, that is, through God's help, making me into a more loving, forgiving, compassionate Christian, and which, I pray, will hold and sustain me as long as I live.'

Jake was looking increasingly alarmed. Emma Greer was still scribbling. And nobody was stopping Lydia.

'I have known God's grace so much more since He has shown me, through the love and support of Colette and other Christians, that He loves me, and has always loved me, as I am, as a lesbian, as He made me, and that, before Him at least, I do not need to pretend to be what I am not.'

Jake kept putting a foot forward, glancing at Lydia, glancing at Emma Greer, and backing away again. She wished he would make up his mind.

'This is why I am resigning from my position as hall officer. I quite simply cannot in good conscience lead the module that is scheduled to be delivered the week after next; it is a direct contradiction of God's teaching as I have encountered it in my study of the Bible and in the Spirit's working in my own life.'

Now Jake did take one pace forward.

'Of course,' Lydia continued as if she had not seen him, 'God works in all sorts of ways, including through the Teaching and Study Committee – and I am bound to respect the guidance of that committee. This is my own decision, led, I believe and trust, by God's Spirit. I am not leaving Fellowship and I will continue to work for the coming of God's kingdom at this university and beyond. Thank you, Jake. Thank you, Colette. Thank you, *everybody*.'

A moment of pure hush. Lydia stepped back from the microphone, bowed her head briefly, and left the podium. Again, she thought she heard a boo from the other side of the room – but no – much nearer, someone was wolf-whistling – good God, it was *Will* – and the whole lecture hall had erupted in applause, and he was on his feet, clapping furiously along with the rest of them, the Richmond row was cheering, and Colette was in tears.

They piled in to the waiting taxis, the Alma Road gang and the Richmond Hall group, and Michaela and Kris and Vicki. Lydia, giddy with adrenaline, watched the city lights pass the cab windows in a blur. She had done it. She had told them. She was twenty-one and she was free. It was not possible, surely. She bounced in her seat, felt Colette take her hand.

'Sorry about embarrassing you,' she said, quietly as she could manage.

'I'll get over it,' Colette murmured. Lydia could just see her smiling.

'Tcha,' Peter said from the front seat as they drew up outside Tiger Eye. 'No red carpet?'

'I don't need a red carpet,' Lydia said, accepting Colette's silent offer of an arm to help her out of the cab. 'I'm walking on a cloud.'

There was a little cluster of people on the pavement, waiting for her. Stuart, clean and brushed-looking. Abby, and Rachel! Mel! And Rose!

'How did it go? How does it feel?' Stuart was asking.

She let herself be hugged and escorted inside. 'It's a relief, mostly. I don't feel like I'm lying to everybody any more, and I don't have to ask my friends to lie for me.'

'I meant being twenty-one,' Stuart teased. 'But seriously, how did it go?'

'She was brilliant,' Peter said. 'It was amazing. You should have been there.'

'Thank you,' Lydia said, cheerfully. 'It – well, I needed to say it.'

Georgia said, 'Indeed. It was a very good speech. You've hoist them with their own petard.'

'Ah,' Lydia said.

Peter said, 'Yes, I noticed that. Nicely done. Sound of a bluff being very thoroughly called.'

'Don't be coy,' Stuart said. 'Tell me what happened, for God's sake.'

'What are they on about?' Rachel asked.

Lydia cleared her throat. 'It's possible,' she said, 'that Jake was expecting me to resign from the whole Christian Fellowship, not just the Teaching and Study Committee. I – this is only going to make sense if you know the ins and outs of the whole Union saga. And it wasn't nearly as deliberate as you two seem to think.'

'Explain?' Abby said. 'I *have* been following your Students' Union thing, so far as is possible via the internet, so I have a reasonable chance of getting it.'

'Oh,' Georgia said, 'it's brilliant. She resigned from the Evangelical Christian Fellowship Teaching and Study committee. She very explicitly did not resign from Fellowship.'

'I think they were expecting her to resign from everything,' Peter explained. 'It does save trouble if these little embarrassments tidy themselves up, you know?'

Georgia continued, gleefully, 'But she didn't. She said in one breath that she was a lesbian, in the next that she was in a relationship, next

271

that their poxy course was unchristian guff, and *then* that she had no intention of resigning from the Evangelical Christian Fellowship.'

'Leaving them,' Peter concluded, 'with the choice of either allowing her to remain a member knowing she's gay, and knowing that everyone else knows that, or kicking her out themselves, and for evermore having a reputation as horrifically homophobic.'

'*Even more* homophobic than we already knew they were,' Georgia said. 'More to the point, that really would give the Union an excuse to come down on Fellowship and stop all their funding forever. They won't do it. They can't afford it. They've got no possible reason to kick her out. She signed the acceptance thingy. She even signed the Statement of Belief. She's a genius.'

'I only wanted,' Lydia said, rather embarrassed, 'everyone to know exactly what was what. And why should I leave Fellowship? I'm still an Evangelical Christian.'

Colette tapped Peter on the shoulder. 'Do you think,' she asked, 'you could round people up and get them to gather around that stage thing over there? I think everyone's here, and it feels like it might be time for cake.'

'Excellent plan.' He strode off.

Colette turned to Lydia. 'Now, pretend you didn't hear that conversation, and come over here with me and prepare to be terribly surprised.'

Georgia called, 'Come on, everybody! Cake!'

Somebody turned the music down.

'Cake,' Colette said, as the guests formed a horseshoe shape around the little podium, 'and also another speech. By me! Help me up, someone!'

'Oh, God.' Georgia leapt up to steady Colette as she climbed onto a chair. 'Careful, you'll snag your dress on your shoe... OK? There you go.'

'Thanks. Can you all hear me?'

They could.

'I'll keep this short,' she said. 'You've already had one speech this evening, and it was better than this one is going to be. For those who didn't go to the Fellowship meeting this evening, you missed the most extraordinary scene I've ever witnessed. My gorgeous, reckless, brave, *insane* girlfriend got up in front of three hundred evangelical Christians and told them that she was in love with me. I fully expected to be lynched.'

Laughter.

She glanced at the palm of her hand. 'As I wasn't, I find myself having to do something only marginally less terrifying, and speak to you. I want to tell you, her friends and her family, how very proud I am of her; how courageous she has been, not just tonight; and with what awesome integrity she has faced the last few months, which to be quite frank have been bloody awful.

'Finally.' She beckoned Lydia, who came and stood next her chair, feeling deeply conspicuous. Colette reached down to take her hand; then spoke as if there were no one else in the room. 'Lydia, my darling, I love you. Happy birthday. Happy coming out day. We've got here, somehow, and I want to keep walking with you to the very end. I said that the last few months have been bloody awful. They have, but they have also been so very wonderful that I would not change them. Only,' she said in a sudden rush, 'I wish Becky could have been here, because she would have loved your speech.'

Lydia, rather flustered, said over the applause, 'I don't think there's room for me on that chair as well. And I don't want to repeat everything I said earlier, only to say again that I meant it. And I love you. And please come down off there.'

While Colette was hopping down from the chair, and being kissed (very thoroughly, to loud cheers from the more drunken guests) by Lydia, Georgia brought the cake out and lit the three token candles.

It was not the most beautiful cake in the world; 'and Congratulations!' had been squeezed in under 'Happy Birthday!' in just the wrong shade of red, and somewhere over the course of the journey it had got rather battered around the bottom right-hand corner. But it was most definitely cake, and Lydia was deeply touched, and had a tear in her eye when she blew the candles out.

Another pair of cabs deposited them back at Alma Road a little while after one in the morning, at which point Lydia, too excited and perhaps too scared to go to bed, decided that it was time to open her birthday bottle of wine.

'I bought it for *you*,' Stuart said. 'You singular.'

But it stretched to six, just about, because Will was very abstemious and said 'when' after only about an inch had got into his glass. He raised it to Lydia, said, 'Happy birthday,' drained it very quickly, and disappeared off to bed. Lydia wondered whether his hangover was already kicking in, or if it was a hangover at all. She decided not to worry about it. He had come to the meeting, and he had come to the party, and she could not ask for more.

Stuart was the next to retire, citing a desire to get more than four hours' sleep. 'Good night, sleep well. And happy birthday! Even though it's not your birthday any more!' He hugged Lydia, then hugged Colette for good measure. 'Hey,' he said, suddenly serious. 'That was brave.' He rinsed his glass under the cold tap before heading downstairs to bed.

He had barely left the kitchen before they heard a pop. 'Bugger! Sorry!' he called. 'That was the light blowing on the top landing. I didn't even mean to touch it!'

'Don't worry,' Colette called back. 'Go to bed!'

'I'll change it in the morning,' Georgia said. 'I can't be arsed rootling around in the cupboard under the stairs at this time of night, and we'll need a stepladder to get to it. You two just be careful when you go up to bed, all right?' She glared at Colette and Lydia.

Peter yawned. 'They'll be fine. Where were we? Oh, yes. Happy coming out day, Lydia. Excellent party. I can't believe you're still sober.'

Lydia grinned. 'I can't believe you're not. When's your selection thing, again?'

'Oh, I've got three days to get over the hangover. A week, if you count the retreat.'

'Good luck,' Colette said. 'I'm sure you'll do well.'

'Thanks.' He hesitated, then said, 'Be happy, you two. Blessings. Literally. What you said earlier – well, Amen to that. And I was thinking that when I *was* sober. I just pray the Church sorts itself out for you. It doesn't deserve you.'

'I will put up with it,' Lydia quoted, though she could not quite remember whom, 'until I find a better, and it will have to put up with me until I become better.'

'Have a hug, you soppy bugger,' Colette said to him, 'and go to bed. I'll send Georgia in with a cold sponge at seven.'

Peter groaned. 'Night, then,' he said, and shambled off to the sitting room.

'Should we get the camp bed out for him?' Lydia wondered.

'Wouldn't bother,' Georgia said. 'He knows where it is.'

'You all right, G?' Colette asked.

'Me? Oh, yes. Feeling a bit wistful, that's all... I was thinking about Becky.'

Colette nodded, her eyes suddenly bright. 'I know. It's very weird, having a party without her. She'd have loved this one.'

'She would,' Georgia agreed. 'And, it's lovely to see you two being happy together. She'd be so pleased. *Is* so pleased, I bet.'

'I do wish you'd stop saying "us two",' Colette protested. 'This was Lydia's party. I'm only collateral.'

'*Are* you.' Georgia drained her glass. 'Well, I'm off to bed. I'll see you two in the morning – considerably later, I hope, than when I wake Pete with that cold sponge.'

Lydia, feeling herself blushing, touched Georgia's hand. 'Just a moment. Thank you, Georgia, for dragging Will along tonight. I know he wasn't entirely happy, and I've got enough raving evo left in me to know why, but I do appreciate his being there.'

Colette said, after a little pause, 'Yes. Particularly given what we were just saying about Becky.'

Georgia nodded awkwardly. 'You're welcome. Night then, both. Sleep well.'

'Well,' Colette said when they were left alone. She exhaled slowly, moved an empty glass to one side, and took Lydia's hand.

'It was a lovely party,' Lydia said. She mopped carefully at a pool of spilt wine with a paper napkin. 'I meant it, you know. Every last word of it.'

'So did I.' Colette shivered. 'Today may be the best we ever get, so far as the Church is concerned.'

Lydia thought about that. 'No. I don't think so. You were right. Things are changing.'

They sat for some moments in silence.

At last Colette said, 'It's more than enough to be going on with. Aren't you just a tiny bit terrified?' She was looking straight at her, and there was indeed a kind of reverent fear in her eyes.

'Petrified. I didn't mean to be that serious,' Lydia admitted. 'But I am, and it's no good lying about it, and I only hope you feel something like the way I do.'

'Always,' Colette said. 'I always will.'

'Yes,' Lydia said. She stood up and shook the creases from her dress. Silently, she held out a hand to Colette. Colette, laughing, rose and kissed it; the old-fashioned gesture surprised and charmed Lydia. 'My dearest love,' she said, and could not continue.

A heartbeat, and Colette had her in her arms, and was kissing the tears from her cheeks. 'I love you,' she said.

Lydia laughed shakily. 'Come on,' she said, 'let's go to bed. We can find the way from here.'

Colette took her hand, and kissed her mouth, and they went up the dark staircase together.

Faith; hope; love: which was enough for now, and perhaps for ever.

Printed in Great Britain
by Amazon